A JAUNTY JAM

A MULBURY MYSTERY

JUNO HARVEY

First published by Mandurang Press 2024

Book cover by Melissa Williams Design

ISBN: 9780645651133 (ebook)

ISBN: 9780645651140 (paperback)

To Anne Murphy, for her support

ONE

Rosemary Exeter stood on the slope leading down from the farm's homestead. From here, she overlooked the little tourist town of Mulbury but from an angle she rarely saw. Goldmarket Square was obscured by the row of buildings leading up to the cemetery on her left, Robert Sparkling's mansion Ravenhome towering over any other. To her right, the veranda that shaded the shops underneath it—Mrs Lionel's The Green Mulbury, Rosemary's The Preserved Mulbury, Jasper's The Read Mulbury, and now Honey B's Teas—was dark and protective against the heat of summer. Rosemary imagined the flock of visitors dipping in and out of the shops in the centre of town, exclaiming over lavender soaps and strawberry jam, then pausing at the locked door of Jasper's dark second-hand bookstore, before heading off to sample chocolate cupcakes. She sighed.

'Mumblemumble?' asked Justin Gentleman, coming over to her with a basket full of the farm's boysenberries.

Rosemary nodded thoughtfully as she tried to decipher what Justin had said. The farmer studied her with concern, his bushy silver eyebrows crumpled together. Perhaps he thought her downcast? 'A bit,' she said.

He nodded. 'Mumblemumble.'

She smiled as she took the basket. 'Indeed.'

They stood together a while longer, the farmer contentedly chewing on a lucerne stalk which thankfully kept him quiet. Rosemary knew she wasn't the only one who couldn't ever work out what Justin said, although she usually grasped his sentiment. The farmer had provided Mulbury and other nearby towns with quality vegetables, fruit, meat and eggs for as long as she had been a resident, and he spent his days mostly alone with no need to develop fine speaking skills.

The summer sun was nearly at its zenith and Rosemary wished she was wearing a broader brimmed hat to better protect her face. She indicated the land below them. 'It's been a lush year,' she said. 'Rainfall is the highest it's been for decades.'

Justin nodded and pulled his lucerne out to point across to his full dam. The sun glinted off its surface, making it difficult to see clearly, but she knew what he meant.

'That's unusual. A full dam in the middle of summer.'

The man nodded again, his wispy hair floating in long strands from under his hat as he did. 'Mumble.' He waved at the paddock full of grass in front of them.

'Yes. Green grass in summer when usually it's dry and crispy by now.' Rosemary tapped her foot on a clump of grass. 'Mrs Lionel says the weather pattern is changing. When she was farming, they would be hand feeding the dairy cows by now.'

Justin grunted and swung his hand towards another paddock where two Friesian cows grazed. To the left of them, a little herd of dairy goats clustered together. Rosemary heard the cackle of chickens from the mobile coop behind the house, and in the distance, a horse whinnied.

'Honestly, Justin, if I didn't love where I live in the middle of Mulbury, I'd be coming out there to camp in your backyard. You have a beautiful property.'

Justin beamed. The smiled transformed his face from grizzled farmer into wondrous landholder. He threw down his lucerne and started talking rapidly, pointing with a bent finger at the various sheds and water troughs within their sight line. 'Mumblemumblemumblemumblemumble...'

Rosemary let his voice blur into the background of her thoughts. Mulbury was having a busy season, with tourists evidently enjoying the slightly cooler summer, and the lush growth in the paddocks and bushland. The Preserved Mulbury seemed forever low on stock, and Rosemary had taken to making jams and pickles at midnight to keep her shelves relatively full. Most nights, she was bone tired by the time she fell into bed, but it was better than lying awake wondering about Jasper Lu.

The tourists knew something was up. 'How long will the bookshop be closed?' asked one woman, a regular visitor to the town, standing in The Preserved Mulbury last Monday. 'I've nearly run out of Fiona McIntosh's.'

Rosemary had managed a smile. 'I don't know.'

The woman frowned and pushed her spectacles up on her nose. 'Don't you have any idea? One month, two? Any more than that and I'll have to go to the city for my books.'

Rosemary opened her mouth for a terse reply but was luckily interrupted by Mrs Lionel who had stepped into the shop. 'It'll be open soon, we hope,' she said to the woman, smiling warmly. 'Jasper is having a holiday.'

'Hmmm,' said the woman, picking up her carry bag full of jars of tomato pickles. 'He's been on a very long holiday.'

He had. Three months. At first, Rosemary could explain it to herself as Jasper needing space to search for his father, with no time to think of anything else. But two months in, and no one had heard a word from him, not even Mrs Lionel, and Rosemary had begun to worry.

'No news is good news,' Gerry had said when she'd last seen him. He'd been holding a bundle of evening gowns made from abandoned school uniforms, with a selection of reconfigured school ties as sashes draped around his neck. 'He'll be back before we know it.'

'Oh, yes.' Patti appeared at that moment, whirling passed her husband clutching padded clothes hangers for the gowns. 'Jasper's too much of a sweetie to disappear without a trace.'

Disappearing without a trace was exactly Rosemary's worst fear, although she knew Patti was trying to be reassuring. She'd left them setting up their new display of upcycled garments without saying another word.

Three months in, and even the sisters at Mulbury Feeds were showing concern. 'We're used to people leaving for months on end,' Holly commented to Rosemary among the cat food pellets. 'Dad did that all the time.'

'But he'd never go three months without ringing.' Hannah rubbed at her spiky blonde hair, making it stand up in tufts. 'He wouldn't go that long without checking on Heather.'

'Daddy,' said Heather, twirling a black feather between her fingers. 'I'm his favourite.'

'Yes, we know,' said Holly crossly.

'Just so *you* know,' said Hannah, grinning at her little sister, 'you are the favourite of us all.'

Heather chuckled and drew the feather down Rosemary's arm. 'I know.' She let the feather rest on Rosemary's hand. 'Jasper's coming back. You'll see.' The feather tapped twice.

Out of the discussions Rosemary had had with her Mulburian friends, it was Heather's words she inadvertently clung to most. Jules and Roman had said the same thing, as had Franco the baker, and even Rakisha was convinced Jasper would appear at any moment, but the wild-haired youngest Hubbard sister, with her extraordinary ability to know things, was the most reliable source of truth.

Only Robert Sparkling, of all Rosemary's friends, said nothing about Jasper. In fact, she hadn't heard him say Jasper's name since he'd left.

'Mum?'

Rosemary snapped back into real time to watch Honey Blossom climb the hill in front of her. In Honey's arms, a sleeping Tallulah clung to her mother, glossy auburn hair glinting in the sun.

'Mumble,' said Justin, grinning.

'Yes,' said Rosemary. 'The most beautiful thing in the world.'

'I hope you're referring to me,' said Honey as she reached them. She lifted Tallulah up a little and smoothed her top down. 'It might have been worth the effort to hear my mother say that.'

'I was talking about-'

'Yes, yes.' Honey patted her mother's arm and smiled. 'I know exactly who you meant.' She turned to face the paddocks leading down to the dam. 'Oh boy, Justin, you have an amazing property.'

Justin nodded. 'Mumblemumble.'

'Why are you here, Honey?' asked Rosemary. 'Shouldn't you be baking?'

'Probably.' Honey rocked the sleeping baby. 'But I suddenly needed to get out and I saw you drive away with your basket.' She nodded at the boysenberries. 'Berry jam?'

'Berry conserve, as Aunt Lilibeth would suggest. Justin's berries are very large and they'd be best broken down.' Rosemary studied her swaying daughter, noting the crisp white dress she was wearing. 'Why did you have to get out?'

'You know.'

'Right. Ronnie's mother.'

'Yep. Ronnie's mother. Pearl.' Honey used one hand to tuck an escaped strand of her chestnut hair back into her ponytail. 'She's a pearler, all right.'

Justin folded his arms. 'Mumble?'

'Yeah, you said it.' Honey shook her head. 'Hard worker, but very high standards.' She glanced down at her dress. 'I was heading out here to see you in my normal working gear when she caught me. I don't know how she expects me to keep this clean with a baby and a tearoom to tend to. One blob of pink icing from a cupcake on this, and I'd look like a...' She waved her hand around.

'A baker?' suggested Rosemary.

'Well, yeah. And what's wrong with that?' She gestured to Rosemary's faded denim skirt and collared blue short-sleeved shirt. 'You wear that when you're making preserves and to serve in the shop.' She waved a finger at Justin. 'And there'd be no sense in you wearing a suit when what you need is a decent pair of coveralls.' She dropped her hand and pulled at the skirt of her dress. 'So, there's no need for me to be dolled up in this.'

'Could be worse.'

Honey sighed, shifting Tallulah across to her other shoulder. 'I know, I know. Pearl has her good points. She had Ronnie, for one. He makes up for every move she does I don't like.'

'How is Ronnie coping with his mother staying in close quarters?'

'He's Ronnie, isn't he? He's perfectly affable.' Honey stroked the baby's head with one finger. 'Sorry, Mum. I shouldn't be whinging. The tearoom is starting to flourish, our new home is set up, and Cuddles has befriended Snowy. What more could I want?'

'Cuddles certainly loves Snowy. His tail nearly falls off from wagging when he sees him.'

'Cuddles loves company, and he's never had a fellow dog in such close range before.' Honey stopped rocking and regarded her mother. 'Snowy must be missing Jasper.'

Rosemary shrugged. 'Snowy is perfectly at home on my couch, much to Sunny's disgust. When she starts grumbling at the poor dog, I take him to Mrs Lionel's so Sunny can reassert herself as top animal.'

'Well, she's been top cat for a long time.' Honey switched her gaze to the land in front of them. 'Have you heard when J-'

'No.'

Honey nodded and rocked the baby. 'Okay, okay. Just thought I'd ask.'

'I am not Jasper's keeper.' Rosemary shifted the basket roughly to her other arm.

Honey kept looking down the hill. 'No, you aren't. Hey, Justin. What's that?' She pointed towards the dam.

The water still sparkled with the strong sunshine, but now Rosemary saw a dark patch on it. It was towards the bank, and partly obscured by reeds.

'Mumble?' asked Justin, starting the trek towards the dam.

Rosemary followed. 'Could it be a cow or a goat?'

Justin shook his head. 'Mumble.'

Honey ran a few steps to catch up to her mother. 'A kangaroo, maybe?'

Justin shrugged.

The hill was tufty with the occasional rabbit-dug hole. Rosemary stepped carefully, mindful of both her basket and the precious bundle in Honey's arms, and Justin was soon in front of them. He lumbered to the dam's edge and stopped. 'Mumble,' he said, as the others came in behind him.

'Mumble indeed,' said Rosemary. 'I'm going in.' She threw off her shoes and waded into the water, hearing indecipherable protests from Justin and a gasp from Honey. She sloshed through the sun-warmed water until she reached the dark shape stuck face-down in the shallows of the dam and hauled it around.

'Mum? What is it?'

Rosemary started back, dragging the mass behind her. 'Honey,' she said. 'Call the police. Tell them…'

'Tell them what?'

Rosemary reached the edge and Justin bent to heave her load onto dry land. As he did, it revealed itself as a balding, grey-faced man in a sodden sport jacket, his neck patterned with bruising. 'Honey,' she said, feeling for signs of life and not finding anything more than the cold, dense texture of a dead man's throat. 'Tell them there's a murdered man in Justin's dam.'

TWO

The police took less than thirty minutes to arrive at the farm. The little group on the water's edge sat in the sun listening to the sirens as two cars hurtled up Justin's unsealed driveway, leaving behind a long cloud of dust. 'Hard for them to go anywhere secretly, isn't it?' said Honey, nursing the drowsy Tallulah.

Rosemary stood and waved her arm. The sun's angle turned the police officers into silhouettes, but she knew their shapes. 'Hello, Geoffrey,' she said as the man arrived. 'Hello, Christopher. You were quick.'

'We were in the district.' The older detective tipped his head to Honey. 'Honey Blossom. And congratulations.'

'Thank you.' Honey smiled. 'But you've met Tallulah.'

'Yes, and she's a little doll.' Geoffrey bent to touch the baby's cheek before straightening again. 'I meant congratulations about Honey B's Teas. Quite a venture to take on with a new little one.'

'Well, you know.' Honey redirected her smile to Rosemary. 'Mum helps. As does Mrs Lionel. Oh, and the

Hubbard sisters, Jules, Patti, Gerry...even Franco, believe it or not.'

'Well, that is interesting. I thought that man never left his patisserie.' Geoffrey pulled his suit coat straight. 'You know Christopher?'

'Hi, Toffee,' said Honey B, hoisting Tallulah up a little. 'How's things?'

'Great, Honey.' The young constable smiled. 'Nice to be here in Mulbury, even if...' He gestured to the dam.

'Never a dull day in Mulbury.' Geoffrey turned to Justin. 'Your farm, Mr Gentleman? Right. What have we got?'

'Mumble,' said Justin, pointing at the dead body, which he'd covered with an old chaff bag. 'Mumblemumblemumble'

'Yes,' said Geoffrey, nodding. 'It's quite a mystery. So, you don't know him?'

Justin shook his head vigorously.

'I see.'

Another police car arrived, and more people moved down the slope. Rosemary helped Honey up and they moved away from the group of investigators to allow them full access to the scene. Justin stayed with them, talking rapidly to Toffee, who nodded at the farmer and took occasional notes.

'We see a lot of him these days,' said Honey, nodding towards the young man.

'Yes.'

'You know, Toffee adores Holly.'

Rosemary frowned. '*Toffee* doesn't suit a police officer.'

'Maybe not, but it suits a boyfriend of a Hubbard sister.' Honey jiggled Tallulah in her arms and then kissed the top of her head. 'Holly thinks the world of him, too. I can tell by the way she talks. I reckon he's the one for Hol.'

'Holly isn't ready yet.'

'Isn't ready for what? A relationship?'

Rosemary glanced at her daughter. Honey's hair caught the light and shone a healthy shoe-polish brown. Tallulah lay easily in her mother's arms, clasping softly at the neckline of Honey's dress. The picture was peaceful, contained. The sisters' world was not so solid. 'She isn't ready to leave Mulbury Feeds.'

'But she said she was.'

'It's easier to say what you think you want to do than actually do it.'

'Spoken like a woman who knows.'

'Yes.'

Honey settled the baby against her shoulder. 'But she will leave, won't she? With Toffee?'

'Yes.'

'And Heather is working more and more with Patti.'

'Yes.'

'Which will mean Hannah will be left with the animal produce store.'

'The store that Robert owns.'

'Owns, but doesn't work in.'

'Yet.'

'Mum, he has the garage as well.'

'Honey, Robert Sparkling has no need to work anywhere.'

Honey shrugged, careful to not move Tallulah. 'Robert isn't an idle person. He'd be working even if he owned half of Mulbury.'

'He's heading that way.'

Honey gave her rich chuckle. 'Well, lucky he's such a nice person.'

'Right.'

Honey gave her mother a sideways glance. 'You do think he's nice, don't you? He thinks you are.'

Rosemary turned to stare directly into her daughter's eyes. '*Nice* is not a word that's commonly used about me, so my assumption is you're making that up.'

Honey laughed again. 'Robert didn't say anything to me, but he didn't have to. He *lingers* when he looks at you.'

Rosemary frowned, but before she had a chance to say anything, Geoffrey strode up the hill to where they stood. 'There's no identification on the deceased. Initial observation makes me think he's in his seventies.' He pointed down the hill to where the man lay drying out in the sun, revealing a muddy tangerine-coloured jacket and dirty moleskins. 'We'll have to wait until we can check our databases for missing people. There is that, though, from his suit pocket.' He indicated a sodden piece of paper lying curled on a grassy tuft halfway down the slope.

'What is it?' Honey went closer, then shook her head.

Rosemary followed her daughter. The paper was torn, leaving it a rough triangular shape as if it was the corner of something larger. It was too wet to make out the half-exposed letters at the top against the dark colouring of the background, but there was a round graphic twisting its way down its edge. She crouched to look underneath. 'An advertising flyer? There's a bullet list of something on the back.'

Geoffrey nodded as Rosemary stood up again. 'We'll know once it's dried out.' He swivelled around to check the workers below. 'We could be a while yet.'

Rosemary nodded. 'Do you need us anymore?'

'Not now. We'll need statements, though.'

'You know where we are when you want us.'

'Come and see the tearoom, Uncle Geoffrey,' said Honey. 'Ronnie would love to see you. And we have Pearl visiting.'

'My sister-in-law is there?' Geoffrey harrumphed into his hand. 'I'll probably send a constable to see you as I have limited time. Ah, how long is Pearl staying?'

'There's no ETD.'

'I see.' Geoffrey gestured to the busy scene in front of him. 'Right, well, back to work.' He raised a hand and went to join his colleagues.

Rosemary and Honey walked slowly to the top of the hill. Tallulah was awake and squirming, and the large basket of boysenberries was awkward in Rosemary's arms. 'I'm glad to be leaving that terrible scene behind,' Honey said, glancing back over her shoulder. 'The police have such a gruesome job.'

'Yes.'

'Did you get the impression Geoffrey didn't want to see Pearl?' asked Honey, stepping carefully over a dried cow pat.

'Indeed. You'd think he'd want to see his brother's wife, particularly if he hasn't seen her much since he died.'

Honey was quiet. Rosemary glanced at her but said nothing. Although you generally chose the person you married, you couldn't choose their family. Rosemary had only met Pearl a couple of times, each one a short visit by Ronnie's mother, with only enough time to see Pearl's desire to be the centre of the conversation. Rosemary had left her well alone but looking at Honey's darkened expression made her wish she hadn't. It might be useful to work out what made Pearl tick.

Honey's white station wagon, emblazoned with a blue

and back striped native bee, was parked next to Rosemary's old blue sedan. Rosemary studied her car for a moment. It was the last remnant of her life with Alasdair and for some reason it was hard to let go. It was so shabby. Maybe it was time to say goodbye?

'I'll see you after, Mum,' said Honey, buckling Tallulah into her seat.

'Right.'

'You've forgotten, haven't you?'

Rosemary shook her head. 'Monday night dinner. Like we always have every Monday with everyone coming along.'

'You've forgotten that it's at our place.'

'Yes. Sorry.' Rosemary held the basket up. 'I'll make boysenberry crumble.'

'Aren't you using those for jam?'

'I'll mix apple in for the crumble then I'll have some left over to make my conserve.'

'I'm rearranging the tearoom to fit everyone in.' Honey straightened and shut the car door. 'We're having tomato tarts.'

'Sounds great.' Rosemary put a hand briefly on her daughter's arm. 'You didn't have to volunteer for this. You're busy enough.'

'Oh, everyone's busy in their own way. Besides.' Honey opened the driver's side door and slid in, grinning. 'It's safer in numbers.'

'What's safer in numbers?'

'Being with Pearl.' She shut the door, started the car, and drove slowly away, waving once to her mother.

Rosemary placed the basket of precious berries on the back seat and prepared to follow Honey down the dusty driveway to the main road. The cluster of police, Justin gesturing madly in their midst, still gathered at the water's edge and no one turned to acknowledge her departure. She let Honey pull ahead so the dust cloud made by the car settled, and then drove down the hill.

The outskirts of Mulbury were pastoral, mostly littered with sheep. In a normal summer, the hills were rocky and dry, but this season had kept tinges of green on the slopes. Magpies flew from tree to tree, squawking to their families, and casual kangaroos lifted their heads to watch the car go past. Rosemary drove into Mulbury, parked her car around the corner near Mulbury Feeds, and walked the short distance to The Preserved Mulbury, the basket of berries swinging at her side.

'Rosemary!'

The familiar voice, usually warm and welcome, had a hint of concern. Rosemary turned to her friend. 'Did you see the police cars?'

'Well, yes.' Mrs Lionel stepped from her shop and went to Rosemary. 'They went straight up the hill and out towards...' The older woman waved her hand in the direction of Justin's farm.

'Justin Gentleman had a man floating in his dam.'

'I take it the man was dead?'

'Yes.'

'Goodness me.' Mrs Lionel fiddled with the collar of her dress. 'Do we know the fellow?'

'I'd never seen him before.'

'Was Geoffrey there?'

'Yes.'

'That's good. They'll get to the bottom of the poor man's demise.' Mrs Lionel smoothed her apron, patting its pockets as if looking for something. 'But how is Justin? I'm not sure how he would react to such an unfortunate event right on his doorstep.'

'He was very vocal.'

'Ah, well, yes. Was he distressed?'

'More puzzled than distressed.'

'Yes, goodness, he would be. He would be. Finding a man in your dam. Most unexpected.'

Rosemary frowned. Mrs Lionel was now twirling a grey curl around one finger, a movement usually associated with Patti or Heather Hubbard or Rakisha, but not the steadfast and sensible owner of The Green Mulbury. 'Are you alright?'

'Me? Am I alright? I'm not the one who saw a dead man in a dam.'

'Dragged.'

'Pardon?'

'I dragged a dead man from the dam.'

'Oh, Rosemary! Did you have to do that?'

'No. Justin could have. But I didn't want Honey to do it.'

'Honey was there as well? With Tallulah?'

'Yes, but I don't think the baby would have noticed anything.'

'But Honey. Is she alright? I know she's your daughter, and unaccountably strong-natured, but the shock of seeing such a thing must have disturbed her.'

'Yes. It disturbed *me*. The Exeter women may be strong-natured, but we do have feelings.'

'Sorry, Rosemary, sorry. Of course, you do, dear.' Mrs Lionel fiddled with the buttons of her cardigan, undoing the top two then doing them up again. 'I didn't mean...'

Rosemary put a hand out to still her friend's. 'Right. What's going on?'

Mrs Lionel gave a wobbly smile. 'What's going on?

You've just had an unfortunate encounter and I'm worried about your souls.'

'Thank you. Your concern is noted. But that's not what's causing you to flap about.'

Mrs Lionel dropped her hand, and for a moment, looked exactly as she normally was: solid, sensible, unflappable. 'Flap about?' she asked sternly. Her hands twitched and she started on the buttons again.

'Yes.' Rosemary put her berry basket down and linked both her hands to Mrs Lionel's. 'Right. Tell me what's going on. Not what's happened at Justin's. What's happened here that's caused you to be so upset.'

Mrs Lionel's lower lip trembled, a sign that made Rosemary's heart jump. 'Well...'

'Well, what? Whatever it is, we can work it out.'

Mrs Lionel squeezed her hands. 'I hope so, dear. I truly hope so.'

'Tell me. What is it?'

The older women took a deep breath in, and let it out slowly, standing straighter as she did so and fixing Rosemary with a look. 'He's back,' she said. 'Jasper's back. But he's changed and I don't know him anymore.'

THREE

Rosemary glanced along the veranda to where the windows of The Read Mulbury remained dark. In Jasper's absence, his online book sales were monitored mainly by Jules and the shop stayed closed. Rosemary became used to walking towards Honey B's Teas and ignoring the heavy door and dull brown blinds that hid so many reading treasures. What she hadn't become used to was the absence of noise through the wall of her home that joined Jasper's. She still strained for a kettle whistling or the thud of books on a kitchen table that was a regular feature of mornings with a bookshop owner as a neighbour. Rosemary let Mrs Lionel's hands go and picked up the berry basket. 'Come in for a moment.'

Mrs Lionel shook her head. 'I won't, thanks. Snowy is inside. Percy is watching him sleep.'

Rosemary smiled briefly at the image of the ghostly Percy eyeballing the ancient Snowy. 'Maybe he's hoping for a new ethereal friend soon?'

Mrs Lionel didn't smile. 'Jasper will be very upset when Snowy dies. I'm sure he'll be along shortly to take him home.'

Rosemary frowned. 'You mean he hasn't come to see his dog?'

'No. He hasn't.' The older woman's voice was firm, the tremor of before gone. 'I wouldn't have even known he was back if it wasn't for spotting that.' She pointed at a car parked along the road. 'It made such a noise.'

Rosemary eyed the black sedan. 'That's not Jasper's car.'

'His is parked behind it.'

'What happened then?'

'He got out of his, and this man got out of the other.'

Rosemary noted the dried mud on the ground near the large car's driver's door. 'A farmer perhaps?'

'I don't know what he was. All I saw was a big fellow carrying a bundle of leatherbound books and a little suitcase.' Mrs Lionel raised her arm to show the man's height, then put her hands out to the side to show his width.

'Probably not a farmer then.'

'He was dressed more like a retired banker, expensive shoes, and a casual shirt with tie.' Mrs Lionel let her arms drop. 'Jasper saw me. He looked right at me! The man said something to him. Jasper pointed at his door. Then they went inside.' She waved at the bookshop.

'That's all? He didn't hug you, or ask after Snowy, or...?'

'He just went inside.' Mrs Lionel clasped her hands together. 'Oh, Rosemary, he looks so different.'

'What do you mean?'

'He's thin, and his hair...' Mrs Lionel gestured helplessly.

Rosemary thought of Jasper's dark hair. The length of it rivalled her own. He had a habit of hooking it behind both ears when he was thinking. 'What about his hair?'

'It's gone. Cut short. It's *harsh*.'

'Right.' Rosemary shifted the basket to her other arm. 'He's thin with short hair. He may not be well.'

'I hadn't thought about that.' Mrs Lionel tapped a finger on her lip. 'Why hadn't I thought of that? It would explain his manner. He was so sick before and had really only just recovered.' Worry creased her face. 'We need to see him.'

'Yes. We will. But not now. Other things have happened. Let's get on with our day first. Geoffrey will be here shortly, I imagine. The police will need witness statements.' Rosemary studied her friend. 'Are you okay?'

Mrs Lionel put her shoulders back. 'Yes, dear. The shock is over. I'm sure there will be a logical explanation to Jasper's appearance.'

Having been Mrs Lionel's best friend for several years now meant Rosemary wasn't fooled. The odd encounter with Jasper had rattled the older woman more than previous events over the last twelve months. His absence had caused her great concern, and his reappearance had done the same. There was still a slight tremble in Mrs Lionel's hands. Rosemary nodded. 'He'll visit us once he's settled. If not, we'll send Snowy in.'

Mrs Lionel chuckled. 'If we can get him off my couch.'

'He does love a couch. Yours, mine, Jasper's.'

'He does indeed.' Mrs Lionel gave her hair a businesslike pat. 'I'm going inside. I'll see you later, dear.'

Rosemary glanced at her watch as Mrs Lionel went back to The Green Mulbury. She caught a hint of citrus as her friend opened the shop door, probably from the range of lemon cleaners sitting on a display table near the entrance. The electronic motion detector frog's frenetic croaking echoed under the veranda until the door shut, cutting it off. Rosemary pushed her way into her own shop, looking around in satisfaction at the glow of ruby coloured jams and golden pickles on her shelves.

Sunny turned to give her a baleful look from her position on the windowsill as Rosemary entered her living quarters and plunked the basket onto the kitchen bench. The tip of the cat's ginger tail flicked up at the noise and she blinked slowly.

'Sorry, Sunny. I thought I'd have most of the day to make jam. Not sure that's going to happen now.'

Through the wall behind the kitchen, voices started, deep and loud. Sunny turned her attention to them, tail flicking once more.

'Jasper's back,' Rosemary said to the cat.

Sunny ducked her head to lick a paw. *No kidding, Einstein,* the gesture seemed to say.

The walls between the four shops under the veranda along Goldmarket Road were only one layer of brick, mostly covered in plaster. Rosemary's kitchen cupboards and laundry buffeted her from much of Jasper's shop noises when she was in her living quarters, but now voices rumbled through, indecipherable in content but obvious in intent. Next door, people were arguing.

Rosemary tried not to listen. She thought about putting music on, or the radio, or even a podcast, but something held her back. The room was stuffy and it was a natural move to open the glass doors leading out to her balcony, the one that joined Jasper's on one side and Mrs Lionel's on the other. The open door let more than fresh air in.

'No, I won't. I can't!'

Jasper's familiar deep voice carried through the open door to his kitchen, across the balconies, and into Rosemary's. She froze, one hand still on her door handle, and waited.

'Well, my boy, it's really not up to you.'

The other voice was much quieter but very firm, as if the person was talking to a recalcitrant child. Rosemary waited for Jasper's response, but he was quiet. Footsteps told her he'd moved from the floorboards of the shop area onto the carpet of his lounge area, a second set following. When the voices started again, they were too soft to decipher.

'Watching the magpies?'

Rosemary jumped. A figure came up to stand next to her, short spiky hair brushing Rosemary's arms as it peered past her through the doorway. 'Hannah. You scared me.'

'Yeah?' The young woman grinned. 'That's a first, scaring Rosemary Exeter.'

'You came into my house and stole up behind me.'

'Yeah, sorry,' said Hannah, not sounding it. 'There's something wrong with the bell above your door. I guess I should have knocked or something, but you know.'

'Do I?'

Hannah rubbed at her head, suddenly serious. 'Good neighbours don't always knock and I've got something important to tell you.'

'Right.'

'The police are here but that's not it.'

'Do you mean Christopher or other police?'

'Toffee doesn't count.' Hannah frowned. 'I mean, he does, but he's here so often that it wouldn't be news. That old policeman is here but he's talking to someone on the path.'

'Right. What else?'

'Rakisha is trying to give the police cups of legume coffee—do you think she's lonely since her sister Silkie left? —but that's not it, either.'

Rosemary said nothing but thought the only way anyone would drink Rakisha's coffee was if it was given away, and even then, you'd have to be desperate.

'The film is out.'

Rosemary studied Hannah, waiting for more. The young woman's bright eyes were fixed on hers. The three sisters were eerily similar in looks, with golden hair and blue eyes, but Hannah was the most energetic. Even now, she moved her feet impatiently and folded and unfolded her arms. It was like watching a spring unfurl. Rosemary shook her head. 'Remind me, Hannah. What film?'

'That woman's film. You know, that woman that made Patti famous.'

'Adelia Lochard? The documentary maker?'

'Yeah, her. Adelia. She got Patti to make costumes for her short films, and that made Patricia's famous, which meant that Patti and Gerry had to expand their business, which meant shifting into the bottom of Robert Sparkling's mansion, which let Honey B's Tearoom open in Patti's old shop, which meant...' Hannah grinned again. 'Which means that now you have your daughter living in Mulbury.'

'Thanks for the potted history, Hannah. I do remember those events.'

'There you go. So, Adelia's film is out.'

Rosemary felt cold wash over her. When Adelia Lochard was in Mulbury, she had an unhealthy fixation on Jasper. More specifically, Jasper's famous writer mother and, even more directly, Jasper's unknown father. Adelia's pursuit of Jasper had been difficult for him, but luckily, she couldn't release any footage until the mystery of the skeleton in Jasper's backyard had been solved. Which it was. 'How do you know it's out?'

Hannah dug around in the pocket of her shorts and pulled out a piece of paper. 'Here.'

Rosemary took the paper and flattened it against her thigh before tipping it to the light to read. 'Where did this come from?'

'It came with a load of lucerne. The delivery man had it in his truck. See?' Hannah tapped the paper. 'It's from Big Town's newspaper. They're having a special showing at the Art House Theatre.'

The flyer was roughly designed in the manner of the volunteer-led picture theatre, with a mocked-up film reel running down its front side. On its back, it listed several obscure films, with 'The Lives and Loves of T. G. G. Duncan' right at the bottom. The screening date was in two days' time.

'Anyway,' said Hannah, perching on the back of the couch. 'It wasn't only that I came to see you for.'

Rosemary put the flyer on her table next to the fruit bowl. 'How can I help you, Hannah?'

Hannah swung her foot back and forth. 'It's Heather.'

Rosemary took an involuntary step forward. 'Is she alright?'

Hannah waved her hand dismissively. 'Oh, yeah. No need to panic.' She shook her head. 'Why do people panic when I mention Heather?'

Rosemary thought of Hannah's younger sister and her reactions in the past to traumatic events. Heather was intuitive, a feature that meant she was sometimes vulnerable to things others didn't even know were happening. 'I'm not panicking, Hannah,' she said. 'I'm just looking out for-'

'Yes, yes, I know.' Hannah's foot stopped, and she stared at Rosemary, seriousness creasing her forehead. 'It's great, you know, having the whole town looking out for Heather.

We do appreciate that. Really.' She sighed. 'Anyway, Heather's fine. But she's working two jobs and it's been a whole month since she did any taxidermy.'

'Right.'

'That's a problem, Rosemary.'

'Yes.' Rosemary pulled out a dining room chair and sat on it, half-turned to Hannah. 'Come to think of it, the last time I saw Heather with a dead bird was before Christmas.'

'Yeah. That poor little honeyeater.'

Rosemary nodded. One of the more interesting traits of Heather Hubbard was her predilection for rescuing whole dead birds from the side of the road where they'd been hit by cars and recreating them into stunning taxidermied forms. It was a talent not always appreciated by people outside Mulbury, although when she displayed them in the animal feed store, they sold well. 'She hasn't got time anymore.'

'That's right!' Hannah's foot tapped again to a furious beat. 'Heather helps out at Mulbury Feeds before breakfast, then she wanders off to Patricia's for most of the day, then comes home and throws haybales around until dinner. She's asleep by eight o'clock, and sometimes we have to help her into bed.'

'Is she happy?'

'Happy?' Hannah slapped her thigh. 'She's ecstatic! She hums along and, you know, does that thing she does.' She twirled a finger around.

Rosemary knew what she meant. Heather could often be seen twirling and humming, sometimes waving to town folk as she went, but more likely quite content in her own world. 'Is there a problem, then?'

'Maybe. Yes. I don't know. I just think she's working too hard and Holly's not doing anything about it.'

'There's a reason I'm not doing anything about it.'

Rosemary and Hannah turned at the sharp voice. Holly Hubbard, hair pulled back in a short, untidy ponytail, stood in the doorway. 'Holly,' said Rosemary. 'I didn't hear you come in.'

'Your bell's broken.' Holly kept her eyes on her sister.

'What is it?' asked Hannah. 'What's the reason you're letting Heather work so hard?'

Holly took a step in. She was the smallest but oldest of the three sisters, and she shared their determined demeanour. 'Firstly, we don't control Heather. She is her own person. She can work where she wants and we can't stop her.'

'But-'

'No buts, Hannah. You know that's true.'

'Yes, okay, I get that, Holly. I just thought you hadn't noticed.'

'Of course I noticed.'

'But it's not the reason, is it?'

'No.' She hesitated. 'No, it's not.'

'What is it then?'

Rosemary saw the small helpless gesture Holly made but Hannah didn't seem to. She stared belligerently at her big sister.

'I need you two to be able to manage without me.'

Hannah scoffed. 'Oh, don't be stupid, Holly. We already do.'

'Not as much as you're going to have to.'

Hannah froze. 'What do you mean by that?' she asked slowly.

Holly opened her mouth to answer, but instead turned and ran out the door.

Hannah was half a step behind her. She yelled, 'You're

impossible at the moment!' and disappeared outside. The door of the shop slammed shut.

Rosemary sighed. Holly's secret was obvious if only Hannah would allow herself to see it. She took up the flyer again, studying the times for the showing of Adelia's documentary, and frowned. She'd seen flyers from the Art House Theatre quite regularly, and never taken much notice except if Mrs Lionel wanted to see a film. It was cleverly designed for a small enterprise, with eye-catching deep colours. Its palette reminded Rosemary of velvet stage curtains. That purple, for example-

She paused, lifting the flyer towards the light and looking at it again. That purple, albeit dry and warm from being stuffed in Hannah's pocket, was the same colour as that of the paper in the dead man's jacket. He'd been carrying around the flyer from Big Town's Art House Theatre.

'And it was the only item he had on him,' said Rosemary to Sunny, who turned her elegant head to her mistress.

A clue, she seemed to say with a swish of her tail.

'A clue indeed.'

FOUR

Robert Sparkling glanced up from the car to see Holly Hubbard walking briskly from Rosemary's shop towards Mulbury Feeds. Hannah exited a moment later, but instead of following her sister, she ran across the road, almost getting skittled by one of the morning's slow-driving tourists, and disappeared past Rakisha's café. As he shut the bonnet, he wondered whether she was headed to Raven-home, his house and Patti and Gerry's upcycled garment shop, or the cemetery at the top of the hill where the sisters' mother was buried. Either way, it was strange to see Hannah leave work during the day, and certainly not at the pace she was going. It seemed like she was deliberately running in the opposite direction to her sister.

He wiped his hands on a rag and threw it into a bin in the garage, peeled off his coveralls, and walked over to the row of shops under the veranda on Goldmarket Road. As he reached Honey B's Teas, the door squealed open, and a woman barrelled out with a sandwich board painted a garish pink and yellow. She plonked it on the edge near the road and dusted it down with a frilly handkerchief.

'That's...new,' said Robert.

The woman glared at him. She had long, faded red hair pulled back in a knot at the back of her head, its wispy wilfulness reminding him of someone. 'Yes, it is.' She studied the sign with satisfaction. 'Just what this place needed.'

'Oh, is Honey selling ice-creams now?'

The look she gave him would have speared him dead had it been a knife. 'No. It's a *tea*room. It sells tea and cake.'

'And coffee.' Robert shrugged. 'Sadly, I'm more of a coffee man than a tea person. Still.' He indicated the sign. 'I thought she'd branched out.'

The woman crossed her arms.

Robert tried a pleasant smile. When that had no effect, he nodded and went into the tearoom.

The narrow area already had customers. Kelly Flanagan perched on a chair near the shop counter, casually reading the newspaper from Big Town. Rakisha stood to the left with her nose almost touching the shelf of bright jams ready for spreading on scones, her tie-dyed layers falling in jagged hems to the floor. The only non-Mulbury customer was a large man sitting by himself at the table closest to the door, tucking into a slab of black forest cherry cake and sipping at a delicate cup decorated with roses.

'Hello, Robert.' Honey leaned over the back of the counter to straighten a few pamphlets advertising an antique show in the next town. 'The usual coffee?'

'Yes, thanks.' Robert leaned down to pat Cuddles on his broad head before the Golden Retriever settled again on his bed next to the counter.

'Cake of the day?'

'I think I'll have a chocolate cupcake today.'

'With bee or without?'

He looked where she was pointing. Two fudgy cupcakes sat on display, one with a smattering of orange sprinkles and the other with a stiff iced blue banded bee that appeared to be devouring the cake before any customer would. 'Without. Thanks.'

'Just be a tick.'

Robert leaned sideways against the counter. Kelly Flanagan gave him a sly smile, and went back to her paper, holding it up slightly so he could see a picture of Honey B's Teas on the front, complete with an unflattering picture of Honey, Ronnie, Tallulah and Rosemary looking unprepared for the photographer. Honey was hoisting the baby up on her shoulder so her nappy was the biggest part of her. Ronnie had his hand on his head, probably trying to flatten his hair but caught in the act of making it stand up more. Rosemary was calm as usual, although a shadow across her face darkened it and made the long, silver-streaked hair across her left shoulder more like a shroud than a carefully tended braid. It was an old photo, one that had been taken by the free rag in Big Town when Honey B's Teas had opened. Kelly had shown it to him before. He guessed she liked it.

'Did you hear, darling?' asked a voice in his ear, making him twitch. A woman stood so close to him her skirts tickled his leg.

'Hear what, Rakisha?'

Rakisha lifted a hand to wipe at the flyaway hair veiling her face, making the beaded bangles on her wrist clash. 'Justin Gentleman has a body, darling.'

For a moment, Robert was tempted to agree. Last time he'd seen the farmer, he'd definitely had a body and was about as far from ethereal as one of his fine cows. But the concerned look on the woman's face stopped him. 'A body, Rakisha?'

'In his dam. Rosemary pulled it out. Honey had Tallulah, you see, and Justin is too...' Rakisha waved her hands around.

'Rosemary pulled the body out?'

Beside him, Honey placed a keep cup on the counter. 'There's your coffee, Robert.'

'You were there, Honey?'

'Yep.' Honey wiped the countertop. 'I'd gone for a drive.' Her eyes went to where the woman with the wispy red hair barrelled through the door, attacking the tabletops with her frilly handkerchief as she went.

'And Rosemary was, too?'

'Getting berries. We saw something floating in the dam.' Honey shrugged. 'Mum is nothing short of practical. In she went and dragged the poor man out.'

'She's okay?'

'Of course, she is.' Kelly Flanagan shook the paper so the front-page family photo wavered, distorting people's faces, and stood up. 'She's the centre of the police's atten-tion, right where she wants to be.'

'I don't think she wants to be there, Kelly,' said Honey mildly.

'Strange, though, how she always is.' Kelly put her cup on the counter. 'Thanks, Honey. Goodbye, Robert.'

'Bye bye, Kelly darling,' said Rakisha.

Kelly walked out without a glance at the dishevelled woman.

'She's so lovely, isn't she?' Honey laughed. 'What a b-'

'Honey Blossom!'

Honey's mouth snapped shut as the woman with the handkerchief stormed up to where she stood. 'Yes, Pearl?'

'There's a *fly* in the display window. Where's your spray?'

'I don't use fly spray, Pearl. There's a swat on a hook near the kitchen door.'

Pearl bristled. 'You expect me to use a *swat* in the tearoom? What a look! Slapping at flies, goodness me.'

Honey scowled. 'Better than spraying chemicals around, don't you think?'

Pearl patted her daughter-in-law's hand soundly. 'Better to get rid of the little blighter as quickly as possible. I know these things. Remember, I once owned a-'

'Café.' Honey slid her hand away. 'Yes, Pearl, I remember you telling me once or twice.' She lowered her voice so Pearl couldn't hear. 'Or a million times.'

'Well.' Pearl patted the counter a few times. 'I will see what I can do.' She stormed back to the window to do battle with the fly.

Robert glanced at Honey. The young woman's face was red, as if she were running around trying to swat a wayward fly herself. 'Are you okay, Honey?' he asked.

'Ten days, three hours and forty-five minutes.'

'What's that?'

'The length of time I have to put up with her.' Honey grimaced. 'Do you think I'll make it?'

Robert laughed but sobered quickly at Honey's sharp look. 'Yes. Of course, you will. You are strong, like your mother.'

'Mum wouldn't put up with this.' Honey tipped her chin towards Pearl, who had climbed into the window display to slap at the fly with her apron. 'She would throw her out the door.'

'Throw who?' Ronnie Edwards was in the doorway to the living quarters, Tallulah in his arms. He smiled at

Robert as he came forward. 'Hello, Robert. Having a busy day?'

'Just steady.' Robert reached over to run his finger lightly over the baby's head. 'Looks like you're keeping busy.'

'I don't think of it as busy.' Ronnie lifted the sleeping baby and kissed her head. 'She's so beautiful.' He touched his cheek to Tallulah before turning to Honey. 'Throw who?'

'Oh.' Honey opened the cake cabinet and stared intently inside. 'I've forgotten what I was talking about.'

'Okay.' Ronnie tipped his head to look down the shop. 'Is Mum alright? She looks like something's wrong. What's she doing?'

'Removing insects,' said Robert.

Ronnie chuckled. 'She's such a stickler for cleanliness. Did you know she once owned a café?'

'Yes. She was just saying.'

'Yeah.' Ronnie rocked his charge. 'I can't remember it. She said it was before I was born. I don't know why she sold.'

Robert picked up his coffee and turned to go, but the large man from the far table stood behind him, blocking his way. 'Sorry, sir,' said Robert. 'I didn't see you there.'

'Didn't see me?' The man put his head back and laughed heartily. 'Hard not to see me!' He patted his girth. 'That was a delicious slice of cake, my girl.'

Honey smiled. 'Thank you. Would you like another?'

'I would indeed. I would indeed!' The man shook his head. 'But not now. I'm heading out for lunch soon with my son. I don't want to spoil my appetite.' He put a heavy hand on Robert's shoulder. 'I hear that this restaurant has a fine city chef who moved to this quaint little country town because of his wife and brought his culinary skills with him. *Capricious*, his name is.'

'Capriccio? You mean Roman Capriccio? The restaurant is called The Leftover Restaurant.'

'That's it, that's it. Funny name but he insists we go, he insists.'

'Your son?'

'Yes, him, always wanting me out of the house and seeing the sights. Funny name, *Leftover*. Could have thought of something more sophisticated, eh? Eh?'

Robert shrugged. 'It's apt. Roman uses produce that wouldn't sell in a modern supermarket but is still good quality.'

'Anyway, anyway. That's where we're going.'

'I wonder if Pearl would like to go,' said Honey. 'Get her out of the house to see the sights.'

The man turned to see who Honey was looking at. 'That fine woman? What a grand idea although she looks too busy, eh? Busy bee indeed!' He chuckled and brought his wallet out, offering Honey his plastic card. 'Thank you for the cake, thank you indeed. I'll be back regularly here during my stay, mark my words, mark my words.'

'How long are you here for?' asked Honey as she processed his payment.

'Not sure, it depends. Yes, it depends. Checking out the place. So quaint, so quaint.' He took his card back. 'Thank you, my girl.' He held his hand out to Robert. 'I'm Kerry Carruthers. Nice to meet your acquaintance.'

Robert shook the man's hand. 'Robert Sparkling.'

A thud from the window display and Pearl retreated, triumphantly holding up her apron like a flag. 'Got it,' she shouted across the café, making everyone turn.

'Great,' said Honey in a low voice.

'Wonderful, eh?' Kerry chuckled at Pearl. 'Can't have flies over the tearoom's possessions. Possessions give a man self-respect, eh?'

'Thanks, Mum,' said Ronnie, heading over to take the apron from his mother. 'We can't have flies... Mum?'

Pearl had frozen in the act of giving her son the soiled garment, her stare transfixed on the big man at the counter.

'Mum!' Ronnie put his hand on her shoulder.

Pearly blinked and shook her head slightly. 'What is it, Ronnie? Really, you do need to get your vermin under control.' She thrust the apron at him and stormed back through the shop to the kitchen.

Kerry chuckled. 'Thank you for the cake, my girl,' he said to Honey. 'Good work, good work.' He slid his wallet back in his pocket. 'Must go. My son is waiting for me. Tootaloo, all!' He bowed to Honey.

'Goodbye,' said Honey. 'Do you know where to go from here?'

'Oh, yes.' The man pointed at the wall. 'In there.'

Honey tipped her head. 'In Jasper's bookstore? But it's not open.'

'He is there, he is. Waiting for me, no doubt.'

'Jasper is waiting for you?' Honey glanced at Robert. 'Do you mean...?'

'Jasper, yes.' The man spun and walked to the door, waving his hand over his shoulder. 'Jasper, yes, yes. Jasper is my son.'

FIVE

Rosemary was deep into jam making when Ronnie rattled in the door and appeared in the kitchen. 'Jumble berry?' he asked, leaning forward to sniff in the rich aroma.

'Boysenberries.' Rosemary stirred, noting the slight change in colour that indicated the conserve was ready.

'Good on scones?'

'Good on anything.' Rosemary put the wooden spoon down and closed Aunt Lilibeth's recipe book on the counter. 'Is it urgent?'

'Is what urgent?

'What you want to say to me?'

'Sort of...'

'One minute.' Rosemary brought her jars from the oven and expertly ladled the sticky condiment into them. Ronnie stood back and watched, one hand in his shorts pocket and the other absently stroking Sunny where she crouched on the back of the couch. The cat watched her mistress, too. Her haughty expression said *Hurry up with that so you can pay attention to me.* Rosemary put the pot and spoon into the sink and washed her hands. 'Now, Ronnie. What is it?'

'Did you know your bell is broken?' Ronnie waved his hand towards the front of the shop.

'That's the sort of urgent thing you want to say to me?'

Ronnie's pale face mottled. 'No, not that. I thought you might want to know, though.'

'Thanks. I do already.'

'Oh, okay. Do you want me to fix it?'

'I can fix my own bell, thanks, Ronnie.' Rosemary put her folded hands on top of the kitchen bench. 'Is Honey alright? Tallulah?'

Ronnie grinned. 'They're beautiful.'

Rosemary shook her head once. Ronnie was every inch a devoted husband, and very misty-eyed over Honey and their daughter. 'That's not what you came here to tell me.'

'No. Oh, no.' Ronnie straightened, taking his hand away from Sunny suddenly. She glared at him. 'It's Jasper. He's-'

'Back.'

'You knew?'

'Mrs Lionel told me.'

'Did she know who was with him?'

'No.'

'His *father*.'

Rosemary took a moment to answer, instead smoothing a stray hair back into place along her braid. 'So, Jasper found him.'

'Yeah. He came into the tearoom.'

'Jasper?'

'No, his dad. Kerry.' Ronnie frowned. 'Didn't look much like Jasper.'

'Why not?'

'He's a big man whereas Jasper's tall and thin.'

'That doesn't mean much.'

'I suppose not. He didn't act like Jasper.'

'And that doesn't mean much either.'

'No, I know. But Jasper's kind and gentle. This man...'

'Wasn't kind and gentle?'

Ronnie nodded. 'Well, I wouldn't have described him as that.'

Rosemary busied herself screwing lids on the jam jars, half an ear on the wall that separated Jasper's living area from hers. She couldn't hear any voices. 'I expect we'll see him soon.'

'One other thing.'

'Yes?'

'Uncle Geoffrey will be in to see you in a minute. He's just-'

'Getting a coffee.'

Rosemary looked up and smiled. 'I didn't hear you come in, Geoffrey.'

The older man grimaced. 'Your bell is broken.'

'Yes, thanks, I know. It's on my list of things to do today.'

'I'll need your statement first.' Geoffrey sat his coffee on the table. 'How are you, Ronnie?'

'Good, thanks, Uncle Geoffrey.'

'Busy enough?'

'Yep, it's busy with the tearoom and Tallulah, and I've still got some private investigations to finish up.'

'Are you giving up your PI licence now that you have other pursuits?'

Ronnie shook his head. 'I thought I'd keep it.'

'Good.' Geoffrey indicated a chair. 'Mind if I sit down, Rosemary?'

'Please.' Rosemary took a tin from the kitchen bench and slid it onto the table in front of the older man. 'Ginger biscuit?'

'Thank you.' Geoffrey took one then glanced at Ronnie. 'I'm going to take Rosemary's statement.'

'Oh?' For a moment, Ronnie looked puzzled, then his face reddened. 'Oh! I should go.'

'Stay if you want.' Rosemary sat down in the chair opposite the detective. 'You might be interested to hear what happened.'

Ronnie sat on the edge of another chair. 'If you don't mind...'

'Up to you, Rosemary. So.' Geoffrey pulled a notebook from his pocket. 'I talked to you at the farm, but if you could relate your morning and what happened.' He smiled. 'It's quite a nice change, taking witness statements. I've sent Christopher over to see Honey but thought I'd talk to you myself. Go ahead.'

Rosemary gave her account of the morning, starting with her trip to Justin Gentleman's farm, collecting boysenberries, and Honey arriving. She got to the part where they'd seen something in the dam and paused.

Geoffrey put his pen down. 'Everything all right, Rosemary?'

'Yes. Just thinking.' She picked up a biscuit but held it in her fingers without eating. 'We saw something, a dark hump in the dam, but it wasn't obvious until we arrived at the edge what it was.'

'Understandable.'

'Only from the point of view that we weren't expecting a body.' Rosemary put the biscuit down. 'That dam isn't in Justin's day-to-day line of sight. That body may have stayed there for a long time.'

'It was caught in the shallows, too, from what you said. Otherwise, it would have sunk and not been discovered for days. Bodies sink once the lungs fill with water. They rise again once they start to decompose.' Geoffrey shrugged. 'Gas creation.'

'He wasn't decomposed.'

'The deceased hadn't been long in the water.'

Ronnie sat back in his chair. 'But what was he doing on Justin's farm? Looking at the cows?'

'Justin's farm is on the sightseeing route, the one that showcases old gold-mining towns.' Rosemary frowned. 'But he isn't open to the public and his fences are solid. I don't think that man was a tourist going for a walk.'

'Hard to say what he was up to.' Geoffrey picked his pen up. 'Tell me more.'

'I didn't feel I could leave him there so I went in and dragged him out.' She looked at the detective. 'Sorry. I should have left him there.'

'You had to make sure he was dead.' Geoffrey tapped the pen on the table. 'Was there anything about the way he was floating I need to know? Debris caught around his legs or his head?'

'No. He was clear.'

'The divers will trawl the dam in case there's something else in there.'

'Or *someone* else.' Ronnie chewed his lip.

'Hmm.' Geoffrey closed his notebook. 'The post-mortem is booked.'

'Do you have any idea who he is?' Rosemary studied his face, noting its implacable expression. 'Or who wanted to see him dead?'

'I am not at liberty to say.' Geoffrey's expression softened. 'Meaning, I don't really know. We have a sad list of missing men. We're seeing whether any dots join up.'

'Right.' Rosemary stood and went back to her jars,

twisting the lids on more tightly. 'I've worked out what the paper in his pocket is.'

'You have?'

'A flyer for Big Town's Art House picture theatre. Do you think it could be a clue?'

'Everything's a clue, Rosemary.' Geoffrey stood as well. 'Even if some clues are clue*less*. Well, you know how to get in touch with me if you think of anything else.' He tucked his notebook in his suit coat and nodded to his nephew. 'Ronnie.'

Ronnie stood quickly, making his chair tip. He caught it with one hand. 'Won't you come and see Tallulah?'

Geoffrey tugged his coat together. 'I understand your mother's staying with you?'

'Yeah, she's helping out for a few weeks.'

Geoffrey hesitated. 'I'm very busy today, Ronnie. I'll visit the tearoom next time I'm here.'

'Okay, Uncle Geoffrey.'

Ronnie led the way out, leaving Geoffrey to give Rosemary a goodbye nod before he followed. She shut the silent door behind her visitors and glanced up. The large brass bell had originally belonged to the primary school before it closed and the children were offered places at the schools in Big Town. Not that it had been used as a school bell for a while, partly because the knocker had fallen off and no one had bothered replacing it. The other part was the school had a dwindling number of students and all the teacher had to do was clap her hands to call them for class. The old building had fallen into disrepair, and it was only luck Rosemary salvaged the bell from its demolition and gave it a new knocker shaped from a brass hook. And now it seemed the knocker had fallen off again.

'But where is it?' Rosemary asked Sunny who'd come to

the front window for a better look at the streetscape. *Don't bother me,* the cat said with a swish of her tail. *Something more important is happening out there.*

Rosemary followed the cat's gaze. The police had gone, leaving the road lined with the usual smattering of tourists' cars. Small groups of people sat in the Square outside The Sweet Potato, Mullings of Mulbury or Franco's Patisserie, munching lunch. In the middle of the Square, though, stood three men facing each other in an uneven triangle. The small man and the large one, Rosemary didn't know, but the one with his back to her, she did. His slender form was so familiar that she put one hand on her mouth to quieten an involuntary gasp. It was Jasper Lu, albeit with hair cropped close to his skull.

As if he'd felt her look, Jasper turned to stare in the direction of The Preserved Mulbury. It would be almost impossible for him to see her behind the shadow of the open blind on the square of glass embedded in the door, but she took a step back anyway. Spying on Jasper Lu was not her style, although curiosity, and something warmer, made her want to burst out in the street and run across the road. Instead, she turned swiftly and went back to check her cooling jam.

When her door opened again, it let in sounds of distant discussion as well as two older women intent on choosing the best pickles. Rosemary helped with their selection, one ear on the noise from the men in the Square. She packed tomato relish into paper bags, failing to hear what one woman had asked. 'I'm sorry, could you say that again?'

'I was wondering how long you'd been here?' The woman indicated her friend. 'We have a jaunt every five years to catch up with our workmates.' She laughed. 'Or who's wanting a change of scenery.'

'Right. I was here five years ago, but perhaps not always operational.' Rosemary handed the bag over. 'Are there more of you from your work?'

'Oh, yes.' The woman nodded towards the Square. 'I'm Milly. This is Lucy.' She indicated her friend looking at the shelves of tomato pickle. 'Karen, Rebecca and Barbara came in yesterday.' She pointed. 'And you can see Kerry and Colin there.'

Rosemary shifted to see out the window. 'Do you mean the men standing with Jasper?'

'I'm not sure who Jasper is.' Milly turned to Lucy but the other woman shook her head.

'Are you staying in Mulbury?'

'Close by.'

'What was your workplace?'

'We worked in the city with vintage car parts in The Jalopy Factory. Have you heard of it?'

'No.'

'You will, once Andrew publishes his history on it.' Milly smiled. 'We always make our reunions somewhere other than the city because so many of us have moved away. We stay in all sorts of places, some of us making it a real holiday, and get together for days like this.' She took her bag and shook her head. 'I must say, Kerry was happy to be coming to Mulbury. He says he found some family connections to the place, which is marvellous. It might settle him down.'

'The tall man is Kerry?'

'That's right. He's the one with his hand on the shoulder of that fellow you called Jasper.'

Rosemary watched as Jasper ducked away from the man and walked back over the road. She heard the heavy sigh of the bookshop door as he opened it, but then...nothing.

The women started walking out, chatting and pointing to the shelves as they went. Rosemary heard snippets of 'strawberry jam is my favourite' and 'seeds stick in my teeth'. She hurried after them. 'Do you think Kerry needs settling down?'

Milly smiled back at Rosemary. 'Oh yes.'

'Why?'

Lucy held the door open as Milly considered Rosemary's question. 'Kerry is a restless soul with what's euphemistically called a chequered past.'

'Meaning?'

Milly's face darkened. 'Kerry's is not my tale to tell, although I'm hoping Andrew's book may show him up. I will say this, though.' She took the door as her friend exited and turned to talk softly. 'Bad things happen to good people.' She hesitated before leaving the shop, the door swinging closed slowly. Rosemary caught her last words just before the latch clicked. 'So hopefully the reverse is true, also?'

SIX

At six-thirty exactly, Rosemary heard a tap on the front window. She glanced at her watch then leaned down from the ladder to wave at Mrs Lionel. 'Be there in a moment,' she yelled through the glass.

The older woman nodded. 'Fixing the bell?' she called back.

'Trying. The old knocker is still missing.'

'Can't you find it?'

'I've looked everywhere but no luck so I've made a new one.'

Bell-fixing was within the scope of Rosemary's talents, or so she had thought, but so far, the new bell knocker refused to swing freely, instead hanging stiffly down as if frozen. She had tried wool and wire, string and ribbon, but something was wrong with the weight of the improvised pendulum which had been hastily shaped by gluing four fifty-cent coins together. Rosemary tapped the bell roughly, and it swung uselessly back and forth, silent as night.

Mrs Lionel tapped on the window again. 'Leave it now. This is heavy.' She held up a pot.

Rosemary clambered quickly down and moved the ladder so she could step through the door, pulling it closed behind her. 'Why do you have that? It's Honey's turn to cook Monday night dinner, and she has my berry crumble.'

'I know. She'll do a fine job and your crumble will be delicious.' Mrs Lionel handed the pot to Rosemary. 'Carry it for me, dear. It's not for Honey. It's for Robert.'

'Robert?'

'Yes, Robert. Robert Sparkling.'

'I know which Robert you mean.'

Mrs Lionel grinned. 'Then don't look so surprised.'

Rosemary lifted the lid of the pot, getting a whiff of summer rich tomatoes and olives. 'He's lucky.'

'Isn't he?' Mrs Lionel took Rosemary's arm and steered her along. 'No, not really. We're bartering services.'

They were level with The Read Mulbury's doorway. Rosemary forced herself not to look in. 'What's Robert giving you in return?'

'He's helping me with my products.'

'Because Ronnie doesn't have the time anymore?'

'That's right. Ronnie has a lot of things on his plate with the tearoom and little Tallulah, and Robert is a big help.'

The bookshop door sighed open and Jasper stepped out, accidentally knocking Rosemary. He caught her as she stumbled to hold the pot upright. 'Sorry,' he said, gripping her by the waist.

For a moment, it was as it had been. Jasper's kind face was creased in worry as he held her, dark eyes wide. Then something came over him, a wave that wiped his face blank and Rosemary found herself staring at a man she barely knew. His sharp haircut didn't help. It revealed a bony head, pale ears, and a long, thin neck studded with shaving rash.

Jasper let her go and stood with his fists by his side.

'Jasper,' said Mrs Lionel, a sight strain in her voice. 'How lovely to see you, dear. It's been such a while, and you haven't come to see me yet.' She cleared her throat and her voice strengthened. 'Or Snowy.'

Jasper swallowed. 'How is he? Has he...?'

'Snowy is fine. He has a new friend in Cuddles and he loves our couches almost as much as yours. He shares Rosemary's with Sunny until the cat gets grumpy which is why he's currently with me.' Mrs Lionel stepped close to Jasper and took one of his hands. 'Snowy misses you, you know. I walk him past here on the way to Honey B's Teas and he whines.' She put her other hand on his. 'We miss you, too.'

Jasper nodded, not looking at either woman. 'I thought I'd get him. Bring him home.'

'You're home now, dear?'

He swallowed. 'For the time being.'

'What does that mean?' Rosemary hadn't meant to sound so sharp. 'Are you leaving Mulbury?'

Jasper didn't answer. Instead, he turned, tearing his hands from Mrs Lionel's, and pulled the bookstore door closed behind him. 'Can I get Snowy now?'

'No, dear.'

He blinked at Mrs Lionel.

'It's Monday dinner at Honey and Ronnie's. You can come along and fetch Snowy later.'

'I'm not going to Monday dinner.'

'Well,' said Mrs Lionel. 'I am.'

'I could just go in and get him while you're at dinner.'

'The door is locked.'

Rosemary tucked the cooking pot under one arm. She didn't believe Mrs Lionel for a second: the door to The Green Mulbury wasn't locked until Mrs Lionel went to bed. Nonetheless, the older woman held Jasper's look until he blinked and gestured uselessly. 'I'll get him tomorrow, then.'

Mrs Lionel's face softened. 'Come to dinner, Jasper,' she said softly. 'We've all missed you, not just Snowy. You don't have to talk about what happened while you were away. Your presence is sorely wanted, dear.'

Jasper ran his hand along his head. Normally, that action would smooth a strand of long, mischievous hair behind an ear, but all it did now was to make him look awkward. Rosemary felt a twang of pain somewhere in her chest. 'Come on, Jasper,' she said. 'Come to dinner. Honey's cooked tomato tarts.'

The door of the bookshop burst open and a large man stepped out. 'Ah, there you are, son. Chatting to the ladies? Of course, of course. Chip off the old block.' He slapped Jasper hard on the back, making him lurch forward.

'Kerry,' said Rosemary.

'Yes, what, Kerry? That's my name. And how, beautiful lady, did you know that?'

'Your work colleague told me.'

'Work colleague? Which one, sweetheart?'

'Milly.' Rosemary narrowed her eyes. '*Sweetheart.*'

Her brittle tone wasn't lost on Jasper as it seemed to be on Kerry. Jasper's face colour deepened. 'Kerry is my father,' he said so quietly Mrs Lionel strained forward to hear him.

Kerry grinned and slapped Jasper again, this time leaving his heavy hand on Jasper's shoulder, gripping it tightly so Jasper's shirt rumpled. 'Yes, he's found me, the scoundrel. Thought I'd got away with it.' He shook Jasper briefly. 'Only kidding! It's not that I was hiding.'

Rosemary studied Jasper's face, which was pale once more. 'What was it then?'

'Oh, time goes too swiftly, don't you think? Jasper's mother and I were close once, and then not. Cycle of life, and all that.'

Rosemary thought back to when Jasper had first discovered the lovely man who'd raised him wasn't his father. His mother was a famous writer incognito, and the dedication in her books was directed at someone unknown, Jasper's biological father. 'Kerry, not Kesper?'

'Kerry, Kerry, yes, that's what they call me. Well, to my face, anyway. Heaven knows what they say behind my back!' Kerry chuckled and leaned towards Rosemary. 'But never Kesper. Where did that come from? Your name is Rosemary, isn't it, love? I bet you get called Rosie.'

'Never,' said Rosemary.

'Ah, well, you should! You're a sweet rose, I can tell straight away.'

Rosemary the rose felt her thorns prickle. Beside her, Mrs Lionel was trying to smile warmly at Jasper, but he wouldn't look at her. Kerry still gripped his shoulder, painfully, by the way Jasper grimaced every now and then. Rosemary hugged the pot to her side, reached over to Jasper and tugged him out of Kerry's grip. 'Nice to meet you, Kerry. Jasper is coming with us tonight. He probably forgot to tell you but this is a pre-arranged event.' Rosemary smiled, all teeth. 'Have a pleasant evening yourself.'

Kerry frowned, his round, jovial face collapsing into dark shadows, but Rosemary kept her hold on Jasper and marched him to the tearoom door. 'Get in,' she hissed, and Jasper pushed the squealing door open and went inside. She held the door for Mrs Lionel, nodded once at Kerry standing on the pavement, and followed her friends in. For good measure, she locked the door behind her.

'Jasper, darling!'

Rakisha was the first to fling herself at Jasper, wrapping cotton-clad arms around him, and burying her head into his chest. Her long, fly-away curls drifted into his face, and he clawed them away. 'Hello, Rakisha.'

'Look, everyone! It's darling Jasper! He's back without Silkie.'

'Your sister has her own life, Rakisha.' Jasper patted her on the back. 'We parted company straight after leaving here.'

'Yes.' Rakisha's voice was muffled against his shirt. 'I do understand, darling. My little house feels empty but I can't fill it with Silkie's rampaging aura.' She pulled back. 'It's so glorious to see you, darling!'

One by one, the others seated at the tables arranged together stood and gathered around Jasper. Roman's smile was nearly buried by his moustaches, but he put both hands on Jasper's face and heartily kissed left cheek then right cheek. Jules followed, lightly stroking Jasper's arms before delivering a softer version of her husband's greeting. Patti bounced around him, her rockabilly dress slapping at Jasper's legs while Gerry shook his hand heartily. Robert Sparkling stretched across the fray to shake Jasper's hand, but Kelly Flanagan angled her way through, shoving Rakisha aside to give Jasper a full bodied, longer-than-essential, clutching hug. Even Cuddles barrelled up to him and nosed his way in for a pat before heading back to his mat behind the shop counter.

'Welcome, Jasper,' said Honey when the small crowd went back to their seats. 'It's great to see you.'

Jasper glanced around the tearoom. 'Look what you've done here. It's wonderful.'

'Honey did it all,' said Ronnie, standing beside his wife and slipping his hand into hers. 'Well, I helped put the teapots on that shelf.' He indicated the long shelf near the ceiling where an array of decorative teapots lined the wall. 'Oh, and I painted. I'm not good at it, but I got it done.'

'It's great, Ronnie.' Jasper smiled briefly. 'All that with a baby as well.'

'We had a lot of help.' Honey indicated the people at the table.

'That's right,' said a voice from the kitchen. 'She certainly needed it.' Pearl appeared in the doorway. 'Fancy taking on a new business with a new baby! Ridiculous. She should have been stopped.' Pearl glared at Rosemary.

Rosemary gave the same toothy smile she'd given Kerry—the one without mirth—to Pearl. The woman seemed oblivious. She patted the tight apron attached to her waist and turned on her heels. 'Honey Blossom.'

Honey let Ronnie's hand go. 'Looks like I'm wanted.'

'Do you need a hand?' asked Rosemary.

Honey looked back over her shoulder at her mother. 'I wouldn't put you through it, Mum.'

Ronnie turned a puzzled face to Rosemary. 'What did she mean by that?'

'Nothing you need worry about.' Rosemary pulled out an empty chair and sat next to Mrs Lionel. 'Is Tallulah sleeping?'

'Yes.' Ronnie turned to Jasper. 'Do you want to see her? She's gorgeous.'

Jasper nodded. 'I'd like that very much.'

Rosemary watched as the men left the room. Jasper was fond of children, she knew that, but the haste at which he followed Ronnie, almost pushing the younger man out of the way, was more to do with what he was leaving behind than what he was going to see.

'He's worried we'll pry,' said Jules, lifting her glass and pointing it towards the kitchen.

'We would not ask Jasper anything that was going to cause him discomfort,' said Roman. 'We are not that pretty.'

'Petty, I think you mean.' Jules drained her glass and set it down. 'Although, I am curious. He came back with his father, so the rumour goes. The father, says another rumour, is nothing like Jasper.'

'But he didn't grow up with the man.' Kelly waved her glass in front of Roman, who filled it obligingly with a sharp Chardonnay. 'We can't expect they would be that similar. Although genes do win out, I hear. Perhaps we're looking at what Jasper is to become?'

'I haven't spent long in the father's company,' said Mrs Lionel. 'However, I don't think Jasper will be like him ever.'

Kelly waggled her glass, making the wine splosh from side to side. 'Made a good impression, did he, Mrs L?'

'He made *an* impression, dear.'

The sound of clashing crockery made them pause. 'Everything's fine,' called Honey from the kitchen.

'It will be,' said Pearl, also hidden from view. 'Once I sort things out here.'

'Oh dear,' said Patti. 'That doesn't sound good.'

Muffled mumbling from the kitchen seemed to agree.

'How long is Pearl staying?' asked Mrs Lionel of Rosemary as the others resumed their conversation around her.

'Long enough,' said Rosemary. 'Honey is being very patient, mainly because Ronnie doesn't notice tension thickening the air. She doesn't want to upset him.'

'As I suppose we shouldn't upset Jasper with not

quickly warming to his father.' Mrs Lionel shook her head. 'I really must give Kerry more time before I judge him.'

'Kerry.'

'Yes, Kerry. That's his name, isn't it?'

Rosemary leaned forwards. 'Do you remember the wording of the dedication Jasper's mother made in her books?'

'No, dear, I do not.'

'I do. "To H, I. J, K." Jasper thought the K stood for Chris, the father that brought him up. Then he discovered the hero of his mother's books was Captain Kesper.'

'What are you implying?'

'Kerry had no idea about the name Kesper.'

'No, he didn't. Should he?'

'Yes, if he's ever read any of T. G. G. Duncan's books. It's convenient, isn't it, that Kerry turns up after watching Adelia Lochard's film and that his name starts with K?'

'Convenient, or just circumstance. How else would he realise that T. G. G. Duncan had a son?'

'How indeed.' Rosemary folded her arms. 'None of us except Jasper has seen the film. We don't know what's in it.'

Mrs Lionel shrugged. 'Easily solved.'

'Yes.' Rosemary smiled at her friend. 'Feel like a trip to Big Town to the picture theatre?'

Mrs Lionel smiled back. 'I'm free when you are.'

SEVEN

Monday dinner was a lovely, but tense, evening. Rosemary came home with a wonderfully full stomach from two servings of tomato tart with mustard sauce, and a large helping of berry crumble with double cream from the dairy cows at Justin's farm. Her head, though, stayed troubled from Jasper's lack of communication and Pearl's over-communication. Jasper had barely said two words, and no one had pushed him. He ate in silence, raised his glass quietly when toasting the initial success of Honey B's Teas, and answered Roman's cheery queries about whether he was enjoying the last long days of summer in monosyllables. Pearl, on the other hand, couldn't shut up.

'Such a big endeavour,' Pearl started. 'A new business with a new baby.'

'I'm coping.' Honey had kept chewing her tart. 'I have Ronnie.'

'Ronnie? I know he's my son, but he's not the brightest diamond in the necklace, is he? Good boy that he is, but...' she'd leaned closer to Rakisha '...rather dull.'

Rakisha had blinked at Pearl, before putting a hand

studded with silver rings on her arm. 'Oh no, darling. Ronnie is a magnificent person! See how he shines? He is gold, darling, gold! Better than diamonds, don't you think, darling?'

Rosemary had never loved Rakisha more, and by the look on her daughter's face, neither had Honey. Nonetheless, Pearl had missed any life lessons about noticing non-verbal clues from others, and continued to feed her thoughts about Ronnie, and the business, and the state of Mulbury in general into the conversation. Rosemary had felt Mrs Lionel's restraining hand on her arm more than once.

'I wonder why she's so negative?'

Although the question had been directed at the cat rhetorically, Sunny lifted her nose in response. *She doesn't have a cat,* the ginger tabby seemed to say as she leaned forward to rub her head on Rosemary's leg.

'Of course.' Rosemary bent to sweep the cat into her arms. 'No one could be pessimistic if they shared a house with an exquisite creature like you.'

Sunny purred loudly. *Precisely.*

As Rosemary prepared for bed, she listened intently for noises next door. Jasper had left after dessert, which meant that he could be already asleep. The quiet was disturbing, though. It was as if Jasper had not come back to Mulbury and that, she decided, would be worse than the current situation.

***

TUESDAY DAWNED BRIGHT AND HOT. When Rosemary opened The Preserved Mulbury, she propped open the door to let fresh air in, scowling at the silent bell as she did. She fetched the step ladder again and was about to climb up to have another go at the pendulum when a voice caught her. 'Excuse me, but could you tell me the way to Patricia's?'

A woman stood outside the door. Rosemary recognised her from yesterday. 'Milly, isn't it? Patricia's won't be open.'

'Oh.' Milly held up a map with dark blue edges. 'That's fine. It's the start of our jolly jaunt.'

'Jolly jaunt?'

She held the map higher. 'You know. A treasure hunt, like a town trawl. When you go from place to place in a town looking for objects. There's always a prize for the person who finds something truly original.' Milly shook the map. 'We are the Jaunty Jalopers on account of where we used to work.'

'The Jalopy Factory.'

'Yes! Such a wonderful place, full of lovely old car parts that refurbished vehicles into very special pieces of motoring history.'

'Sounds interesting.' Rosemary indicated her blue sedan parked on the street. 'It's not quite a jalopy.'

Milly laughed. 'Hang on to it for much longer and it will be.'

Rosemary gave the car a stern look before focusing on the woman again. 'You trawl towns, I see.'

'Yes, we get points for collecting items from each place marked on the map.' The woman folded the map and put it in her pocket. 'Colin made it up but I don't know what he based it on. The shop he's marked as Patricia's is called something else now.'

'Honey B's Teas.'

'That's it. Only I think that will ruin the game. Colin's making us collect an upcycled handkerchief from Patricia's. But now that Patricia's is a tearoom, it doesn't make sense.'

'Patricia's is along the road here.' Rosemary pointed to her left. 'You can't miss it. Biggest building there. Look for the sandwich board on the footpath.'

'Thank you.' Milly held out her hand.

Rosemary shook it. 'I'm Rosemary Exeter.'

'Thank you, Rosemary. You have a very fine shop.' Milly peered inside The Preserved Mulbury. 'Do you make all that produce yourself?'

'Yes.'

'Marvellous.' Milly sighed. 'I would like to do something creative like that myself, perhaps with plants. I'm a keen gardener.'

'Then do it.'

Milly's eyes widened. 'But I barely get a chance to do my own garden, I've got so many other things on my plate looking after my big old house.'

'You always will have things on your plate.' Rosemary studied the woman before her, noticing the double rings of pale blue under her eyes. 'You need to take the plunge or you'll be dead before you know it.'

'Well,' said a calm voice from the footpath. 'We're all on that track.' Mrs Lionel glared at Rosemary before smiling kindly at Milly. 'Forgive Rosemary. She's as blunt as a hammerhead shark.'

Milly shook her head before chuckling at Rosemary. 'Blunt you may be, but you're right. The years are catching up with us all. Why, some of the Jalopers are nearly eighty years old now!' She shook her head again. 'I'm not that old, but if I don't start to do things for myself, I'll spend the rest of my life doing the bidding of others, including the never-ending task of keeping an old house.'

Rosemary gave a curt nod. 'That's the way.'

Milly raised her map and walked off towards Patricia's.

'Honestly, Rosemary.' Mrs Lionel patted Rosemary's arm. 'Some restraint would be a good idea.'

'She wasn't offended.'

'Lucky for you.' Mrs Lionel watched as Milly cut through the Square and disappeared around the corner of The Sweet Potato. 'What's she doing, anyway?'

'Going on a treasure hunt, apparently. She belongs to a group of ex-workers who find it amusing to spend their time visiting towns and making up competitions. A jolly jaunt, she called it.'

'It sounds very collegial.'

'Kerry is among them.'

'Goodness, can't imagine him on a jolly anything.' Mrs Lionel chuckled. 'Oh, I am getting grumpy in my older age! Are our shops on the map?'

'I don't know.'

'Just in case, I'm going back to check my stock. They might be after something specific so I need to know what I've got.'

Rosemary frowned. 'You know exactly what you have or don't have on your shelves.'

'Yes, well.' Mrs Lionel tucked her cardigan around her shoulders. 'I best be prepared. And I've got to pack up Snowy's things.'

'Ah. I get it.'

'Get what, dear?'

'You're really waiting for Jasper.'

Mrs Lionel tipped her head at Rosemary before walking away, calling back over her shoulder. 'Well, aren't we all?'

It was true. Rosemary climbed the ladder to the bell, contemplating why it was taking her so long to fix the troublesome thing. It would be more sensible to take it down and work on it at the shop counter, but that would not give her the viewing advantage of being up a ladder at the front of the shop. She untied the makeshift pendulum again, listening intently for any action from next door.

Nothing eventuated anywhere for quite a while. Just before lunch, a car pulled up, spilling the three women Milly had named Karen, Barbara and Rebecca onto the pavement under the veranda. Behind them, another car pulled in. The man Rosemary recognised as Colin stepped out, along with Lucy who had visited her shop with Milly. They joined the others who were starting to argue furiously, each clutching a Jaunty Jaloper's map. The noise rose as if a flock of corellas were flying overhead.

Rosemary came down the ladder and packed it away, then went to her shelves to do what Mrs Lionel had said was sensible, checking the stock in case pickles were part of the visitors' jaunt. Two women headed into Honey B's Teas while Lucy and another stood a little distance away with Colin, speaking earnestly to him. He shook his head, took the map from Lucy, and gestured around at Jasper's closed shop. From the confused look on his face, it was clear he hadn't expected a few things about Mulbury.

Colin was still scratching his head when the door of The Read Mulbury flung open, sighing loudly, and Kerry stepped out. A pace behind him was Jasper, looking paler than ever despite the bright day. 'Ladies,' said Kerry, moving quickly forward to embrace both women at once. 'Lucy, Karen, gorgeous, gorgeous. You're ready for the day, I see. Good, good. Got that little map our mate Colin set up?'

Colin rolled his shoulders. 'It took quite a lot of time to create it, Kerry.'

'Did it now? Did it indeed?' Kerry gave the women he

was holding another squeeze, making Lucy cringe and Karen giggle, and let them go. 'But you look puzzled, my friend. Is there an issue?'

'The map doesn't show what the town is like.' Lucy held her map to Kerry. 'It's not Colin's fault. I know how hard he worked on it.'

'Yes, yes, I guess you would. You had to do all the household chores while he was creating it!'

Lucy stepped back and waved the map again. 'We can't find Patricia's and the bookshop is shut. Andrew won't like that. Although maybe he's not coming? I haven't seen him yet.'

Karen rolled her eyes. 'Andrew doesn't always do what he should, does he? He's probably hightailed it somewhere else.'

Lucy shook her head. 'He wouldn't just not turn up.'

Karen studied her nails. 'Maybe he knew the bookshop was closed. It would be typical of him to go to another town where a bookshop was open.'

'We can solve the little problem with the bookshop, ladies.' Kerry turned and took Jasper by the arm. 'Here is the owner, recently back from a special treasure hunt of his own.'

'Oh,' said Colin. 'Do you do town trawls as well?'

'Not that kind of treasure hunt, Colin, old boy. Jasper here was on a hunt for his *parentage*.'

Colin frowned. 'Is there a map for that?'

From Rosemary's viewing vantage through the open shop door, the way Kerry's face darkened reminded her of how summer storm clouds could quickly cover the sun. Then he brightened, the clouds pushed away. 'No, Colin. Jasper was on the hunt for *me*. I am Jasper's long-lost father.'

There was a long beat of silence as the crowd of Jalopers studied Jasper as if he was a specimen in a museum.

'I didn't know you had any children,' said Colin. 'Did you?'

Kerry chuckled loudly. 'Colin, Colin, Colin. We all did things in our younger day that have repercussions later in life, eh?' He slapped Jasper on the arm. 'Here he is, my repercussion.'

Rosemary waited for someone to protest Jasper's labelling but the group continued to stare at him. She was about to charge outside when Lucy spoke. 'How lovely,' she said unconvincingly. 'How did you find each other?'

'Oh, Jasper is famous! He's had a film made about him.'

'Not me.' Jasper's voice was husky. 'About my mother.'

'About Jasper's mother but more so about Jasper. He was *discovered*, as they say. In coming to film a bunch of old clothes, Adelia Lochard found out Jasper was the son of a famous writer and he didn't know it!'

'You didn't know your mother or your father?' said Colin.

'He knew his mother but not how others knew her. Poor lad.' Kerry thumped Jasper again. 'His family had lots of secrets and he was the last to know. Luckily, I saw the film and came to his rescue.' He chuckled again. 'Jasper, son of T. G. G. Duncan and son of mine. Extraordinary!'

'Adelia Lochard is an amazing documentary director,' said Lucy. 'You are very lucky to have her as a filmmaker.'

'It didn't feel lucky at the time,' said Jasper so quietly Rosemary could barely hear him. 'It felt like being stalked.'

'Ah, Jasper, you card!' Kerry gave Jasper a last thump then plunged his hands into his trouser pockets. 'Anyway, ladies.' He swept his arm out to encompass the women of the Jaunty Jalopers and winked at Colin. 'Jasper's shop is reopening today so you'll have a chance to fulfil your treasure hunt dreams.'

'That's good,' said Colin, glancing down at his map as Kerry sauntered into the bookshop. 'This one was Andrew's idea. He's such a bookaholic.' He shook the paper. 'We need to buy a book from the classics section that's different to everyone else's. The older the better. That's so Andrew ends up with lots of books to read because he knows no one else will read anything they collect.'

'Swings and roundabouts,' said Karen, rummaging through her shoulder bag and plucking a nail file from a yellow manicure kit. 'We'll all end up with a bunch of something from this because I don't see you wanting to keep the organic seed neck warmer from The Sweet Potato.' She filed briskly at a pristinely shaped nail and slid the kit into her bag while blinking coyly at Colin.

Two women wearing the same velveteen leisure suits and garish green running shoes as Karen came out of Honey B's Teas clutching take-away coffees. They joined the group, handing Karen a large cup, and laughed as Colin scowled. 'True, I'd prefer a scarf if I had a cold neck,' he said, and peered around. 'Where is Andrew? Lucy rang him but he didn't answer. Barbara, have you seen him around here?'

'I haven't seen him today. He's probably holed up somewhere writing that ridiculous memoir of his,' said the tallest woman of the crowd who sported a bleached updo and a scowl. 'And we would see him if he was around, wouldn't we?'

'Oh, yes.' Lucy smiled. 'Andrew can be spotted a mile away.'

'Why is that?' asked Jasper. 'Does he carry a book around with him?'

'Probably. But that's not the reason.'

'It's what he wears,' said Barbara. 'Andrew Valencia always has an orange blazer on. It's his little joke on his name. Valencia oranges, get it?' She rolled her eyes. 'Quaint, but tiresome. You'd think with that little eccentricity, the man would be entertaining. No, he isn't.'

'Not at all,' said Karen.

'Totally, utterly boring,' said Rebecca, plucking an invisible thread from her sleeve. 'No fun at all, even when fun is right under his nose.'

'Or sitting at the desk next to him.' Rebecca giggled. 'Or going for a walk with him.'

'Rebecca,' said Barbara, snorting. 'You're such a card!'

'Shall we get our next treasure?' Karen said, holding her cup up to point at The Read Mulbury. 'We'll get this dull one over and done with.'

Rosemary left the Jalopers as they poured into the bookshop behind Jasper, stepping down from the ladder as the bookshop door sighed closed, and reaching for her phone. When she got Geoffrey, she turned her back to the door.

'What is it, Rosemary?'

'I've found out the name of your John Doe,' she whispered. 'It's Andrew Valencia.'

EIGHT

Rosemary kept to herself inside The Preserved Mulbury while she imagined the police going to work on the identity of the drowned man. Outside, the Jaunty Jalopers went on their way from business to business, clearly revelling in the hunt, going by the amount of laughter accompanying them. Jasper stayed within The Read Mulbury and now Rosemary could hear the familiar sounds of the bookstore coming to life. The blinds on the front windows went up, a trolly of tattered books was wheeled out to the pavement as giveaways, and the vacuum cleaner roared briefly.

In Jasper's absence, the Mulburians had kept his online book sales going, but The Read Mulbury was primarily a bricks-and-mortar shopfront with very low traffic on the internet. If the residents of Mulbury had a dollar for every time a disappointed customer had turned away from the closed doors, the whole town would be paved in gold. Mulbury needed a bookstore. 'More specifically,' Rosemary said to a graceful Sunny perched on the shop counter, 'Mulbury needs that particular bookstore owner.'

Sunny blinked. *Or you do,* the flick of her tail seemed to say.

Rosemary rubbed vigorously at a sticky patch on a jar of apple jelly. 'I survived without him for three months,' she said crossly.

Sunny said nothing but lay down, tucking her paws neatly under her chin.

The three brightly coloured women from the Jalopers came in and out of The Preserved Mulbury to buy jars of zucchini pickles and boysenberry jam. Rosemary wondered what the treasure hunt sheet had said about her shop until Rebecca left her map on the shop counter. Next to The Preserved Mulbury it read: *Are you in a pickle or a jam? Choose both to spread on bread.* There was an arrow pointing towards Franco's Patisserie, where the busy man sold special sourdough loaves.

The only thriving business that wasn't on the map was Mulbury Feeds, a clear omission on the part of Colin, who probably didn't realise that the animal produce store was now a garden centre, albeit of the pea straw and mushroom compost kind. Had they known the work colleagues would be coming and buying so much, Holly and Hannah could have done a display of pots or seedlings or indoor plants.

As if she could hear Rosemary's thoughts, Holly Hubbard pushed open the silent door and stormed up to the shop counter. 'Rosemary,' she said. 'Your bell is still broken.'

'Yes.' Rosemary took in the unruliness of Holly's short ponytail and the streaks of dirt down her shirt. 'Did you come here to tell me that?'

'What? No!' Holly ran a hand over the top of her head then yanked the hair tie out. 'Everything is a mess.'

'I assume you're not talking only about your hair?'

'My hair?' Holly glanced at the hair tie in her palm. 'I couldn't really care less about my hair. It's Heather.'

'Right.'

'You've heard?'

'I've heard she's working a lot.'

'A lot? She's working too much. She hasn't-'

'-done any taxidermy for ages.'

'You know that?'

'It's another thing I've been told.'

'Okay. Good. Well.' Holly scratched her head then scooped her hair back into a ponytail that was worse than before. 'It's got worse.'

'How so?'

'Hannah thinks it's my fault. I don't think it's anyone's fault. It just *is*.'

'What is just *is*? Why has it got worse?'

Holly put both her hands flat on the counter and leaned forward. 'It's worse because Robert wants to put someone on to help us.'

'That sounds sensible.'

'But, Rosemary, it's our family business!'

'Owned by Robert.'

'Yes, but, well, maybe....'

'Not maybe. He bought it.'

'I know that!' Holly sighed. 'I know that,' she said more quietly. 'I also thought this might happen.' She looked up at Rosemary, a glint of a tear at the corner of one eye. 'And I'm being ridiculous. It is his business and he can do what he likes but he never suggests anything that doesn't come from us.'

'Until now.'

'Yeah. Until now.'

'Holly.' Rosemary stretched out her hand and tapped

the younger woman's arm. 'He's doing this to help you. But if you're unhappy about it, you need to talk to him.'

'I'm talking to you.'

'I'm not Robert.'

'No.' Holly touched Rosemary's sleeve briefly. 'But you help us.'

Rosemary thought for a moment. 'This isn't about Robert hiring someone to help you, is it?'

Holly straightened. 'What? Yes, it is.'

'Partly, I imagine. It's more that you're leaving Mulbury Feeds and you don't know what to expect.'

Holly's mouth opened slightly but the retort that would have normally rushed out didn't appear. 'How do you know?'

'Holly, it's been in your eyes well before you met Toffee. And now you have him, you don't want to be tied down to the store.'

The younger woman took her hands from the counter and plunged them into her shorts pocket. 'Toffee has a transfer.'

'They're moving him away from Geoffrey's unit?'

Holly nodded. 'Yes. He's got a chance for a promotion but it isn't in this state. It's 3000 kilometres away west.'

'That's a long way.'

'It's about as far as Dad is away but in a different direction and you know how much Dad visits.'

'I haven't seen him since he sold Mulbury Feeds.'

'Yep, that's right. It will be difficult going such a long way away.'

'But you will go with Toffee.'

Holly dipped her head. 'Yes. But I'm torn! I don't want to leave Hannah and Heather. I'm their...'

'Big sister, who has the right to make her own life.' Rosemary gave Holly a small smile. 'They will be okay, you know.'

'I know, I know. I've gone over this in my head for so long I know all the pros and cons.'

'If you don't take risks, there are no rewards.'

Holly looked up, matching her smile to Rosemary's. 'That's profound.'

Rosemary shrugged. 'Mrs Lionel said it to me once.'

At the mention of their friend, Holly's smile dropped. 'How can I leave Mrs Lionel? What if she...?'

'Mrs Lionel is fit and well,' said Rosemary firmly. 'She may be my oldest friend—literally—but she is also one of my fittest. She would be horrified if you delayed going until she was-'

'Don't say it!' Holly clutched at the sides of her head. 'You'll make me change my mind.'

'Your mind is made up then.'

Holly let her hands drop. 'Yes, it is. Toffee's leaving next week and I said I'd follow.'

'Right. Does Robert know? Theoretically, you have to give him a certain amount of weeks' notice. He's your employer.'

'I do?' Holly frowned. 'All these rules and regulations when you work for someone else.'

'Robert may already know, which is why he's thinking of hiring you some help.'

'I think it's more that he knows Heather is spending so much time at Patricia's.' Holly paused then looked at Rosemary earnestly. 'Oh, and Rosemary?'

'Yes?'

'You would let me know if I had to come back quickly. For any reason. You would, wouldn't you?'

'If that's what you want.'

'Yes. Yes, it is.' Holly's smile was wobbly. 'It would help if I knew that.'

'Then of course.'

'Okay. Right.' Holly stood straight, her face serious. 'Off I go to think about how to tell the others. Thanks for your help.'

'I only said what you knew anyway.'

Holly walked towards the door, turning slightly to say, 'I know, but I needed to hear it.' She reached the door and pulled it open. 'You know, you really need to fix this bell. It's too strange not to hear it jangling.'

Rosemary sighed as Holly disappeared along the path to Mulbury Feeds. It wasn't the comment about the bell, it was in anticipation of Holly's conversation with her sisters. Hannah would be upset but not surprised, but Heather could react terribly. The younger Hubbard sister felt things deeply, and those depths were sometimes unfathomable.

The cluster of Jalopers had moved into the Square to partake of fine cuisine from Franco's Patisserie and eclectic fare from The Sweet Potato, Kerry joining them with a bag full of goodies from Honey's tearoom. For the less adventurous, there was always Mullings of Mulbury where Kelly served stock standard slices and decent coffee. Or so Rosemary was told. She'd have to be three-quarters dead to buy a coffee from Kelly Flanagan.

In the relative quiet of Goldmarket Road, the door of The Read Mulbury sighed open and Jasper appeared in the view through the window. He swung a dog leash from one hand as he walked past The Preserved Mulbury without a glance inside. Rosemary hesitated, then shot after him. 'Jasper,' she said.

He stopped but didn't turn. His back was narrow and familiar, but Rosemary still couldn't reconcile his short hair.

From behind, the hair was close-shaven until halfway up his head where longer strands of black curled slightly. As she watched, his shoulders lifted slightly as if warding off a blow and she had to resist running over to him to put an arm over them.

'Jasper,' she said softly. 'What's going on?'

She didn't expect an answer but he stepped around until he faced the window display of cheery berry jams arranged on a pink satin runner Patti had created out of a pillowcase. 'I found my father,' he whispered to the jars.

'Apparently.' Rosemary stepped down onto the pavement. 'He's an interesting man.'

Jasper nodded once. 'He found me.'

'I heard that.'

Jasper looked at her. She tried not to show how shocked she was, but his eyes were dull and his cheeks were pale as milk. He blinked slowly. 'I should be complete.'

Rosemary went to his side and took his arm. 'Jasper, something is terribly wrong. What is it?'

'I should be...'

She shook his arm slightly. 'You should be what? Happy? Resigned? Satisfied? Maybe all those *wants* were in your head when you left Mulbury, but I don't think that's where you're at.' She clutched him harder. 'Jasper, this is *wrong*. You can feel that.'

He dropped his head. 'It must be right.'

Rosemary squeezed his arm and let it go. 'Why? Just because he says he's your father-'

'He is, Rosemary. He is. He can prove it.'

'How?'

'He-'

A door shrieked open and Honey came belting out of Honey B's Teas. 'Mum! Come here!'

Rosemary ran to her daughter. 'What is it, Honey? Is Tallulah all right?'

'Yes, yes. Tallulah's fine.' Honey grabbed Rosemary's arm and pulled her towards Honey B's Teas. 'But Pearl isn't. Come on.'

Rosemary glanced back at Jasper only to see the clip of the dog leash disappear into The Green Mulbury before Honey hauled her into the tearoom.

Pearl lay under a table clutching a teapot to her chest.

NINE

The tearoom was relatively empty after its deluge of morning tea consumers. Only Gerry sat at one of the tables, a blue geometrically patterned teacup held poised before his mouth as he stared at Pearl, Cuddles beside him quietly whining. Ronnie crouched near his mother and tugged at the teapot in her hands. 'Come on, Mum,' he said gently. 'Give it to me and I'll help you up.'

'No, Ronald.' Pearl's voice was high. 'It's too valuable to be here.'

'I understand,' said Ronnie, glancing at Honey and shaking his head slightly. 'I've said you can have it. You can have any of the teapots in here. Cups as well, if you like.'

Pearl's hand whitened over the pot. 'I want this one.'

'And you've got it. Now.' Ronnie shuffled back a bit. 'Can I help you up?'

'I'm quite comfortable here, thank you.' Pearl sat the teapot upright on her chest. 'Leave me, Ronald.'

Ronnie backed away and stood up. 'I tried,' he said to his wife.

'Yes, I see that. I tried, too.' Honey took Rosemary's hand briefly. 'You have a go, Mum.'

Rosemary knelt but kept back from Pearl. 'How did she get down there?'

'She sort of dived.' Ronnie rubbed his head, making his sandy hair stick out. 'I had just sat the teapot on the bench and she grabbed it. Next thing I know, she was under the table.'

'She doesn't look comfortable,' said Gerry, lowering his cup. 'That floor is hard.'

Rosemary slid towards Pearl. 'Are you comfortable under there?'

Pearl turned her head slightly. 'No. I'm not.' She moved her head back. 'That's not the point.'

Rosemary beckoned to Ronnie. 'A pillow, Ronnie. Make it two. Let's make your mother comfortable.'

Ronnie ran to the lounge and came back with two fluffy cushions. 'How are these?' he said, handing them to Rosemary.

'Let's see.' Rosemary tucked them under Pearl's head. 'Better?'

'Thank you. Much better.'

'Would you like a blanket as well?'

'No, thank you. I'm quite warm.'

Rosemary shifted so she was leaning on one hand. 'Tell me more about the point.'

'What point?'

'You said before that this was not the point. So, what is the point?'

Pearl kept her gaze to the underside of the table. 'Why should I tell you?'

'Because I'm listening.'

At that, Pearl rolled her head on the cushion and locked

eyes briefly with Rosemary before turning back. 'The point,' she said, 'is that this teapot came from my café.' She held the pot away from her chest for a moment, exposing its retro blue floral pattern. 'I gave it to Ronald and Honey Blossom as a wedding present.'

'I remember.'

'So, you see the point.'

'You don't think it should be in the tearoom.'

'It was a gift. You have to keep precious possessions safe.'

'I'm sure Ronnie and Honey will put it back in their kitchen for family use only.'

Pearl scowled. 'How can I be sure? I won't be here forever.'

'You have my word, Mum,' said Ronnie.

'Mine, too.' Honey crouched. 'And we'll be sure to pass it down as an heirloom to Tallulah.'

Pearl tapped her finger on the pot. 'You promise to keep it safe?'

'Promise,' said Ronnie and Honey together.

Rosemary waited until Pearl gave a short nod. 'Ronnie.'

Ronnie knelt swiftly and took the teapot from his mother. 'I'm taking it into the back room straight away.' He stood awkwardly, cradling the pot. 'Then I'll help you up.'

'I don't need your help, Ronald.'

With unusual skill for such a round woman, Pearl pushed herself backward, using the cushions as a skid, until she was clear of the table. She then rolled on her side, sat up, tugged her skirt down and stood. 'Well,' she said, looking around at the near-empty tearoom and smoothing her fine hair back into its wispy bun. 'I'll start the morning's dishes.' She followed Ronnie into the living quarters.

Rosemary stood as well, scooping the cushions up and handing them to an open-mouthed Honey.

'What was that all about?' Honey said as she took them.

'Safeguarding family treasures?'

'Hardly.' Honey shook her head. 'There are half a dozen cups from Ronnie's paternal grandmother in this room, and we take good care of them.'

'No doubt you do.' Rosemary patted Honey's shoulder. 'This teapot had obvious meaning.'

'Even so, she went under the table!' Honey hugged the cushions. 'This is strait-laced Pearl we're talking about, not Rakisha who I would expect to like being under a table if only to say hello to the wood it's made from.'

'I agree. More Rakisha than Pearl.' Rosemary crossed her arms and tapped her fingers on her sleeve. 'Have you ever seen Pearl do anything like this before?'

'She's a bit nervy sometimes but I've never seen her under a table. Maybe Ronnie has.' Honey lowered the cushions. 'I'll ask him later.' She looked at Gerry. 'You won't say anything except to Patti, will you, Gerry?'

'Not a word.' Gerry wiped his mouth and stood. 'We're all able to have a little meltdown or two without deserving comment from strangers.'

'Thanks, Gerry. You are sweet.'

'So Patti tells me.' Gerry grinned broadly. 'And she should know. Thank you for the tea, Honey. I'll be going.'

'Tea and cake are on me today, Gerry.'

Gerry pushed his chair back, gave Cuddles a reassuring pat on the big dog's head, and squeezed himself through the tearoom tables to place money on the counter. 'I wouldn't hear of it, Honey. You have a business to run. My advice is to take the money when you can.' He raised his hand and made his way out.

Honey stuck the cushions under one arm and went to collect Gerry's empty cup. 'Sorry to disturb you, Mum. I saw that you were talking to Jasper. He looks frail, a bit like he was when he was sick.'

Rosemary nodded.

Honey paused on her way back to the kitchen. 'Are you alright, Mum? You must have missed Jasper a lot, and now he's back but...' She shrugged.

'I'm fine, thank you, Honey,' said Rosemary stiffly.

Honey put the cup on the counter and threw a cushion at her mother who caught it deftly. 'Don't *I'm fine* me, Mum. Go back to Jasper and talk to him. Find out what's wrong with him.' She frowned. 'He's not sick again, is he? Did you ask him?'

Rosemary threw the cushion back. 'I haven't had the chance to say more than a few sentences to him.'

'What? Go now then!' Tallulah's waking cries filtered into the tearoom and Honey turned automatically. 'I have to go. Let me know what happens.'

Rosemary made her way out of the tearoom, leaving Honey to handle the various domestic crises happening in the area behind the café. As the door closed behind her, Rosemary stood for a moment on the step. In front of her, the Square was dotted with groups of happy tourists, some sitting comfortably on the ground next to the entanglement that formed a barrier around The Exceptional Tree standing magnificently in the Square, while others occupied the chairs and tables set out in front of The Sweet Potato and Mullings. The pavement in front of the shops under the veranda was empty except for the display books near The Read Mulbury. The sun blazed in an uninterrupted blue sky, serving to make it a lazy late summer day with a stillness that hinted at the end of things.

Rosemary walked slowly past the windows of the book-shop but no one was inside. Likewise, The Preserved Mulbury stood empty except for Sunny positioned in the window. She tapped the glass in front of the ginger tabby, and Sunny lifted her nose for a moment, then went back to her vigil. Rosemary went on to The Green Mulbury and pushed the door open, setting the frog into an electronic croaking spin. Its noise didn't seem to alert anyone, and Rosemary ventured into Mrs Lionel's living area before she caught sight of her friend.

Jasper stood with Mrs Lionel and a panting Snowy on the balcony. They were looking into Mrs Lionel's yard or, Rosemary thought, maybe they were leaning on the top rail for somewhere to park their elbows. She went to the back door and slid the screen open as quietly as she could, but Snowy heard her and staggered around on his arthritic legs to wag his tail at her entrance.

'Ah, Rosemary,' said Mrs Lionel, turning away from the rail. 'Time for a cup of tea.' She put a light hand on Jasper's arm, then left him, stepping carefully into her home. 'Give me ten minutes to make a few sandwiches, too.'

Rosemary kept her eyes on Jasper. 'There's no need-'

'Ten minutes,' Mrs Lionel whispered. 'See what you can do.' She gestured at the floor—beckoning Percy inside, no doubt—and shut the screen door firmly.

Rosemary bent to pat Snowy's greying head. Jasper still had his elbows on the rail, and stared outward as if he was at sea. She walked up beside him and copied his stance. 'Are you sick?'

He made a small movement of his shoulders. 'No. Why do you ask?'

'You look sick. You're pale and thin.'

'Have you heard me coughing?'

'No.'

'Seen me breathless?'

'No.'

'Heard me groan?'

'Jasper. It was a simple question.'

Now he turned to her. 'Rosemary, I'm not sick.'

She faced him. 'Explain, then, why you seem a shadow of your normal self.'

'Do you want me to explain my curse yet again?'

Rosemary closed her eyes briefly. Jasper's fixation on his family curse was a very sore point in their relationship. 'Your curse has made you thin and pale.'

'It's contributing.'

'What's the other reason, then?'

He hesitated then went back to staring out over Mrs Lionel's clothesline.

'Jasper? Come on.'

A magpie carolled suddenly, making them both look up. Its strong warbling seemed to make Jasper's mind up. He straightened. 'The other reason is I found my father.'

'Right.' Rosemary waited.

'He's not what I thought he was.'

Rosemary pictured Kerry, his robustness and bluster. 'People are rarely what you think them to be.'

'He's not what I imagined my mother...'

Rosemary nodded. 'Your elusive mother.'

'Yes, elusive'

'Yes. Elusive and secretive. You imagined that an even more secret lover would be someone more...more what?'

Jasper gave a ghost of a smile. 'Secretive.'

'Right.'

Jasper sighed, a weary, can't-be-bothered-anymore sigh that lingered in the hot air. 'She detoured from my adoptive father who was a lovely man, gentle and kind. He brought us up without favour, which I understand for Helena and Iris, but he even loved me.'

'You are quite loveable.' As soon as she'd said that Rosemary wished she could snatch the word back. Jasper's face lit with hope which faded as she shook her head and said, 'Any family man would love you as a son, Jasper.'

He turned away from her to look across to their joined balconies. 'It's odd my mother would have had any sort of affair, cherished or not.'

'You can't know what your mother's action meant.'

'No.'

'Maybe she didn't.'

'Didn't what?'

'Have an affair.'

He glanced back at her. 'What are you talking about?'

'Kerry's not your father.'

'But he came out of the woodwork after I'd been looking for so long!' Jasper gripped the railing. 'Helena said she'd found a man who could be my father.'

'Did Helena say the man was Kerry?'

'She didn't know. She'd found this reference to a man in one of Mum's diaries where she kept her notes for her books. It was her first mention of Captain Kesper, and Helena has this vague memory of a man who used to visit. She thought maybe he was an agent of some kind or at the very least a type of salesman. Helena tried tracking him down by looking at Mum's phone book contacts. She thought she'd found a match.'

'Maybe it was a trick of Helena's? She's not always been nice to you.'

Jasper shook his head. 'She's bossy. A bully, sometimes. But I believed her and she truly sounded genuine. The contact she'd found had all the right credentials but we tried tracking him down and it was as if he'd disappeared.'

'And when did Kerry turn up?'

'After the documentary showed in the city. Adelia made me go to the premiere.' Jasper's face reddened. 'It was excruciating. The only people there were those that wanted to kowtow to Adelia. No one was interested in the story. Not that I wanted them to be.'

'Except Kerry was. Very interested.'

Jasper dropped his head. 'He approached me a few days later. He isn't the person Helena found in the phone book but I don't have any reason to believe he isn't who he said he is. I mean, what would he gain by pretending to be my father? I'm not rich or anything.'

Rosemary leaned on the rail and stared down into Mrs Lionel's garden. Her tomato plants were a riot of growth, studded with fleshy red tomatoes perfect for sauces. 'He wants you to do something,' she said finally, pushing away from the balcony's edge. 'I heard you arguing.'

Jasper kept his head down and chewed on his lip.

Two balconies up, Kerry burst suddenly onto Jasper's balcony, his phone held fast to his ear. He spotted Rosemary and Jasper, lifted a hand in sudden recognition, and shot back into the bookshop.

Rosemary frowned. 'What does he want you to do?'

It didn't seem possible, but Jasper paled further. 'He wants me to sell the firsts.'

'The firsts?'

'You know, Rosemary. My mother's firsts.'

Rosemary thought of the cabinet behind the shop counter where Jasper stored precious finds. 'The first edition, first print run copies of your mother's books?'

'That's them.'

'They're worth a lot of money.'

'Yes.'

'He won't get that money, though. It's yours.'

Jasper put his hand in his jeans pocket to pull out a piece of paper. 'My mother said they were his.'

Rosemary took the paper. 'A letter?'

'From Mum to...my father.'

'Are you sure it's genuine?'

Jasper pointed to the bottom where a decorative signature sliced across the page. 'Yes. I've had it checked. And before you call on Robert Sparkling the fountain pen fanatic to check the ink, I had that checked as well. It's of the time and genuine.'

Rosemary studied the letter's quality, then switched to what it said. 'Your mother is bequeathing Kerry her firsts.'

'Yep.' Jasper lifted his face to the sky, as if trying to catch the sun's warmth. 'It's not the money because I was never going to sell them. They were Mum's books, special books.' He sighed. 'I don't want to let them go.'

Rosemary resisted the urge to hug him. The tension from his absence was still there, and she didn't want to have the gesture rejected. 'Something is not right here, Jasper. A man does not just come out of the woodwork and know about you and those special books of your mother's.'

A ghost of a smile flashed across Jasper's face as he turned to her. 'Weird things happen all the time. I had a skeleton in my backyard, remember?'

'That turned out to be logical. This is different. Don't do anything yet.' She put a hand on his arm. 'Right? Nothing.'

He let her hang on for a moment, then slowly pulled his arm away, leaving her hand in mid-air. She clamped it to her side. 'What are you going to do, Rosemary? No, really, what will you do?' He tugged the letter from her and walked back inside, clicking his fingers at Snowy, who followed him willingly. 'You can't fix everything, you know.'

Rosemary stayed on the balcony and heard the click of the shop door indicating he'd left. Mrs Lionel hurried back through the doorway, a plate of cheese and pickle sandwiches in her hand. 'What happened? Is everything alright?'

'No, it certainly isn't. Kerry says he has the right to sell T. G. G. Duncan's firsts.'

'But they're Jasper's!'

'So we thought.'

Mrs Lionel lowered the plate so it balanced on the balcony rail. 'What to do?'

'We have to find out the truth. I cannot believe Kerry is Jasper's father.'

'Jasper's been searching for so long, he's not going to take this kindly. If you're the one to discover an awful truth, he may not ever speak to you again.'

Rosemary studied her friend's concerned face. 'Or it may bring him back to us.' She smiled grimly. 'A wise woman once told me if you don't take risks, there are no rewards.'

Mrs Lionel nodded, her frown deepening. 'Indeed.'

TEN

Gerry stood in the same spot he'd been in fifteen minutes earlier, absentmindedly spacing coat hangers. He felt Patti's gaze on him from behind the rack of repurposed puffer jackets as he worked his way down the row and back again, moving each one by a millimetre.

'Gerry?'

Gerry moved another hanger. 'Mmm?'

'What would you like for dinner, sweetie?'

'Ooo, I'm not sure.' Patti sounded distant, and he could barely hear her over the scrape of hangers on the metal rod of the rack.

'We have leftover chicken casserole. How would that do?'

'Mmm.'

'Or you could make pasties.'

'Mmm.'

'Perhaps I could get some emu eggs from Justin and make a cheese and emu egg omelette.'

'Mmm.'

'We could have jumping jellybeans for dessert.'

'Mmm.'

'Or meteor crumble. We haven't had that for a while.'

Gerry frowned. Had she said something odd? Patti sometimes did. He decided to keep neutral. 'Mmm.'

Patti skittered around the rack until she was side by side with Gerry. 'Gerry.'

'What is it, my love?'

'Justin Gentleman doesn't own any emus.'

'Doesn't he?'

'And I ran out of meteors three months ago.'

'That's a shame.'

'Gerry!'

He startled, knocking the rack, and making coat hangers clash awkwardly, disturbing their regimental row. 'Patti! You gave me a fright.'

'That's because you're miles away and not listening to me.' Patti hugged her husband's arm. 'What on earth are you thinking about?'

'Am I thinking of something?'

'Yes! Either that or you're asleep on your feet.'

Gerry grinned sheepishly. 'Although I have been known to sleep in any position I find myself in, I'm not asleep at the moment. I *am* thinking of something.'

'What, Gerry? You're making me very curious.'

Gerry looked around the interior of Patricia's. Since they'd taken over most of Robert Sparkling's mansion's ground floor, it was harder to know how many customers they had. There were garments in the little rooms leading off the main hall, with the more voluminous pieces arranged in the ballroom beyond. Robert's generous offer to share Ravenhome meant that Patricia's was now a shop that rivalled any large city boutique, except there was no other boutique in the country where you could buy an evening gown made from cycling shirts that had been found in various countryside gutters. 'Do you feel like a cup of tea, Patti?' Gerry said, tipping his head towards the kitchen at the back of the ballroom. 'I don't think we have any customers at the moment.'

'Not customers, Gerry. *Friends.*' Patti let Gerry's arm go and kissed his cheek. 'All our customers are our friends.'

Gerry followed Patti as she skipped towards the kitchen. Although he felt he should disagree with Patti on principle, he found no reason to. No one ever said anything rotten about Patricia's, and people who'd purchased garments came back for more. It was marvellous, but not surprising. Patti was a creative genius and everyone's friend.

They took cups of tea to their resting place under one of the ballroom's gigantic windows. The view was of the hill rising to the cemetery at the top of Mulbury and was angled so that the road was barely visible. It was another advantage of Ravenshome, spacious but still connected to the buzz of town. At the end of the day, Gerry and Patti could walk up the hill and around the back of the cemetery to their cottage within minutes.

Patti balanced her teacup on the windowsill. 'Come on, Gerry. What's going on?'

'I'm thinking about Pearl.'

'Pearl? Ronnie's mum?'

'That's the one. I told you how she went under the table with the teapot. It was so odd, I'm wondering why someone would do that.'

'It could have been an accident, Gerry. She may have tripped and fallen under the table.'

Gerry shook his head, making his teacup rattle in its saucer as it balanced on his knee. 'No. It was too graceful. Honestly, Patti, it was like she was a dancer.' Gerry held up one hand and swooped it across his round tummy in an interesting imitation of a prima ballerina.

Patti followed his movements, raising her arm to imitate him before letting it drop heavily. 'She was scared, Gerry.'

Gerry startled, the tea spilling slightly. 'Really? How do you know that? You weren't even there.'

Patti leaned forward and put her hand on Gerry's knee. 'Gerry, I don't have to see someone in distress to know they *are* distressed. Do you remember where I was working before I married you?'

'Very distinctly, Patti. You took care of older people in that attractive care home in the mountains.' Gerry smiled. 'You loved that job. You were very good at it.'

'I did love that job.' Patti gazed over Gerry's shoulder and her eyes misted. 'It was very humbling to be among people who'd lived long lives. They had lots of stories to tell.'

'I'm so sorry you gave it up to be with me.'

Patti sat up. 'I didn't give it up. I went to my next destination. *You*, Gerry. You were my next life chapter.'

Gerry felt his eyes prickle. 'Gosh, Patti, that's beautiful of you.'

'It's the truth, sweetie. And I didn't give up the job in the sense of forgetting everything about it. Those people live in my heart and my head, even if most of them would be gone by now.' She squeezed his knee and let go, reaching for her cup. 'What I was going to say, though, was some of the people I cared for started to change as they got older. Their memories played tricks on them. Some imagined they were back in the past, and some of those memories weren't kind.'

'What do you mean, Patti?'

'We had veterans in the care home, and people who'd been born in war-torn countries. At times, horrific memories would surface, and people would be frightened. Then they would act the way that Pearl did.'

'They hid under tables?'

'Sometimes. Wouldn't you, if you thought danger was coming?'

Gerry scratched his bare head. 'I don't know, Patti, because I've been lucky. I've never been in danger.'

'But you can imagine hiding, can't you?'

'Yes, I can imagine that.' Gerry lifted his cup and drank the rest of his tea. 'I'd been thinking about other reasons why Pearl would descend under a table, but being frightened hadn't crossed my mind.'

'But what were you thinking, sweetie?'

'Silly things, really, like maybe she'd tripped and slid and was trying to save face.'

'But still managed to hang on to the teapot?'

'It seems unlikely, doesn't it?' Gerry sighed and put his cup on the windowsill. 'Do you think the teapot had anything to do with it? She hung on to it as if it were very precious.'

'Maybe.' Patti's feet tapped a little dance on the floor as she thought. 'The sight of it may have triggered something. Or perhaps it was completely unrelated. I really can't say because I don't know Pearl at all.' She leaned back in her chair and waved her arm at the display of garments behind her. 'We've been so busy, Gerry, I feel like we're not catching up with people like we used to.'

'I think it's because we've moved shop. We really only see Robert and Heather from day to day.'

Patti shook her head. 'Let's change that. Let's make sure we go to Honey B's to fetch cake and coffee at least every other day.'

Gerry put his hand on his rounded stomach. 'Splendid idea, Patti.'

She laughed and reached out to take her husband's hand. 'Speaking of Heather, how do you think she is?'

Gerry glanced round the ballroom but Heather had gone back to Mulbury Feeds for lunch. 'I think she's wonderful.'

'Oh, she is a fabulous worker, but how is she in herself?'

'Contented, I think. Don't you?'

'I think she loves her work, both here and at the animal produce store. Do you know, she asked me the other day about dressmaking for special occasions?'

'Does she want to help you with the upcycling?'

'I don't think it was that. Something was on her mind; I couldn't work it out.' Patti hummed for a moment. 'She doesn't rest much, does she?'

'But, my love, neither do you!'

'It's different, Gerry!' Patti stood up and spun around so her flouncy dress smacked into Gerry's face. 'I'm creating! I don't feel like it's work when you're producing garments for someone to love.'

'Maybe Heather wants to do that, too.'

Patti stopped twirling and put her hands on her mouth. 'Gerry, you are so very observant.'

Gerry blinked. 'I am?'

'Yes!' Patti set off across the ballroom, leaving Gerry racking his brains for signs of his cleverness. He heaved himself up, took their cups and saucers, and went to wash them. He could hear Patti in the little storeroom under the stairs, pulling at boxes of thread. A clatter of steps in the hallway caught his attention, and he wandered off to serve potential customers—friends!—leaving Patti to whatever she was up to.

The cluster of women in the hallway caught sight of him and pushed forward, making him stop in his tracks. 'Hello?' he said. 'Can I help-'

A tall woman with her hair swept upwards held up her hand. 'Handkerchiefs.'

'Pardon me?' Gerry couldn't help noticing that three of the group wore the same workout clothes, right down to their bright running shoes. Their outer layers were pristine, which would have made Gerry think that workouts for this group consisted of lifting coffee cups to their painted lips except for the traces of brown mud on their shoes. Maybe they were walkers, the sort that kept a slow pace so they could continue to talk?

The woman waggled a piece of paper at him. 'Hello? You sell them? They must be made out of...' she consulted the paper '... sheets.'

A dark-haired woman dressed simply in a straight skirt and cream blouse moved forward. 'What Karen means, and what we all want, is a handkerchief made from recycled material.'

'Upcycled.'

'Upcycled?'

'My wife prefers the term *upcycled*. She says she's taking useful things and making them better in a different way.'

'Well, that is lovely.' The woman stuck out her hand. 'I'm Milly.' She shook Gerry's hand and indicated the others behind her. 'We're the Jaunty Jalopers. This is Rebecca, Karen and Barbara. We're on a treasure hunt.'

'Really? You're looking for treasures?'

'Metaphorically speaking, yes.' Milly showed him a piece of paper with the map of Mulbury on it. 'The map's wrong, because you've shifted shop, but I think we can still get what we came for.'

'Certainly.' Gerry turned to point into a room to his left. 'Small items are in there, including haberdashery and millinery.'

'Lovely.' Milly smiled broadly at him and led the women into the room, where loud chatter started and filtered out into the hallway.

Gerry started back to where Patti still rummaged in the storeroom but a voice stopped him. 'Ah,' it said. 'Ravenhome. Magnificent and expensive to maintain, wouldn't you think?'

A large man stood in the hallway, his bulk blocking the light through the door. 'You're Kerry, aren't you?' Gerry asked. 'Jasper's father.'

'Yes, yes, all that.' Kerry stepped forward. 'And an interested tourist to boot. Lovely mansion, eh? Lovely, lovely. Worth a quid, eh?'

'I don't know, to be honest.' Gerry looked at the wall which still needed another coat of paint. 'Robert's been kind enough to lease this part of it to us, even though he's renovating. He's a very nice chap.'

'Is he now? A lovely rich chap by the sounds of it. Well, that does make a change, eh?'

Gerry frowned. 'I don't know many rich chaps so I can't say.'

Kerry laughed, the bellicose sound echoing around the hallway. 'You're unlucky, you're very unlucky.' He stopped laughing abruptly and moved forward suddenly. Gerry stepped back. 'And what is he really like, this rich chap who owns this abode? Happy, is he?'

'Well, yes, I would say so, although I wouldn't be so bold as to speak for him.'

'Wouldn't you?' Kerry clapped Gerry on the back, shunting him forward a step. 'So, you wouldn't know if he was wanting for anything? Lost father, perhaps?'

'I believe he has a father. No wants that I know of.'

'Shame, shame.' Kerry bent over Gerry and put a hand on his shoulder before giving him a large wink. 'I do like to fulfil a want.'

Gerry stretched back so Kerry's hand slid off and nodded. 'Yes, helping people out can be very satisfying.'

'Yes, yes, you get it!' Kerry laughed again and prodded Gerry's arm. 'Helping people can be *enormously* satisfying.'

Gerry frowned. By *satisfying*, he meant the wonderful way supporting Patti in her designing or helping Roman chop up carrots in the restaurant made a real difference to their day-to-day lives. The way Kerry said it was more like helping people was linked to something much more sinister.

The women came out holding squares of cotton and Kerry let them pass in their wave of excitement at locating their current treasure. Patti emerged to help with their purchases, leaving Gerry to place the handkerchiefs in little linen tote bags. Kerry retreated rapidly outside, and Gerry felt unexpectedly relieved. The women filed out, although Milly came to briefly side with Gerry.

'Whatever you're thinking about that man,' she whispered to him before she went outside, 'is correct.'

Gerry shook his head. 'How do you know what I'm thinking?'

'You have that look some people have after they've been talking to him.' Milly grimaced. 'Anyway, have a lovely day.' She trailed after the others.

'Still thinking about Pearl, sweetie?' asked Patti, linking her arm through his.

'Not particularly, although I do think she needs thinking about.'

'Let's talk to Honey and Ronnie. Maybe we can help them figure it out.'

Gerry nodded. Now that was the sort of helping he was good at.

ELEVEN

The screening of 'The lives and loves of T. G. G. Duncan' wasn't until after the shops on Goldmarket Road were closed, but Rosemary took a chance that the Wednesday senior citizen buses would be loaded and gone by four o'clock so they could shut early. She locked The Preserved Mulbury and rapped on the door of The Green Mulbury. Mrs Lionel stood in the middle of her shop, leaning over what Rosemary presumed was Percy, and straightened at the noise. 'Coming,' she said.

Rosemary stood back as her friend came out the door and pulled it closed. 'How is Percy?'

Mrs Lionel gave her a sideways look. 'He's missing Snowy, I think.'

Rosemary peered through the shop window to stare at the empty floor. 'How can you tell?'

'I just can.' Mrs Lionel adjusted the brooch she'd pinned to her dress. 'He has a lost look about him.' She held up her hand as Rosemary went to say something else. 'Before you comment, understand that, to me, my dog is as clear to me as Snowy is to Jasper and Cuddles is to Honey.'

Rosemary nodded. 'Right. Sorry.'

'Apology accepted. Now.' Mrs Lionel looked back along the pavement. 'We have to wait for Heather.'

'Heather's coming?'

'Yes, she is. I asked her this morning when she came in to buy wool wash. She was delighted.'

'I'm surprised she wanted to take the time out from her many jobs.'

'Heather doesn't regard any of her work as mere jobs. In any case, she twirled when I asked her.'

'Twirled.'

'You know.' Mrs Lionel swizzled her hand around. 'As only Heather can do.'

'Right.'

They stood companionably in the shade of the veranda for a few minutes until Heather appeared in Goldmarket Square on her trek back from Patricia's. Rosemary smiled as the young woman approached. Heather's long curls draped across her arms as she walked lightly across the gravel, and she flicked them back with a swift shrug. There was something about the carefree way Heather carried herself when she was happy. It was like watching a ballet dancer flit across the stage, or a bird dance along a branch.

'Rosemary,' Heather said as she stepped under the veranda. 'Mrs Lionel.' She wrapped the older woman in her arms. 'Beautiful Mrs Lionel.'

'Lovely Heather,' Mrs Lionel said, rubbing her hand on Heather's back. 'Looking forward to the trip?'

'Big Town.' Heather scrunched her face up. 'I prefer Mulbury. But Jasper's film is calling us. Is he coming?'

'He went to the premiere,' said Rosemary. 'I don't think he enjoyed it that much.'

Heather nodded solemnly and swung around to look

the old blue sedan parked next to the kerb. 'You have the only car among us.'

'No.' Rosemary walked to the car and unlocked it. 'You have one, too.'

Heather waltzed over to the back door of the car and slid in. 'Holly will take it when she leaves.'

Rosemary glanced at Mrs Lionel and whispered, 'Heather knows?'

'Apparently.' Mrs Lionel eased herself into the front passenger seat.

Rosemary went to the driver's side, glanced at the humming Heather, and slipped in beside Mrs Lionel. 'She said that quite happily,' she said quietly.

'As you always say,' said Mrs Lionel, matching Rosemary's low volume, 'Heather is tougher than she looks.'

Rosemary started the car, frowning at the sudden burst of black smoke from its exhaust, and turned it around to go down the road to Big Town. Robert Sparkling stood outside his mechanic's garage studying the engine of a tourist's four-wheel drive, and looked up as she went past. Mrs Lionel waved, and he raised his hand in mutual greeting before pointing at the back of Rosemary's car. 'I think he's telling you something,' said Mrs Lionel.

Rosemary grunted. 'I know exactly what he's telling me.'

'Rosemary's car is nice,' said Heather, patting the back of Mrs Lionel's seat. 'But it's nearly dead.'

Rosemary gritted her teeth. Heather was correct but this was no time to think of trading Alasdair's car in for something better. Adelia Lochard's documentary might hold the key to Jasper's situation, but what that was remained a mystery. Kerry had been at the same premiere as Jasper, and it had been the catalyst for his revelation. A coincidence? She didn't believe in coincidence.

'I haven't been to Big Town for quite a while,' said Mrs Lionel, nodding at the view through the windscreen. 'I see the unusually wet season has kept most of these paddocks green.'

Rosemary glanced at the land alongside the car. It was different to where Justin's farm was, a flat plain instead of undulating hills. Mobs of sheep grazed near the fence line and the occasional horse flung its head up to watch as the car went by. It wasn't long before they hit the outskirts of the town. Housing development stretched into the paddocks and Rosemary wondered how long it would be before the sheep had brick veneer houses as neighbours.

'It's getting bigger,' said Mrs Lionel.

'Big Town will be Huge Town,' said Heather, chuckling to herself.

'So long as Mulbury stays the same size,' said Rosemary. 'I'll be happy with that.'

They drove into the middle of town and parked along the street. While Rosemary worked out the parking fee, Mrs Lionel and Heather went along the footpath looking in shop windows. Rosemary joined them at a bookstore franchise.

'It feels odd looking at all these new books,' said Mrs Lionel, tapping the window. 'I know Jasper has a few, but his preloved ones are much more inviting.' She stepped back. 'Is there a second-hand bookshop in Big Town?'

'Not specifically,' said Rosemary. 'I'm sure you can find old books in opportunity shops. That's why people travel to The Read Mulbury.'

'I think the attraction is more than the books.'

'What do you mean?'

'Jasper is the attraction,' said Heather, looping her arms

through Rosemary's and Mrs Lionel's. 'He knows what people want.'

'And what would that be?' asked Rosemary.

'They want stories they can lose themselves in. He chooses those books for them.'

Rosemary looked over Heather's head to Mrs Lionel as they made their way down the street. 'You think Jasper is the main attraction.'

'Of course, dear,' said Mrs Lionel, studying the contents of a window display of scented soy candles. 'Just as Patti is the main attraction for customers of Patricia's, and Jules and Roman attract people to The Leftover Restaurant.'

'Right.' Rosemary took a few more paces before she spoke again. 'Do you think he's still the attraction now that he doesn't seem himself?'

'He hasn't lost his ability to provide unique service for his customers.' Mrs Lionel frowned. 'At least, I don't think he has.'

Rosemary thought about the flow of people in and out of The Read Mulbury. Despite having been closed for three months, it didn't seem to be suffering now that it was open again. People went in and almost all came out clutching a bag full of books. However Jasper appeared to the residents of Mulbury, he still had his strong knowledge of all types of books to share with readers. She relaxed a little at the thought.

They reached the re-purposed town hall picture theatre half an hour before screening time. The massive wooden entrance doors were propped open, so they went inside where it was cool. A dozen or so people were already there enjoying an icy beverage from the community-owned kiosk, and Rosemary ordered iced tea while the others found a table to sit at in the corner of the room. While she waited,

Rosemary scanned the area and came face to face with a large promotional picture of a woman wearing a low brimmed hat and enormous sunglasses. Despite her disguise, the shape of her nose and her long dark hair made Rosemary think immediately of Jasper. There she was, T. G. G. Duncan.

'Gorgeous, isn't she?' The kiosk volunteer placed three glasses of tea on a tray and pushed it carefully towards Rosemary.

'Hard to tell.'

The volunteer laughed. 'I suppose it is! But wait until you see the documentary. That Adelia Lochard is an amazing investigator. She's found photographs and footage people have never seen before.' He leaned closer. 'I hear that T. G. G. Duncan's son lives in a little town nearby.'

Rosemary raised her eyebrows. 'Right.'

'I think it's Ambervale.' He gave Rosemary a wink. 'I might go there on the weekend to see if I can find him.'

Rosemary smiled briefly as she took the tray back to the table. Ambervale was in the opposite direction and a few hours' drive away from Mulbury, which felt comforting. The image of Jasper being swamped by fans disturbed her. 'Thank you, Rosemary,' said Mrs Lionel as she took a tea. 'Did you know we can take our drinks inside? We'd better do that or we won't get a couch.'

'A couch?'

Mrs Lionel chuckled. 'They have couches instead of seats. Come on.'

They carried their drinks to the hall's entrance, showed their tickets to the usher, and went inside. The old hall was filled with rows of neatly spaced couches, all with a handy table on either side. Mrs Lionel headed to a floral three-seater in the middle and placed her drink down before seating herself comfortably among some velveteen cushions. She patted the space beside her and Heather plonked herself down, holding her drink high. Rosemary was more careful, lowering herself onto the soft seat before glancing around. Most of the couches held chatting women, none of whom she recognised. It was a cosy setup. By the time the curtains rolled back on the wooden stage at the front, and the film's dedication started, Rosemary felt she could stay quite happily on the couch all night.

But the first few minutes nearly changed her mind.

Suddenly, they were back in Mulbury, following Jasper as he walked up the hill towards the cemetery. He was slow and kept folding his long hair behind his ears. Every now and then, there was a glimpse of someone's arm as they walked beside him, but the rest of their body was never shown. Rosemary knew without a doubt that it was her. Adelia Lochard had filmed them during the time Jasper was recovering from his illness, and they had walked regularly to build his strength up. Although she knew he was weak from nearly dying, the narrator—a faceless, deep-voiced man who sounded like a newsreader—spoke of Jasper as a sad, lost man without true knowledge of his mother, and Jasper's demeanour did nothing to dispute that.

'Just watch,' hissed Mrs Lionel across Heather's head as Rosemary shifted in irritation. 'We're here on a fact-finding mission, not as a film critic.'

Rosemary nodded but the next sixty minutes was a hard slog. The documentary was about the writings of T. G. G. Duncan, and repeatedly showed shots of the first editions discovered by Jasper as if they were a collection of gold nuggets, but focused on the secret she kept from her children. Child, really. Although Helena and Iris were mentioned as Jasper's sisters, there was no footage of them except for a blurred photograph showing the full image of T. G. G. Duncan in her hat and sunglasses, holding the hands of two young girls while a smiling man in the background carried a little boy. It was Jasper and the father who raised him.

It may have been a well-researched film full of never-before-seen scenes, but Rosemary winced at its emphasis on T. G. G. as a deceitful, cunning mother who deliberately kept her life as an author and its huge success from her family. Worse, right at the end, came the revelation Jasper had a different father, 'the K in T. G. G. Duncan's book dedication to her family, the last mystery of T. G. G. Duncan's life. Surely it must be her Captain Kesper'. Loud, dramatic music followed.

Rosemary turned to Mrs Lionel and found her friend and Heather staring intently at her. 'Correct me if I'm wrong,' Rosemary said. 'Kerry doesn't strike me as a Captain of any kind.'

'People change,' said Mrs Lionel. 'Kerry may have been quite dashing when he was a young man. And perhaps less...knowledgeable.'

'He may have been but that's long gone from his personality.'

'Kerry is not Jasper's father,' said Heather, playing absently with the fringe of her cushion. 'He is not gorgeous enough.'

Rosemary frowned. 'Although I agree about the lack of gorgeousness with Kerry, it's not evidence enough he is *not* Jasper's father.' She stood, straightening her dress. 'How are we going to prove otherwise?'

'Easy,' said Heather, helping Mrs Lionel from the depths of the couch. 'Kerry will let Jasper know in the end.'

Rosemary was quiet as she led them back to the car.

Behind her, Heather chatted amiably with Mrs Lionel. It would have been on the cards to dismiss Heather's statement without further thought, but Rosemary was wary of ignoring anything Heather said. Kerry telling Jasper he was not his father would be the best outcome, but how were they going to get him to admit it?

TWELVE

Holly Hubbard stood in her bedroom, surveying her wardrobe. The neatly hanging clothes were almost uniform: long-sleeve shirts, cargo pants, and poly-fleece tops designed for the freezing winter temperatures. Even her summer clothes spelled *work,* consisting of sensible polo shirts of earthy colours and matching shorts. In the far corner of the rack, two summer dresses in bright florals were so out of place she wondered how they got there. In a thrill of happiness, she remembered buying them at a city shop on one of her trips away with Toffee. Wearing them felt liberating, as if the stress of constantly worrying about lucerne bales didn't exist.

And it really didn't exist much anymore. Since Robert had purchased Mulbury Feeds, the Hubbard sisters were no longer owners but employees. They still worked as hard as ever in the flourishing animal feed and garden store, but the late evening concerns of invoicing and debt-chasing weren't hers alone. Robert took care of the business side, leaving the sisters to make the store as wonderful as possible. But Holly still worried, partly about whether the business would survive and act as a family legacy but mostly so that her younger sisters—the irascible Hannah and the ethereal Heather—had ongoing work.

'What are you doing?'

On cue, Hannah came into Holly's room and plonked herself on the bed.

'Do you have to sit on my quilt in your work clothes?'

Hannah glanced down at her shirt. Straw clung to her buttons and there were patches of dirt checkering its front. 'Yep,' she said. 'Work clothes are all I've got.'

Holly turned back to her wardrobe. 'Boy, do I understand that.'

'You're packing, aren't you.'

Holly heard the catch in Hannah's throat but decided she couldn't take that on at the moment. 'I'm deciding what to take.'

'You won't take everything. There'll be no need.'

Holly came and sat next to her sister. 'I'm not intending to come back, Han.'

'Yeah, but you might. You might have to. Toffee might turn out to be someone you can't stand.'

'He won't.'

'But he might!'

Holly took Hannah's hand. 'He might. But I really, really doubt it.'

Hannah put her other hand on Holly's, gripping it tightly. 'I know. So do I. I just wanted you to say that you'd come back if you had to.'

'Well, that's a no-brainer. Of course I would. And, Han, you know I'll be back to visit as much as I can.'

Hannah dipped her head. 'I know you'll try, but you'll be so far away.'

'There are these things called aeroplanes...'

Hannah laughed. 'Yeah. I might even go on one to see you.'

'Promise you will, Han.' Holly squeezed her sister's hands. 'Promise that you won't spend all your life in the produce shed and forget to look up. And bring Heather with you.'

'Okay, okay. I'll visit.' Hannah shrugged. 'I guess I can now that Mulbury Feeds is Sparkling Enterprises. Robert will have to work out who can take over while we go on holiday.' She chuckled. 'Holiday! I can't believe I even know what that word means!'

Holly smiled, giving Hannah's hands one more squeeze before letting go and standing to contemplate her drab selection of clothing. 'You know, Toffee tells me it gets really hot where we're going. And there's no such thing as frost.'

'Unheard of.'

'That's what I said.'

'I need more climate-appropriate clothes. Maybe I should visit Patricia's?'

'So, you want to go from work-hardy shirts to ones made out of neglected Girl Guide uniforms?'

'Maybe not uniforms, but she does a good skirt out of tablecloths.'

'Maybe Heather could make something for you.'

Holly reached up into the top of her wardrobe and brought down a suitcase. 'Do we need to talk about Heather?'

'We always talk about Heather. She's the centre of our existence.'

'Yeah, I know. I didn't really mean that. She seems to be taking the news of me leaving really well.'

Hannah nodded. 'Yep.'

Holly slapped the suitcase down onto her bed. 'Don't you think that strange?'

Hannah grinned. 'Are you upset that she's not going to miss you?'

Holly put her hands on her hips and gazed out of her bedroom window to the corrugated iron shed housing the animal feed. 'I'm not upset...but I am surprised.'

'Yeah.' Hannah lay back on the bed. 'To tell you the truth, I'm amazed. We've always been together. When Mum died. When Dad left.' She swallowed but continued in a strong voice. 'When we thought we were going to lose Mulbury Feeds. We are a team.'

'We're still a team,' said Holly firmly. 'We'll always be that.'

'Yeah, I know. But this is a change.' Hannah joined her hands together, holding them over her chest before pulling them apart abruptly. 'It's a break in the chain.'

'No, Han, not a break.' Holly sat on the bed again, pushing the suitcase onto the floor so she could lie on her stomach next to Hannah. 'Can I tell you how I see it?'

'You will anyway.'

'True.' Holly propped herself up on her elbows and touched the tips of her fingers together. 'Our family is like a sphere. We're at the heart of it, the iron core, if I'm going to push the metaphor.'

'Push away.'

'The three of us stand with our backs to each other so we can look outwards.'

'You've really thought about this.'

'Shut up and listen, because I have. Now.' Holly stretched her hands away so her fingertips were no longer touching. 'Right next to us, in the next layer, are the people we love. Dad. Mrs Lionel. Toffee. Mum's essence.'

'Right.'

'And in the next layer...' Holly widened her hands. 'Rose-mary, Jasper, Patti and Gerry, Roman and Jules, Robert, Rakisha. Maybe Kelly and sometimes Franco. Beyond that are our faithful customers, and those who've helped us along the way. Financial advisors. Maybe some of our teachers.'

'Heather's birds.'

'Taxidermy doesn't really fit in this picture.'

Hannah smiled. 'Yeah, okay. I get what you're trying to do.'

'No, I don't think you're totally getting it, Han.' Holly brought her fingertips together again. 'The centre will hold. You watch. It will.'

Hannah's face took on an uncharacteristic grimness. 'I hope so, Hol. I'm really happy for you, envious actually that you found Toffee. But I'm a bit scared, too.'

Holly studied her sister for a moment. 'Han, you haven't been scared of anything in your whole life.'

'I was scared when Mum died.'

'Okay. Except for that horrendous time...' Holly shut her eyes for a second. 'Since then? You are formidable.'

'Yeah?' Hannah's face relaxed into a grin. 'You think so? You're not saying that just because you're going?'

'No, I'm not.' Holly tucked a strand of Hannah's tufty hair behind one ear. 'I look to your strength. I always have.'

Hannah stretched. 'It's my superpower.'

'It is. Now.'

'Now what?'

'We've got some other things to think of. Practical things.'

'Oh boy.' Hannah sat up. 'You're always thinking of practicalities.'

'That's my superpower.' Holly swung around and sat on the edge of the bed. 'You'll need more help when I leave. Robert will see it to, no doubt, but you need to have a say in who it is.'

'Why? It's Robert's problem.'

'Because whoever it is needs to fit in to our way of doing things. Robert may *own* the business, but we *know* the business.' Holly re-organised her short ponytail. 'For example, they need to understand Heather.'

'Very important, yep.'

'But they also need to do the things I usually do. Tracking stock. Ordering. Taking deliveries.'

'I can do that.'

'Yeah, I know, but your talent is the day-to-day business in the shed. And throwing hay bales around.'

'We all do that.'

'True, but you have the best knack.'

'What you're really saying is I'm best doing the grunt work while someone else does the office stuff.'

'That's it in a nutshell.'

'Okay. Can do. Unless you want to do some of that remotely?'

'What do you mean?'

'Well, it doesn't matter where you are these days if you've got the internet. You could still do orders, eh?'

'Except for one thing.'

'What?'

Holly took a deep breath. 'I don't want to.'

Hannah pulled herself up to sit next to her sister. 'You... don't want to.'

'No.'

'Are you saying...' Hannah rubbed at her head, making

her hair stick out on one side. 'Are you saying you don't want anything to do with Mulbury Feeds anymore?'

'Han.' Holly put an arm around her sister. 'I want to take a break. You've known that for a while. Going away with Toffee gives me a chance to do that.'

'But what will you do while he's out arresting people?'

'The police do more than arrest people.' Holly shifted Hannah closer to her. 'As you well know. I'm going to try something new, something different.'

'You're going to get a job somewhere?'

'I don't know. I can't imagine working for someone else. Maybe I'll start another type of business. Don't know yet. I've got some money saved. I can have some time off to think about things.'

'A nursery business.'

'Why do you say that?'

'You were the one who started our garden centre. Maybe you could do plants and stuff as well as compost and soil.'

'We'll be living in a rented house. I won't have a place like this.'

'Plants, then. Sell them from the house.'

Holly shrugged. 'Maybe.'

Hannah was quiet. She reached for Holly's hand hanging loosely over her shoulder and tugged at her fingers. 'Are you scared?'

'Scared? Why?'

'Well, I think the reason I can keep going here after Mum died and Dad left and Heather has her little fits of whatever she does, is that I have this place. There's always something to do and I'm good at it. I am a master hay bale thrower.' She chuckled. 'I'm formidable because I'm *grounded* here.'

Holly nodded. 'I hadn't really thought about it. Maybe I will be scared. I have no idea. I have never lived anywhere else but in Mulbury.'

'I'm scared just thinking about not being here.'

'Funny. I'm not.'

'It's because you have Toffee.'

'You think?'

'Yeah. I more than think. I know.' Hannah stood up, catching Holly's arm as she did. 'I guess you'll see, right? And if you're scared to death, you can always come back here. I won't sell your bed.'

'Gee, thanks.'

Hannah laughed. 'I might wear your clothes, though. Except that you're too small.' She reached out and grabbed a moleskin coat from the wardrobe. 'Although, I've always wanted this and it's too big for you.'

Holly snatched it back, holding it out to study the worn fabric. 'This coat and me have gone through a lot.' She handed it to Hannah. 'But you can have it except for when I need it. And you forget I'll be back to visit.'

'Okay.' Hannah slipped the coat from its hanger and folded it over her arm. 'I'll mind it then.' She peered inside the wardrobe again. 'Hey, didn't you have some dresses of Mum's in here?'

Holly moved some coat hangers. 'Yeah, I did. That long skirt and her silk dressing gown the colour of warm milk.'

'I loved that dressing gown. Where is it?'

'Maybe Dad took them when he left?'

Hannah scowled. 'Typical of him to take things without asking.' She grinned suddenly at her sister and tapped a finger on her lips. 'Do you think we should do the recruiting of a new person rather than Robert?'

'We should tell him we're going to in case he's got someone in mind.'

'Someone who already lives here?'

'Like who?'

'Gerry? Jules?'

'They're busy with their own things. And, besides, you need someone who can do some outside work. As much as I love Jules, she's too elegant to get covered in dust and straw. And Gerry...' Holly thought of the cheerful, round man.

'Probably not Gerry.'

'I don't have anyone in mind.'

'Okay. Let's keep our eyes out for someone.'

A loud buzzing from the kitchen made them both leave the bedroom, Holly's coat wrapped firmly over Hannah's arm. The buzz came from the service bell in the animal produce shed. 'I'll go,' said Holly, and ran out the door, through the yard and into the shed.

The sudden plunge into the dim shed made it impossible to see who was standing in the shop area, although Holly could make out the person hold a heavy bag of dog food.

'Hello,' she said, coming to a halt near the cash register. 'Can I help?'

'Hello,' said the customer. 'I'm going to take this home for my dog.'

Holly blinked. The customer was an older woman, but she easily held the big bag in her arms. 'Sure. Can I help you with that?'

'No.' The woman held up the bag so Holly could scan the barcode. 'This is nothing compared to what I usually dead lift.'

'You dead lift?'

The woman laughed. 'Strength-training keeps us oldies

going, love. Without it, we're just a bag of disintegrating bones and a pathetic shuffle. Also, it keeps me entertained. Got to fill those empty days with something worthwhile.'

Holly nodded, completed the transaction, and smiled at the woman. 'Are you here visiting?'

'Yes, I'm here as part of a group.' The woman tucked the bag under one arm and held out her hand. 'I'm Milly.'

'Holly.'

'Lovely to meet you, Holly.' Milly smiled broadly and walked briskly back towards town, the bag of dog food under one arm as if it was a load of feathers.

Holly watched her go, chewing her lip. It was a shame when people reported they had empty days when other people didn't have time to think. She lodged the thought in her head to mull over later as another load of hay arrived.

THIRTEEN

Since their time on the balcony, Rosemary had not seen Jasper. After they spoke, he'd gone back to his shop with downcast head and heavy footsteps. Rosemary sat behind her shop counter and rubbed Sunny behind the ears. 'Where should we start with Kerry, do you think?' she asked the cat, who fixed her gaze on her mistress. *You have an investigator in the family, don't you?* the look seemed to say.

'Of course.' Rosemary tickled Sunny one more time then left the shop, turning her sign to *Back in 5 pickly minutes*. The door closed silently behind her, a quiet reminder of the absent knocker.

Honey B's Teas was a hive of activity. The sculptured bees astride the cupcakes zoomed about the room on saucers borne by Honey and Ronnie, with Pearl standing guard at the till, drumming her fingers erratically on a pile of freshly ironed napkins. Kerry sat at a table near the wall devouring cake, oblivious to the surrounding activity. Rosemary watched him but he was intent on eating.

Honey beckoned her with a crooked finger. 'Give us a hand, Mum? Just for a few minutes?'

Rosemary nodded and headed for the urn to make pots of Darjeeling and Earl Grey tea. Pearl eyed her as she went by. 'Too much for this family to take on,' she said loudly. 'I said so.'

Rosemary gave Pearl a mirthless smile and sailed past Cuddles on his mat to the kitchen where it was comforting to bang around a few trays. The difference in constitution between Pearl and her amiable son was very difficult to reconcile. Honey's face as she came into the kitchen to fetch more cutlery echoed the same thoughts. 'Seven days and five hours,' Honey muttered to her mother.

'Easily done,' said Rosemary, placing a jolly pirate-themed teapot on the tray and carrying it out to a waiting customer.

Once everyone was served, Rosemary went back to the kitchen where Ronnie was washing dishes. 'Can I ask your advice, Ronnie?'

Ronnie's face, usually pale, lit with a checkerboard of red and white. 'Me? You want to ask *me* for advice?'

'That's what I said.' Rosemary frowned. 'Will you give it to me? You seem hesitant.'

'Me?' Ronnie shook his head vigorously, making his strawberry blonde hair stick out in all directions. 'I'll help you if I can. Of course, I will. I just never thought you'd ask someone like me.'

'Of course, I'd ask someone like you. You're a private investigator, and good at his job.' Ronnie's face blazed, making Rosemary wonder if he wasn't feverish. 'Are you alright?'

'Yes, yes, it's the hot water.' He lifted his hands out of the suds, steam rising from his forearms. 'Er, how can I help?'

'Jasper's father. Kerry. You've met him.'

'He comes in here for cake.' He tipped his head towards the tearoom. 'He's here now.'

'Right. What steps would you take if you were investigating him?'

'Investigating him?'

'Yes, Ronnie. What steps would you take as a private investigator beyond what I can do already by searching the internet?'

'Oh. Ah.' Ronnie put his soapy hands on the edge of the sink and frowned. 'Well, when I'm investigating someone, it's true I initially run through what I can on the internet. I check social media sites for the person's name, and then read their comments and maybe check out some of their contacts. People don't realise how much information they put on social media. You can piece together quite a lot about them and their family, and what they get up to.'

Rosemary shook her head. 'Kerry doesn't seem to have a social media presence.'

'You checked different versions of his name?'

'Kerry, Kerri, Ciarraí. Yes, checked.'

'Okay, well, some people don't, especially if they're...' Ronnie's face mottled.

'Older,' said Rosemary.

'Not a digital native, is how I put it.'

'And if the person doesn't have social media?'

'Their name sometimes comes up in relation to their work.'

'Kerry resigned some time ago. He's nearly eighty years old.'

'Probably unlikely, then.' Ronnie shrugged and put his hands back in the sudsy water. 'It's so much easier with younger people. You can build great profiles from the traces they leave in cyberspace, right down to what they eat for breakfast. If they do eat breakfast.'

Rosemary nodded impatiently. 'What else would you do?'

'Anything I can think of. Surveillance if necessary.'

Rosemary thought of her efforts to hear Jasper and Kerry through the walls of her living quarters. 'Right.'

Ronnie washed a few plates and stacked them on the drying rack. 'There are loads of ways you can find out information but I tend to follow my nose.'

'What do you mean by that?'

'Well, if I get a lead, no matter where it comes from, I keep on it until it's either useful or useless.'

Rosemary picked up a dry tea towel and started on the plates. 'That bit I do understand.'

'I have to say, Rosemary,' Ronnie gave her a lopsided grin, 'if you wanted, you would be a great private investigator. You do follow your nose.'

Rosemary placed a dry plate on a pile of similar gold-trimmed ones. 'Yes. I guess I do.'

Ronnie wiped at his face, leaving one soapy sud stuck to his fringe. 'Can I help with anything else?'

'No.' Rosemary glanced back into the tearoom which was emptying of happy cake eaters. Kerry was pushing his way through the door, laughing heartily at a poor woman caught against him in his exit. He rubbed her shoulder vigorously and stepped away towards The Read Mulbury. 'You've been very helpful. Thanks.'

'Any time.'

Thumping footsteps sounded, and Honey hurtled past Rosemary into the kitchen, her face screwed up with lips tight.

'Are you alright?' asked Ronnie as Honey grabbed a clean glass and filled in with water.

'Yes.'

'You don't look alright.'

'Don't I?'

'No. You seem a bit tense.'

'Do I?' Honey drank her water and sluiced the glass in the sink before sitting it roughly in the drainer. 'Do I just.'

'Yes, you do.' Ronnie put a hand on his wife's arm. 'What's going on?'

Honey hesitated, staring intently at Ronnie. 'Listen.'

'I am listening, Honey. I listen to you always.'

'Not me! Listen.' Honey shrugged her shoulder towards the tearoom. 'Listen to that out there. Why does she do that?'

Rosemary and Ronnie turned together to face Honey B's Teas. Scrapes and thuds indicated that someone was tidying chairs, if not a little roughly. A tablecloth flew across the air and landed near the doorway to the kitchen. Another sailed to land close by. A series of napkins did the same and lay scattered like fallen birds on the floor. Cutlery clinked and crockery clunked. 'Pearl is cleaning up,' said Rosemary. 'Quite vigorously, it seems.'

'Yes, she is, and *vigorous* is not how I describe it.' Honey grabbed Ronnie's arm. 'Please speak to her. She's your mother. Tell her that we don't have to change *every* tablecloth *every* time. Some of those napkins weren't even used! She's creating more work and we have enough to do. She gets these moments of frenzied activity and it's driving me nuts!'

Ronnie's brow furrowed. 'She's trying to help, Honey.'

'I know, I know, I know.' Honey shook his arm. 'Oh, I know, but it isn't helping. It's making more work. We were managing fine, weren't we? Even with Tallulah. Even with baking cakes every day. We were fine.' Honey rubbed her eyes. 'Not now. I am exhausted.'

'Well, maybe Mum's right.' Ronnie stroked Honey's cheek. 'Maybe this is too much with a little baby and everything.'

Honey moved her grip to his hand. 'No, Ronnie, she's *not* right. We were managing beautifully with Tallulah and the tearoom. I had even gone back to baking one novelty cake a week. We were fine. We were. Until she came to *help.*'

Honey's voice had slowly risen in range and volume as she'd spoken. The last word echoed around the kitchen, masking the sound of Pearl coming to stand in the doorway. Honey noticed her mother-in-law at last and put one hand to her mouth as the other stretched out towards the older woman.

'Pearl, I didn't mean...'

'I heard you, Honey Blossom.' Pearl's arms were full of haberdashery but it didn't hide the red of her face. 'I see that I'm not welcome.' She let the tablecloths fall. 'That is, as they say, easily fixed. I will pack my things and leave within the hour.'

Ronnie glanced at Honey. 'Mum, no, it's alright. Please stay. We love having you here. Honey is...'

'Exhausted?' Rosemary kicked a fallen tablecloth off her foot. 'Correct?'

'Mum, shhh.' Honey reached across the linen to put a hand on Pearl's arm. 'Please, Pearl, I'm so sorry. I am tired, and I don't know what I'm saying.'

Pearl jerked her hand away from Honey, hitched up her skirt, and high-stepped across the pile. 'No. I understand.

You don't want me. I will go.' Her chin was high as she left the kitchen to enter the spare room.

'Oh, no.' Ronnie shook his head. 'This isn't good.'

'Sorry, Ronnie.' Honey blinked rapidly. 'I didn't mean to be so harsh.'

'I know.' Ronnie smiled wanly at his wife. 'But I do understand. Mum can be-'

A screech from the spare bedroom made everyone jump.

Ronnie was first to its door. 'Mum! What the-' He stepped inside. 'You've got the teapot again.'

Rosemary hurried after Honey as she ran forward and looked over her daughter's shoulder to see Pearl huddled under the little desk Honey kept in the spare room. A teapot's spout poked out from her arms as she cradled it.

'I put the special teapot on the desk this morning,' said Honey. 'I thought she would like to see that we weren't using it to serve customers.'

Ronnie crouched next to his mother. 'What are you doing, Mum?'

'Sitting,' said Pearl in a clear, firm voice. 'Waiting.'

'Waiting for what?'

Pearl shook her head and hugged the pot closer. Ronnie sat back, rubbing his hands on the carpet. 'I don't know what's going on.'

'Let Mum in, Ronnie.' Honey pushed Rosemary forward. 'She helped last time.'

Ronnie wriggled backwards as Rosemary went to the desk and sat cross-legged next to Pearl. 'Are you alright, Pearl?'

It was difficult for Pearl to move, so small was the space under the desk, but Rosemary saw the slight nod. 'Yes, thank you.'

'You seem to be worried about the teapot.'

Pearl let her arms relax a little so the teapot was exposed. 'Not now. I have it.'

'Do you need to hide it for some reason?'

Pearl blinked at Rosemary, showing eyes too wide for the usually scowling face. They weren't focused on Rosemary, but somewhere over her left shoulder. After a moment, Pearl leaned towards Rosemary and whispered, 'They mustn't know.'

'Ronnie and Honey?'

Pearl nodded and offered the teapot to Rosemary. 'See?'

Rosemary examined the pot. It was of its time with a happy decoration of large blue and orange flowers. 'It's a lovely pot.'

Pearl shook her head, loosening strands of hair from her bun. 'No. It's dangerous.' She leaned closer. 'It's what they came for.'

'Who?'

Pearl tapped the side of her nose. 'Them. But they won't get it. It's my possession. I'll hide it properly this time.' She took the teapot from Rosemary and turned away, rattling the desk legs as she tucked the teapot behind it. With great awkwardness, she slid her jacket off and covered the pot before finally crawling out from the desk and standing up. 'Right.'

'Right?' said Ronnie. 'What do you mean, *right*?'

'I mean, right, let's go.' Pearl smoothed her hair back and tucked her shirt neatly into her skirt. 'We have a tearoom to run, Ronald. Don't you realise that?' She marched from the room.

Ronnie's eyebrows rose. 'What the-' He crouched down, crawling awkwardly under the desk to retrieve the teapot.

'Mum,' said Honey, her hand outstretched to Rosemary. 'What's going on?'

'Something, that's for sure.' Rosemary stood as well, putting her hand out to help Ronnie up. 'Something that we need to find out.' She tapped the teapot. 'Ronnie, it's something *you* need to do.'

Ronnie blinked. 'Me?'

Rosemary gave him a brisk pat on the arm. 'Something happened to your mother and it involves this teapot. Follow your nose and find out.'

Rosemary left Honey and Ronnie whispering furiously in the kitchen, and Pearl skilfully setting tables, and exited the tearoom. A small crowd gathered under the veranda and she scanned it for signs of Jasper with no luck. The bookshop's outside displays were set up, which seemed a normal, therefore good, sign. She stepped through the throng, recognising Milly standing at its edge among her group of Jaunty Jalopers. 'Hello,' Rosemary said. 'Sorry if you were trying to buy something. I'm going in now.'

Milly shook her head. 'We weren't waiting for service,' she said.

Rosemary stopped. The group—three women dressed similarly in active wear and fluorescent lime green shoes, and Colin and Lucy in sensible sun-protective shirts and trousers—was talking among themselves. Lucy had a handkerchief pressed against her eyes. Karen, Rebecca and Barbara clutched at each other, their faces pale.

'Right.' Rosemary surveyed the Jalopers. 'Is something going on?'

'We've just found out Andrew Valencia is dead. They

found him in a dam a long way from where his car was parked in a roadside stop.'

'Ah.'

Milly turned a watery gaze to Rosemary. 'You don't sound surprised.'

'I didn't know your friend.'

'But you did know he was dead.'

'I suspected so. He wore orange sport coats, didn't he?'

'Yes. You heard that?'

'I did. And the man found drowned in Justin Gentleman's dam wore an orange jacket.'

'That wouldn't make him Andrew necessarily but they identified him easily enough.' Milly gave a sob before taking a big breath and letting it out slowly. 'Andrew, drowned! It doesn't make sense.'

Rosemary went to stand closer. 'Apart from the fact drowning is awful, why doesn't it make sense?'

Milly dabbed at her eyes with what Rosemary recognised as one of Patti's creations crafted from an old bed sheet. 'Andrew was a kind man, a quiet soul. He wrote poems for us on our birthdays and gave us books as presents.' She sniffed. 'They weren't always appreciated. I didn't even appreciate them! I mean, what was I going to do with a book called "Steam-driven tractors and their many uses", although he did explain the book was somewhat rare and therefore quite precious.'

'You haven't explained why drowning doesn't make sense.'

'Oh, well.' Milly shook her head. 'Andrew had a particular aversion to water. He nearly drowned as a child in a makeshift boat his father made. Andrew would never be within cooee of a dam. He would be much too scared. He wouldn't even go to the beach.' Milly shook her head. 'It doesn't make sense.'

'What if he went there with someone else?'

Milly pursed her lips, thinking. 'He liked walking. I mean, he *really* liked it. He hiked everywhere. When we were at work, he set up the Wednesday Walks. Every Wednesday lunchtime we'd walk around the old part of town, looking at people's gardens. Andrew said it was good for team spirit, and it was. I felt better afterwards, the ladies got a chance to show off their latest gym fashions, even Colin was smiling once we'd finished. Nearly everyone came along.' She sighed. 'I suppose he could have been walking with someone but he still would never go close to a dam. Not on purpose.'

'Have you asked your friends whether they were with him?'

'I don't have to.' Milly tucked the hanky up her sleeve. 'I'm sure no one knew he was even here or they would have said. Lucy and I thought he was late or wasn't going to come. Sometimes he got busy with his books. He was a collector, you know, anything rare or different. His taste was eclectic. Recently, he'd started buying up old unused leatherbound journals.' Her face crumpled. 'We were cross with him for being so late. We had no idea he had arrived. If only we'd known, this may not have happened.'

Rosemary patted the woman on the arm. 'There's no use thinking that. He may have drowned anyway.'

Milly blinked. 'You are uncommonly frank.'

Rosemary frowned. 'Mrs Lionel often suggests that.'

'I suggest what?'

Rosemary looked around to where her friend stood outside The Green Mulbury, smiling at Milly sadly. Rosemary tapped herself on the chest. 'You say I'm frank.'

'Frank? I think I've used the word *insensitive*.'

'Right.'

Mrs Lionel stepped forward to face Milly. 'I'm so sorry about your friend, dear. It must be such a shock.'

'It is! So very shocking.' Milly pressed the hanky to her eyes again. 'We usually have such a jolly jaunt, but this one is turning out to have a number of terrible outcomes.'

'A number?' Rosemary glanced over at the crowd who were still muttering among themselves. 'What else has happened?'

'Oh, nothing of real consequence now we know about Andrew.'

'Tell me anyhow.'

Milly tucked her hanky away again. 'Colin's map was all wrong, and he hates that. It made him quite grumpy. That takes the fun out of the hunt.'

Rosemary almost rolled her eyes but caught the look Mrs Lionel threw her and stopped. 'Terrible. Anything else?'

'Kerry always puts a downer on things.'

Rosemary stood straighter. 'Why?'

'He's...loud.'

'Bombastic.'

'Yes, and opinionated. He made Colin feel worse than he should. That affects Lucy, Colin's wife.' Milly waved her hand at the tall, thin woman next to her husband. 'So, they haven't had fun. And then there's the inevitable competitiveness of the packing room ladies.'

'The packing room ladies?'

'You know: Karen, Rebecca and Barbara.' She gestured to the women in the brightly coloured shoes, who clutched each, talking rapidly in low voices. 'They worked in dispatches. We called it the packing room.

Thick as thieves until it comes to men, cooking and our jaunts.'

'They compete for men?'

Milly grimaced. 'They went to school together and have vied for the attention of every boy they knew since forever, including any male that ever worked for us. They're all single again, so it doesn't help.'

'And the cooking?'

'They make desserts.'

Rosemary tipped her head to one side. 'Doesn't everyone?'

'Not these desserts. Bombe Alaska, tiramisu, black forest cherry cake. Every day at work, there was another. They insisted everyone partake. Colin has diabetes, for heaven's sake, and yet they wanted him to eat their fare and then judge the best. They're bossy.'

'Bullies.'

Milly tipped her head, and her face screwed up. 'Yes. I guess that's what you'd call them.'

'And the jaunts?'

'Each of the packing room ladies wants to win the treasure hunt. It's caused much friction and occasional injury in the past. They can get quite nasty.'

'Why do you do it?'

Milly shot a look at Rosemary. 'Why do I do what?'

'Why do you have these jaunts if they're so fraught?'

'Well, it's not every year that one member drowns!'

'Rosemary's sorry,' said Mrs Lionel, nudging her friend.

'Yes,' said Rosemary. 'I'm sorry to remind you of Andrew, but is every one of your reunions so entrenched in drama?'

Milly busied herself for a moment with smoothing a slight crease on her skirt. 'Drama. Yes, I guess that's what it is.' A smile ghosted her face. 'When we were younger and working long hours together, it seemed much easier. I guess we were busy and didn't have the time to take things too seriously. We all had other worries: children, aging parents, volunteer committees. When Jalopy closed, we scattered. I got a job in a library. Others picked up bits and pieces. We felt the separation quite sharply, which is why we decided to have these reunions. But it seems that the reunions became the focus of some people's lives, a chance to remember how young and strong we were, working in an innovative, celebrated company. Nothing else in our lives was ever that exciting again, or so it seemed to some.'

'What about you, dear?' asked Mrs Lionel. 'What did you think?'

'I don't seek excitement.' Milly smiled tiredly. 'My library job finished and I didn't seek another. I like going to the gym, walking my little dog, and coming home to a peaceful house where a cup of tea is never far away.' She grinned suddenly. 'Now that makes me sound like the most boring person in the world!'

'No, it doesn't.' Rosemary glanced over the Square to where Mullings of Mulbury sat shaded by the Exceptional Tree. 'I know much more boring people.'

'The others want a bit more excitement than you need, by the sounds of it.' Mrs Lionel touched Milly's arm. 'Why don't you come into The Green Mulbury and I'll make you a cup of tea? I have a new mix with citrus rind and thyme you might like.'

'Thank you.' Milly turned to the crowd of Jalopers but they were still murmuring. 'I'll take you up on that.'

'What about you, Rosemary?'

'No thanks.' Rosemary nodded towards The Read Mulbury. 'I'm going in there.'

Mrs Lionel took Milly's elbow and steered her towards her shop, glancing back at Rosemary as she did. 'Need a book to read?'

'I'm always looking for a good story.'

Mrs Lionel's short laugh followed Rosemary as she pushed open the heavy door to the bookshop and stepped inside. The noise of the crowd almost disappeared as the door closed, replaced instead by the hush that always seems to accompany rooms full of books, as if the very air was quietly reading.

Rosemary threaded her way through bookcases and dump bins to the shop counter but no one was there. The door of the glass cabinet against the wall housing Jasper's mother's much-treasured firsts was slightly open, but the books were in their usual position. She went to the door of the lounge room and spotted Snowy asleep in his favourite upside-down position on the couch but no humans. 'Jasper?' she called softly, making Snowy thump his tail in greeting. No one answered.

The kitchen was a mess of dirty dishes and abandoned pots of jam. It gave the room a homely feel, but Rosemary wasn't fooled. The table, crammed with books and papers and pens, was littered with cake crumbs, and a cold cup of tea sat on a leather journal. She shifted it, frowning, and picked the book up to wipe its cover. Jasper would never sit a cup on a notebook that old even if, as she noted, it was blank. She put it back down and scanned the room. The back door was slightly ajar, and at last she could hear a voice.

Kerry stood on the back porch, talking rapidly on his phone and looking out into Jasper's backyard which was a jumble of weeds, leaves and dog bones. Rosemary pressed her face to the glass of the door and spotted Jasper standing in the debris of his yard hanging out washing on the single line he had strung across it. His back was to her, and his raised arms showed a glimpse of his thin torso as his T-shirt lifted. She frowned. He was too angular, all sharp edges. It was disturbing.

Kerry finished his call and closed his phone just as Rosemary stepped out onto the boards of the balcony. 'Rosemary Exeter,' he said, his arms outstretched. 'Good, good. I was wanting to catch up with you, yes indeed.'

Rosemary stopped short of his intended embrace. 'Why?'

'Well, goodness, you know the news, eh? Poor Andrew. Poor man. Drowned! Can you imagine?' Kerry came closer and Rosemary crossed her arms to ward him off. 'And he was such a dear friend of us all.'

Rosemary shrugged a shoulder towards the bookshop. 'It's quite the gossip out there.'

'Everyone is in shock. Such a tragic, tragic event.' Kerry shook his head. 'He was a quiet man, didn't quite fit into the Jalopers, you know? Too quiet.'

'Was that a problem?'

'Oh, you know.' Kerry shot out a friendly punch that skimmed Rosemary's arm. 'Still rivers run deep, eh? Anyway, anyway. I hear *you* found him. You kept that secret, clever girlie.'

'Not a secret. I wasn't sure the man I found was Mr Valencia.'

'Well then.' Kerry stepped even closer and Rosemary took another pace back until she was against the wall of the house. 'You'll be able to tell me all about it.'

'He was in a quantity of water.'

Kerry flicked his hand. 'Is drowning the conclusion the police have arrived at? Andrew drowned?'

'I doubt the police are letting much out at the moment.'

'What do you think?' Kerry leaned forward. 'You saw him. You know how he *was*, if you understand me. How he looked.'

'He was very wet.'

Kerry narrowed his eyes before laughing raucously. 'Such a card, Rosemary Exeter!' His laughter stopped. 'Anything else?'

'Rosemary.' Jasper appeared at the top of the balcony steps, the empty washing basket dangling from his hand. 'I didn't hear you come in.'

'No.' Rosemary moved sideways to clear herself from Kerry. 'Your whole display could disappear and you wouldn't hear a thing. I was coming to invite you both for dinner.'

'Dinner?' Kerry smiled as if he'd never heard a better word. 'Dinner? Yes, yes, we'll be there. Tonight? Six-thirty? Or would you like us earlier?'

Rosemary checked with Jasper. He nodded. 'Six-thirty is fine. See you then.'

She turned to leave but Kerry caught her arm and drew her close. 'You'll be able to tell us more then,' he said in her ear, making the skin prickle on the back of her neck.

She leaned in close to his ear. 'Only if you do,' she said loudly before walking out, leaving Kerry rubbing the side of his head.

FIFTEEN

'You want me to come to dinner as well?'

Mrs Lionel stood in The Preserved Mulbury with a container of eucalyptus dish washing liquid and a cardboard box of rose-scented soap clutched in her arms.

'Is that a problem?' Rosemary took the goodies from her. 'And are you back to making your own soap? Ronnie was helping you to stop you lifting heavy buckets so Robert should be doing the same.'

'He usually does, but he's busy today.' Mrs Lionel flexed her fingers and rubbed them together. 'Heather helped me.' She held up a hand. 'I know, you're going to ask how Heather has the time, but she makes it. She's very dear to me.'

'I know, as you are to her.'

Mrs Lionel smiled. 'We chat. She tells me what's going on with the produce store and Patricia's. And how the other girls are. It's lovely.'

Rosemary indicated a chair in her dining room and Mrs Lionel sat gratefully. 'And how are her sisters?'

'Heather says they're worried about her.'

'So I hear. Is she worried that they're worried?'

Mrs Lionel shook her head. 'Heather knows it's a sign of their affection.'

Rosemary put the kettle on and arranged a teapot. 'Do you think she's working too hard?'

Mrs Lionel took a while to answer. 'Heather has an extraordinary capacity to fill her day. She wouldn't call it work.'

'The others are worried that she's not doing her taxidermy anymore.'

'I asked her about that.' Mrs Lionel took the tea Rosemary offered. 'She said the birds can wait. She has a *project*.'

'What project?'

'Now *that* she didn't say.' Mrs Lionel sipped then put her cup on its saucer. 'Anyway. That's Heather. You want me to come for dinner.'

'Yes. Jasper and Kerry are our guests.'

'That sounds lovely. What are you cooking?'

Rosemary went to the fridge and peered into its mostly empty space. 'Good question. Justin has some produce I ordered. Looks like I'm heading to his farm shortly.'

'I'll come with you. He has lavender for me he's been drying in his shed.'

'Okay. Now?'

'Why not?'

The women drank the last of their tea and headed for Rosemary's blue sedan. Mrs Lionel struggled to open the door so Rosemary did it for her, helping her friend into the passenger seat, noticing how worn the cover was. The car hadn't been cleaned for some time but the layer of dust couldn't hide the broken knobs on the dash or the crack in the windscreen starting to creep towards the roof.

Mrs Lionel patted the door as they got going. 'It's been a good car, this.'

'Right.'

'It was Alasdair's. I remember the first time I saw it driving into town.' She smiled at Rosemary. 'You were in the seat I'm sitting in now. You looked determined.'

'I did?'

'Yes. Later, when I learned more about you, I knew it was your normal grit.'

'Grit.'

'Yes, grit.'

'You make me sound like an oyster.'

Mrs Lionel chuckled. 'You had a lot of determination to begin with and that only increased when Alasdair disappeared.'

Rosemary turned the car onto the open country road, wary of kangaroos in case they bounded unexpectedly along the road, and took a moment to answer. 'Determination and grit are what gets us through. You're an example of exactly that. After Mr Lionel died, you opened a green cleaning shop when you also had a chance to do nothing.'

Mrs Lionel nodded, her gaze on the undulating hills with their grazing sheep. 'Doing nothing does not sit well with me, just as it does not sit well with you.' She switched her look to Rosemary. 'Which is why you're having Jasper and Kerry to dinner.'

'I'm being neighbourly.'

'Yes, and also determined.'

'Determined?'

'To find out more about Kerry.'

Justin Gentleman's farm came into view on the left, and Rosemary slowed to turn onto the bumpy gravel driveway. They wound their way to the top of the hills where Justin's homestead and his tumble of sheds stood. As she parked the car and got out, Rosemary glimpsed the dam where Andrew Valencia had been discovered. It glinted in the afternoon sun.

'Mumblemumblemumble,' called Justin from the barn, holding aloft a hessian bag.

Rosemary helped Mrs Lionel with the car door again, and they walked to where Justin stood. 'Thank you,' said Rosemary, taking the bag from the farmer. 'I was hoping I could get eggs as well?'

'Mumble.' Justin pointed to the chicken pen down the hill.

'I'll wait here, dear,' said Mrs Lionel, reaching for the bag and peering inside. 'Beautiful vegetables, Justin. You could make frittata, Rosemary.'

'Excellent idea.' Rosemary followed Justin as he lumbered away. 'I'll see if Justin has any berries left.'

'Mumble,' answered Justin, which she took to mean yes.

As the farmer gathered a dozen eggs fresh from nests, Rosemary looked around her. The crime scene of just a few days ago was a distant memory, overshadowed by the gorgeous blue-sky day, and the swathe of green grass on the summer paddocks. Two Jersey cows stuck their heads over the fence to watch, and she walked over to scratch their tufty blonde faces. If she hadn't known how hard Justin worked, the farm would seem like paradise. Maybe it still was, in a wholesome, sweaty way.

'Mumblemumble,' said Justin as he came over to give her the eggs. He waved a basket. 'Mumble?'

'Yes, please.' Rosemary wasn't quite sure what she'd agreed to, but trailed after Justin as he headed towards a fenced-off section of the gardens behind the house. It was a relief to see him stoop to pluck strawberries from their neat mounds. 'I'll help.'

They worked side by side for a few minutes before Rosemary paused. 'Justin, can I ask you something?'

'Mumble,' said Justin, nodding.

'When we found that man in your dam, did you notice whether there was anything out of place? A broken fence or trodden on plants or flattened grass areas?'

Justin straightened, groaning a little as he stretched his back. He shook his hand at the hill in front of them, Rosemary following his gaze. The dam was part of a large paddock that could house livestock but more often was left empty. Justin had explained before, with lots of hand gestures and leg actions, how the cows and sheep pugged the water's edge too much, threatening to destroy the dam's banks. He only let them in to get the grass down. A pump pushed water up the hill to the troughs in the other paddocks. 'Mumble,' Justin said, pointing at a spot on the far-left side. 'Mumblemumble.'

Rosemary strained to see where he was indicating. The fence line showed its age, with leaning posts and saggy wire. A new white band of electric tape had replaced the older style barbed wire, and the animals soon learned not to push on it. In the very corner, where the fence swept behind the dam, she saw the tape hanging free. 'The electric fence is broken.'

Justin nodded. He moved his pointing finger to the right-hand side of the far fence. 'Mumble.'

Rosemary saw another section of tape unattached from the post. 'It's broken there as well. Did your cows do it?'

Justin shook his head and took a step towards the Jersey cows. 'Mumblemumble.'

'They've been in different paddocks. So, you don't think it was kangaroos or something else?'

'Mumble.' Justin shook his head.

'Did you tell the police?'

Justin frowned. 'Mumble.'

'Sorry, of course you did. They would have scoured the area, looking for footprints or any clues to what happened. Did they find anything?'

'Mumble.' Justin stomped on the spot, leaving deep boot marks in the dust.

'Okay, lots of footprints. Do you think that the tape was broken by humans?'

Justin made a scissor action with his fingers.

'It was cut? But it's electric tape. Whoever cut it would have got a shock.'

Justin chuckled, and pointed to his cows before doing an elaborate show of explaining to Rosemary once the animals knew the tape was electric and had been attached to the battery that gave the tape its sting, it wasn't necessary to leave the battery on.

'The cows are smart enough to keep away from it?'

Justin grunted and grinned.

'Got it. No shock for whoever cut it.'

The farmer slid his hat off to wipe at his brow, exposing wiry tortoiseshell hair that could have done with a trim before squashing it back on. 'Mumblemumble,' he said, imitating someone pushing through an obstacle. He tapped the ground with his foot.

'Will you show me?'

Justin started immediately down the hill. Rosemary dumped the strawberry basket on the ground and went after him, waving vaguely at Mrs Lionel. Justin opened the gate to the dam paddock and closed it carefully once Rosemary was through. Taking her elbow, he steered her through a line of sedges alongside the dam and headed for the far-left corner. Rosemary studied the area as she trotted alongside him, noting the tufts of grass among the strands of green, and the steep dam bank rising to her right. The ground was spongy underfoot. 'Mumble,' said Justin, stopping abruptly at the fence line.

Rosemary squatted and put her hand on the clumps of grass at the foot of the fence before looking through the saggy wire to the paddock beyond. White tape hung down, its end square and neat. 'Is it easy to cut electric tape? It has strands of wire threaded through the plastic.'

Justin shrugged and made strong scissor actions.

'So, a pair of sharp scissors or something similar? Nothing too special?'

Justin shrugged.

'Whatever it was, someone came prepared. Or had it on them already.' Rosemary knelt and pushed her hand under the tufts to feel the ground. It was soft and pitted. She parted the grass and sat back. A clear footprint showed, not a boot mark but something with little circles in it. 'What do you think happened?' she asked Justin, glancing at the heavy boots she knew he wore all the time. 'This is not your footprint.'

Justin knelt beside her, groaning a little and rubbing his knees. He reached stiffly through the fence and showed her other hidden footprints under the grass. They were a mess of circular markings, and it was difficult to make out another single significant print. He stabbed his finger at the ground, leaping it over the top wire, and poked the air to indicate the trajectory of something heading along the top side of the dam where the bank flattened to ground level.

'Someone walked along here after cutting the fence?'

He shrugged again, standing slowly, and wiggled his fingers.

'Lots of people?'

'Mumble!' He pointed again at the footprints.

Rosemary crawled to the fence and looked through to see that the footprints continued along the side of the dam.

Justin set off along the top of the dam, and Rosemary jumped up to follow him. He stopped at the next corner of the fence and lifted the tape at that end to show its end was jagged, as if it had ripped off. 'Mumble.' He stabbed his finger down.

Rosemary knelt again and lifted blades of grass away to reveal a trampling of footprints, this time from heavier footwear with deep crevices rather than little circles. She scoured the ground through the wire and found similar. 'People came into the paddock at the other corner.'

He nodded.

'And people went out this way?'

Justin frowned a little and stabbed his finger down again.

Rosemary leaned down further, stretching the blades of grass right away from the ground underneath. Pugged into the ground at the base of a tuft was the rounded toeprint of a large shoe. 'Someone else went out this way? Someone different from the crowd that came in.'

Justin snatched his hat from his head and twirled it in his fingers before cramming it back on and giving Rosemary a satisfied wink.

SIXTEEN

Rosemary was quiet as she ferried Mrs Lionel back to Mulbury. The image of the footprints sat uncomfortably in her head but she couldn't work out why. Mrs Lionel sat beside her without comment except to say, as they pulled up, 'Strawberry mousse.'

Rosemary turned the car off and looked at her friend. 'Pardon?'

'For dessert.' Mrs Lionel pointed at the basket of lush, fragrant berries on the back seat. 'Jasper will love strawberry mousse.'

'He will? How do you know?'

'Because you make it.'

Rosemary studied the older woman, but Mrs Lionel was easing herself from the car. She gave Rosemary a little wave and headed to The Green Mulbury, grinning.

Rosemary made strawberry mousse in between tending to customers and collecting jars from her cellar for a batch of Aunt Lilibeth's strawberry jam from Justin's leftovers. The table was set and everything ready for a dinner party to start soon after the guests arrived by the time Mrs Lionel came in with a plate of fudge. 'I had to bring something,' she said over Rosemary's protests. 'Jasper loves fudge.'

'Because you make it.'

The two women smiled at each other.

Six-thirty came and went.

Rosemary spent far too long polishing wine glasses before placing them carefully on the table. Mrs Lionel sat in a dining room chair and stared pointedly at the glasses. 'You'll wear them back to sand granules.'

Six forty-five.

Rosemary picked up the glass closest to her again, avoiding Mrs Lionel's raised eyebrows. 'A smudge,' Rosemary said, rubbing at the rim of the glass.

Six fifty.

Mrs Lionel stood, plucked the glass from Rosemary's hand, and gave her a mild push towards the kitchen. 'Make me a cup of tea. One for you, as well.'

'Tea?' Rosemary wandered over to the kettle but didn't turn it on. 'Are you sure? We haven't had dinner.'

'Valerian tea, thank you.'

'It'll make you sleepy.'

'The valerian is for you, not me.'

'I don't want to be sleepy.'

Mrs Lionel came behind the kitchen bench and rummaged in the pantry for the right tea cannister. 'Not sleepy, just calmer.'

'I don't need to be calm.'

The older woman shook her head slightly. 'Then stop acting like you do.'

Rosemary flicked the kettle on with a sigh, glancing at the clock as she did.

Seven o'clock.

'He's never late,' she said, lifting two cups from the cupboard.

'He was never late *before*.'

'Before?'

'Before Kerry.' Mrs Lionel smiled as she leaned back on the bench. 'BK.'

'BK.' Rosemary chuckled. 'Right.'

The tea was still brewing in its pot when sharp raps at the shop door sounded. Before Rosemary could respond, the door opened quietly and heavy footsteps sounded on the floor. Kerry appeared in the doorway, his bulk taking up most of the space with his head just clearing the top architrave. 'Rosemary Exeter!' He grinned as he saw Mrs Lionel. 'Dorothea Lionel! My two favourite Mulbury girls!'

Mrs Lionel put a swift hand on Rosemary's arm before she could retort that no one in the room had been a girl for a long time. 'Kerry Carruthers. Lovely to see you.'

Rosemary grunted hello, looking beyond Kerry to where Jasper's thin silhouette stood. He raised his hand at her. 'Come in, then,' she said gruffly. 'Sit.' She hesitated. 'You're late.'

'Are we? Are we now?' Kerry made a show of looking at an imaginary watch on his bare forearm. 'Jasper's fault, all Jasper. He had a devil of a time finding something clean to wear.'

'You did?'

Jasper stepped in the room as Kerry pulled the chair out at the head of the table and plunked himself down. He was dressed in all black, jeans and T-shirt and a dark overshirt Rosemary had never seen before. He was a complete contrast to Kerry's casual business outfit, shirt with tie, pressed trousers and darkly polished boots. 'I need to get up to scratch with my housework,' he said. 'It's taken a bit to get the shop back to working order. And…' He pointed his chin at Kerry.

'That's right, poor fellow.' Kerry scratched at his chin as he studied Jasper. 'Works all day and night with those dusty old books. Hardly has time for his old dad. I've had to develop my own interests.'

'And what would they be, dear?' Mrs Lionel moved back to the table with her tea but not before pushing Rosemary's towards her.

'Usual stuff for a man my age.'

'You'll have to explain further.' Mrs Lionel sat next to Kerry, indicating Jasper should sit on her other side. 'I haven't known a man your age for quite some time.'

'Really now, Dorothea!' Kerry gave her a lewd wink. 'That surprises me.'

Mrs Lionel smiled politely. 'You were saying…?'

'Usual stuff, yes. Calligraphy, trout fly tying, carving wood. You know.'

'I don't see you actually doing anything like,' said Jasper, taking the wine that Rosemary poured. 'I see you constantly on the internet.'

'Well, yes, yes. How else do I know how to tie flies? Or how to write a beautiful letter? Or even, dare I say it, how to whittle? It's all on the net these days.' Kerry tapped the side of his nose. 'Got to learn these things before you can put them into action.'

'I see.' Mrs Lionel sipped her tea. 'I bet you learn a lot that way.'

'And not only about flies.' Rosemary took the frittata from the oven and set it in the middle of the table. 'What other things have you learned?'

'From the old net? My goodness, let's see.' Kerry drummed his fingers on the table. 'Many things, many,

many things. Lives of famous people, exploits and adventures, art and antiquities.' He grinned at Mrs Lionel. 'Old things. They're quite interesting, don't you think?'

Rosemary braced herself so she didn't lunge across the table. 'You collect art and antiquities?'

'Sometimes, you know. Whatever comes my way when I'm surfing the old net.'

'I guess it gives you quite interesting topics to talk to the other Jalopers about,' said Mrs Lionel, picking up her cutlery.

'Oh, I wouldn't bother talking to them about much at all.' Kerry tipped his wine into his mouth. 'I check in with them at these reunions, see how their fortunes are going, but they aren't people of substance, you know. That Colin, for example, generous with his wallet but utterly guileless. No interests beyond his wife, and Lucy's focus is on keeping Colin neat and tidy. Totally uneducated in the ways of the world. And those girls in the packing room, I mean, what a group of airheads! They're like a pack of stupid hyenas intent on their next feed. What would they want to talk about? Silly things always vying for some man or other's attention.'

'What about Andrew Valencia?' Rosemary slid into a chair and began serving. 'Did he, for example, like art and antiquities, too?'

Kerry laughed. 'I'm afraid dear Andrew was not so sophisticated. He saw books as the only items of value. The original bookworm, he was. Always going on about some book or another, or their authors or some such thing.' Kerry leaned back in his chair. 'Silly old fellow was our Andrew. Books, books, and more books.' He tipped forward. 'Rosemary, Rosemary. What have we here? Looks delicious.'

'Frittata with Justin Gentleman's summer veg.' Rosemary gave Jasper an extra piece. 'Hardly top-class cuisine. Nourishing, though.'

Jasper smiled at her briefly as he picked up his fork.

'What sorts of books did Andrew collect?' Mrs Lionel asked.

'Oh, now, let me think.' Kerry took a large mouthful of his dinner and took time to chew and swallow. 'Can't think of anything specifically now.' He chuckled. 'Ones with pages in them!' He chuckled again. 'You know, funny old boy he was.'

'Milly said he was a collector of rare books.'

'Did Milly say that?'

'Yes,' said Rosemary.

'If Milly said so, then it must be true.' Kerry tapped the side of his nose and winked at Rosemary. 'Milly is one of those old girls who believes she knows everything about everyone.'

'Old girl indeed,' said Mrs Lionel mildly into her dinner.

'Oh!' Kerry put his hand on Mrs Lionel's shoulder and gave it a squeeze. 'Not to worry, of course I don't mean *you're* one of those old girls. Milly's type is more...nosey, I'd say. Always asking questions. Always pestering.'

'Well.' Mrs Lionel patted Kerry's hand before lifting it away. 'People with inquisitive natures have interesting personalities. Ones I quite prefer.'

'Really?' Kerry frowned briefly before a wide smile took over his face. 'That shows the difference between you and me. Me? I prefer people to stick to their own business.'

Kerry's last words echoed around the dining room and took a moment to settle. Rosemary ate her meal and watched him. Stiffness sat on his broad shoulders until he noticed her looking. He laughed, shrugged, and tucked into his food as if he hadn't eaten all day. Jasper, on the other hand, was grey and spent far too long slicing his food before delivering it to his mouth where he chewed for an extended time before swallowing.

'And how long are you staying in Mulbury, Kerry?' asked Mrs Lionel into the silence.

'Not sure, not sure. Waiting to see what happens next with my son, Jasper.'

'Why?' Rosemary put her fork down. 'What is supposed to happen?'

Jasper paused with a fork halfway to his mouth. 'He means what happens with Mum's books. The firsts.'

'Her lovely books!' said Kerry loudly. 'The ones she wrote. The *famous* ones.' He tapped his nose again. Rosemary resisted the urge to grab his finger.

'Her books?' Mrs Lionel paused, her knife in the air. 'Those cowboy books?'

Kerry stopped mid-chew. 'She wrote Westerns? I don't think that's right, Mrs L.'

'Space cowboys.' Jasper kept his head down and carved at his meal. 'Speculative fiction.'

'They were bestsellers!' Kerry started chewing again. 'They sound quite awful but someone out there must have liked them. A *lot* of people out there must have liked them.'

Rosemary watched as Kerry helped himself to more. 'You said they were lovely books.'

'Well, you know, I meant they are *now*. *Now* that they're worth something.' Kerry waved his fork around. 'Simply lovely books!'

'You've never read them.'

'Me? No, no, heavens no. I'm not a reader.'

'That's odd.'

'Not so odd. Lots of people have never read a book in

their lives!' Kerry took a large mouthful and swallowed without chewing. 'Can't imagine what a waste of time it is to be one of those people who read a book a week.' He shook his head.

'Very odd.'

Kerry rested the edge of his hand on the table, his fork suspended with a quivering mass of egg on it. 'You keep saying that, Rosemary,' he said. 'Why do you keep saying that?'

Rosemary put her utensils down. 'T. G. G. Duncan was a writer. She dedicated her books to her family. Her son owns a bookshop. It's odd, don't you think, you aren't a reader when she dedicated books to *you*.'

Silence fell as everyone paused. Sunny came out of the bedroom, sniffed the air, and stalked back into the bedroom with her tail up like a banner. *It's your game,* her retreating posture seemed to say.

'Not odd,' said Kerry finally, smiling at Rosemary with the sort of grin she normally associated with a dog baring its teeth. 'Opposites attract, so they say, yes indeed. We were madly in love.' He pointed his fork at Jasper. 'Enough to produce this one. Not that I knew about it, oh no. No, no.' He poked the fork towards Jasper's arm. 'I would have stuck around, I would have. If I'd known. Oh yes indeed.'

Jasper slid his arm back away from the offending utensil and went on eating his meal without looking up. Kerry turned back to his and for a moment there was nothing except the scrape of knives on plates and faint chewing noises.

'It's very sad about your friend Andrew,' said Mrs Lionel, placing her knife and fork neatly on her finished plate. 'You worked with him for so long. What was he like as a person?'

'Andrew?' Kerry screwed up his face as he chewed. 'Quiet chap. A bit strange. The sort of enigma that made the ladies curious. But you heard about his dress sense? I mean, really. Orange sport jackets!'

Rosemary poured herself half a glass more wine. 'And he collected books.'

'The trouble with people that read is that they think there's a story in everything. Can never take anything at face value. Always got to...' Kerry put the last of his meal in his mouth.

'Always got to what?'

Kerry swallowed, put his cutlery down heavily, and pushed his plate away. 'Always got to question things. You know? You could say to him that you'd had a lovely weekend, and he'd say, "What was lovely about it?"' He frowned. 'Difficult to have a plain conversation with him.'

'Was he interested when you told him about Jasper?'

'Oh, yes, everyone thought that was marvellous! I told Andrew first, you know. I ran into him very soon after seeing the documentary and making that marvellous discovery.' Kerry slapped Jasper's shoulder again. 'Such a marvellous happening!' He gripped Jasper's shoulder. 'I must say, though, I was disappointed in that woman's reaction.'

Mrs Lionel glanced at Rosemary. 'What woman, dear?'

'Milly, of course.' Kerry leaned towards the older woman and tapped his nose. 'Another reader, you know.'

Rosemary put her glass down. 'Why? How did she react?'

'With questions! She baled me up afterwards.' Kerry made his voice high-pitched. '*How do you know it was you, Kerry? How do you know T. G. G. Duncan didn't have another special friend? How could you have not known you had a son?*' He lowered his voice and took another mouthful of food. 'I mean to say. They were very rude questions, rude, intrusive. But typical. Milly and I never really got on. I must say...' He gave a short laugh 'When Milly turns up to any of our reunions, I'm a bit disappointed. Rather disappointed and a bit cross. I would prefer the old girl stayed at home but she has nothing else to do. Woman needs a hobby.' He helped himself to the last piece. 'I didn't bother explaining things to her.'

'Perhaps you could explain them to us,' said Mrs Lionel, sipping her wine. 'Describe how it was you realised your life was going to be enriched by finding such a wonderful man is your son.'

Jasper raised his head and smiled at Mrs Lionel.

Kerry let his fork clunk on his plate. 'Oh, yes, so glad you asked! It was a wonderful discovery, wonderful! I sat in that theatre and felt realisation wash over me. Jasper has been looking for his father for so long without even a little cooee from anyone. It was obvious that the time was right, in all sense of the words.' He leaned forward. 'It struck me. I had found the man to call my son.'

'Enriching, indeed,' said Rosemary.

'Quite, quite. Rich.' Kerry gazed for a moment at the far wall, a faint smile on his face. 'So. That's my story.' He blinked, leaned forward, and eyeballed Rosemary. 'What's your interest in my son?'

'He is one of my best friends.'

'Ah, indeed. Nothing more? No wish to be more than friends?'

Rosemary risked a glance at Jasper but he was earnestly finishing his dinner. 'Friendship is enriching.'

Kerry laughed loudly. 'So, you're after riches as well, Rosemary Exeter. Perhaps you too are interested in books?'

Rosemary felt her shoulders relax. 'Of course, I am.'

'Oh, don't be boring.'

'Boring?'

Kerry tapped the table. 'Not *books* in a I'm-going-to-have-a-cup-of-tea-and-read-a-book. Special books. Precious books. *Collectible* books.'

'No,' said Rosemary. 'I'm not into books that way. I'm a consumer of words.'

'Well then. Perhaps you should be.'

'It's obvious that you find collecting enjoyable, Kerry,' said Mrs Lionel, straightening her knife and fork on her plate. 'How big is your collection of books?'

Kerry looked at Jasper. Jasper stared at the big man for a moment then held up four fingers. Kerry pointed at them. 'That big.'

'Oh. Not so big.'

'Well.' Kerry shrugged. 'I see no need to hold on to them once I have collected them. I move them on.'

Rosemary leaned forward. 'You're buying more books from Jasper.'

'Buying books from my son? Goodness, what sort of person do you think he is, Rosemary? Selling books to his father? No. He wouldn't do that. Besides, he doesn't need to do that.' Kerry crossed his arms and grinned at her. 'Perhaps you don't know your friend as well as I thought.'

Rosemary felt Jasper's gaze on her but didn't return it. 'Or perhaps I know him *better* than you think.'

Sunny walked into the room again, stalking around the table and springing up on the windowsill, staring intently at the table and its tense occupants. She twitched her tail, distracting Rosemary. *Careful,* the cat seemed to be saying. *Keep calm.*

Rosemary sat back and raised her glass at her guests. 'Here's to everyone here getting to know people better.'

'Here, here,' said Mrs Lionel, relief softening her voice. Jasper followed suit.

Only Kerry hesitated. After a split second, he lifted his glass to match Rosemary's. 'Here's to you trying,' he said so quietly that the clinking of glasses almost hid it.

Rosemary smiled and answered equally as quietly. 'And I will.'

SEVENTEEN

The dinner ended quietly, with Jasper and Kerry making an exit straight after strawberry mousse with no offer to do the dishes. As unusual as it was for Jasper to not offer, Rosemary forgave him for he tried to go home first, probably hoping Kerry would stay on. Kerry, though, was like a piece of chewing gum stuck on Jasper's shoes and stood right after Jasper did, trailing him out the door. Rosemary shooed Mrs Lionel home after them and spent a contemplative hour cleaning up before heading for an early bed with Sunny curled by her side. Her final decision before sleep was to try and get Jasper alone again so she could talk properly to him.

Over the last three or so summers, Rosemary could count on Jasper being on the balcony outside his kitchen on most mornings. He'd be watching Snowy as the old dog snuffled his way around the backyard in the morning quiet, and Rosemary occasionally handed him a mug of tea over the railing. She ventured out the morning after the dinner and stood waiting on her section of the wooden veranda, but when the door to the kitchen eventually opened, it was only the old dog that wandered out, making his stiff way down the stairs to Jasper's dry backyard. 'Jasper?' called Rosemary softly, but no one answered.

Snowy spent a good twenty minutes making sure the backyard was as he had left it the day before and came back up the stairs one at a time, wagging his tail once as he spotted Rosemary before ambling back inside. The door to the kitchen closed and she was left with two cooling mugs of tea. 'Well,' she said to Sunny waiting for her in the doorway. 'Waste of time, that was.'

Sunny walked delicately out onto the wooden boards and sat by her mistress to overlook foraging magpies among the trees in Rosemary's yard. *Not sure what you expected,* her swishing tail seemed to say.

'I thought Jasper might come out and tell me more about what's going on.' Rosemary bent to scratch the ginger tabby's neck. 'I'm relying on his need to tell me, aren't I?'

Sunny stood, rubbed her chin on Rosemary's shin, and stalked back inside.

Rosemary drank the lukewarm tea and followed the cat. It was probably too much to expect from Jasper. He was, after all, a man who thought good things about everyone and had been totally taken in by Kerry from the beginning. If Kerry was lying, it would hit Jasper hard. Then again, if Kerry wasn't lying and he really was Jasper's father, it surely would be a huge disappointment after waiting so long to find out who his real father was. It was sometimes better to let sleeping dogs—and secrets—lie.

The day dragged onward with no signs of Jasper or Kerry until the shops opened. Rosemary waited by her front window until she saw the first of Jasper's outside book displays, a padded trolley full of romance novels, appear on the pavement. She shot outside and stopped. 'Gerry?'

Gerry let the wheelbarrow down, puffing out a large

breath as he did. 'These are heavier than I thought,' he said, lifting a book up to reveal the torso of a muscular man on its cover. He turned it at Rosemary's raised eyebrow, and quickly dropped the book among its companions. 'By heavy,' he started, 'I meant...'

'The weight, not the content,' Rosemary finished for him.

'Yes, that's right. Thanks.'

'Where's Jasper?'

'Oh.' Gerry wiped his hands on his shorts and gestured towards the inside of The Read Mulbury. 'Kerry rang me quite early. He asked if I'd mind opening this morning as he and Jasper had something to do out of town.'

'What was it?'

'What was what?'

'The thing they had to do.'

'Now that they didn't say.' Gerry frowned and drummed his fingers on the trolley handle. 'He just said they had to go today.'

'Both of them were doing this activity?'

'I guessed that was the case or one of them could have opened.'

'What time was that?'

'They rang about seven o'clock.'

Rosemary nodded. Later than when she'd stood uselessly on the veranda. She'd probably been in the shower when they'd left.

Gerry glanced at a car full of women pulling up at the kerb. 'I'd better keep going because Kerry said they were expecting the Bronte Book Club this morning and I suspect that's them.'

Rosemary nodded as the women piled out of the car and hurried to The Read Mulbury. Gerry held the heavy door open for them and they streamed in clutching tote bags decorated with the silhouette of Patrick Bronte's painting of his sisters. As the little man went to follow them, Rosemary grabbed his arm. 'Kerry didn't give any hints about where they were going, Gerry?'

'No. Not a clue.'

'And when will they be back?'

'I'm not sure, Rosemary. I said I'm available all day.' Gerry smiled. 'It's so lovely having Heather around to help as it means I can help others. Like today.' He indicated the shop. 'Like now.'

She let him go, and he hurried after the women, leaving Rosemary to ponder the absence, once again, of the book-shop owner as she went back inside The Preserved Mulbury.

Despite, or perhaps because of, the Bronte Book Club, the morning was quiet. The late summer sun decided to scorch the air of any moisture and as the day went on, Rosemary cranked up the ceiling fans and put a jug of lemon tea to cool in the fridge. Through the wall, she heard Gerry's cheery chatter and the occasional excited muffled tones of customers purchasing book bundles. Goldmarket Road remained bereft of familiar cars.

At five minutes before closing time, as Rosemary toted up the day's slim takings, Gerry pushed his way through the silent door. 'I'm heading off now, Rosemary. Jasper texted to say they'd been held up and weren't yet on their way back and to close anyhow.' Gerry placed two linked keys to Rosemary. 'Jasper left these for me on top of the door sill this morning. They're best left with you.'

'I'll get them to him. Was it a good day?'

Gerry smiled. 'Undoubtedly! I suspect I make a good bookseller.'

'Gerry, you're a *people* person. You make people feel good. You'd be a good *anything* seller.'

Gerry's round face glowed. 'Oh, Rosemary, that's very nice of you. I don't expect it-' His colour deepened.

'You don't expect praise from me?'

'Well, you know...'

Rosemary shrugged. 'I only give praise to those who deserve it.'

Gerry's cheeks nearly caught fire. 'Right, thanks, gosh. I'd better get back to Patti.' He turned to go, then swung back again. 'Once again, I must say, Heather Hubbard is a treat to work with. Thank you for that good idea.'

'Heather was an obvious choice as Patti's assistant.'

'Obvious to you. I'll admit to some reluctance, what with her...' Gerry waved his hand around.

'Heather is unique.'

'That she is. And very creative. You should see-' Gerry clapped his hand over his mouth. 'I can't say,' he said, his voice muffled.

'Right. Heather is working on a project.'

Gerry's hand dropped. 'You know?'

'I know it's a project but not what the project is.'

'Ah. Well, I'm not exactly sure, either.' He swivelled to go but again turned back. 'Did you know that Holly is leaving soon?'

'No need to whisper, Gerry. It's just us.'

'Yes, well, it's a secret, isn't it?'

'I think most of Mulbury knows so it's a bad secret.'

'I don't think Heather knows.'

Rosemary thought of Heather's happy face as the younger woman went about her work. 'She does.'

'Really? She doesn't look sad enough.'

'Heather is tougher than others imagine her.'

'But look what happened when her father was away that time!'

'It wasn't that her father was away, Heather was feeling someone else's pain. Holly is leaving for a happy reason, not a sad one. Heather will be fine.'

'Well, I hope you're right, Rosemary. You usually are.' Gerry turned once again but this time made it out the door and along the path to disappear from Rosemary's view.

She locked the door behind him and lowered the blinds. Sunny was on the counter when she went back, sniffing derisively at the set of keys Gerry had left behind. The cat stepped daintily back as Rosemary picked them up. 'It's alright, Sunny. They're Jasper's.'

Sunny put her ears back, leaped to the ground, and ran lightly back inside the living room.

Rosemary stared after her then held the keys out to catch the light streaming in from the skylight. Jasper's big front door key was indeed on the wire loop, as was his cellar door key, although he never locked it because he used it more for storage than hiding anything precious. Not that he had anything particularly precious, he said, except his mother's first edition, first print books and he liked to display them at the back of the shop with any other book he thought special.

She closed her hand gently around the keys, pulled out her phone with her other hand, and dialled Jasper's number. It went straight to voice messages. She ended the call without leaving any.

A sharp rapping on the door made her look up. Through the gap between the blind and the window edge she saw a face peering in before it disappeared and the rapping started again. 'Hello?' said a voice through the door. 'Hello? Please?'

Rosemary shoved the keys in her pocket and opened the door. 'Milly?'

'Rosemary! Mind if I come in?'

It wasn't really a question, as Milly almost ran inside, her bag swinging roughly against her side. 'Can I help you?' Rosemary asked, holding the door open.

'Close it!' Milly blinked, as if startled by the sound of her own voice. 'I mean, could you please close it?'

Rosemary did, keeping her eyes on Milly. 'What's going on?'

'It's Kerry.'

'He's back?'

'Back from where?' Milly shook her head. 'You mean, he's not here?'

'He's not next door.'

Milly relaxed a little before her shoulders went stiff again. 'It doesn't matter where he is, does it? He could be anywhere and it would still be happening.'

'What would be happening?'

'It's Colin, mainly. It's nearly always Colin. I don't know why he doesn't leave the man alone.'

Rosemary folded her arms across her chest. 'You aren't making sense.'

'Aren't I? Oh, I thought you'd know...'

Rosemary resisted the urge to sigh. 'Know what?'

'What Kerry does. What he's always done. What he shouldn't do but he does.'

Rosemary waited but Milly seemed lost in her own contemplation of Kerry's doings. 'What does Kerry always do?'

Milly shook her head and tutted. 'He cons people, Rosemary! Repeatedly, if he gets the chance.'

'You're saying he conned Jasper?'

'Well, it wouldn't surprise me. I don't have any hard evidence about that. He has conned Colin, though. Again.'

'In what way?'

Milly dropped her bag to land at her feet. 'Well, I'm not sure. But Kerry must be involved.'

'Involved in what?'

Milly took a deep breath in and let it out slowly. 'Colin's been taken into the police station.'

'What for?'

Milly looked at Rosemary with open, teary eyes. 'I think they're blaming him for Andrew Valencia's death.'

'And who should be blamed?'

Milly blinked. 'It's obvious, isn't it? Kerry.'

Rosemary waited but Milly was twisting her hands together and didn't say anything else. Outside, the road was empty except for a laughing couple who slid into their camper van and drove off slowly. 'I didn't see any police out there?'

Milly peered past her. 'Oh, it didn't happen here. Colin, Lucy and I are staying at the same bed and breakfast about ten kilometres away. I was driving out when two police vehicles turned up. I tried to go back but they blocked me. All I saw was Colin being led away and Lucy following. She texted me.' Milly held up her phone. 'See? *They are taking Colin in for questioning about Andrew's death.*'

Rosemary frowned. 'Lucy was sure that's what they were doing? On what evidence?'

Milly's mouth fell open. 'What do you mean?'

'People do not get questioned without evidence. What do the police know?'

'Not enough! Can't they see that Colin wouldn't hurt a fly? It's Kerry they should be dealing with.'

Rosemary let Milly's shouting die down and took the

woman by the arm. 'Come with me. We'll have some tea and try to figure this out.'

Milly shook her head. 'No, no, I really think we should do something.'

'We can't figure out what to do unless we know exactly what we're up against.' She steered Milly into her living area. 'And we will.'

Milly sat at the dining table and put her hands flat on its dark wooden surface as if clinging to a lifeline. 'I'm not usually like this.'

Rosemary set the kettle on. 'Like what?'

The older woman rubbed her hands along the table's surface. 'Well, I guess you might think me overly dramatic.'

'Concerned.'

'Pardon?'

'You sounded concerned. You don't like Kerry.'

'Oh, it's not a matter of liking him...' Milly gave a quick grin. 'Actually, I'm not sure why I'm apologising. I *don't* like Kerry. I never have. He has a bad aura about him.'

'Have you been talking with Rakisha?'

'Is that the lady with the unusual tasting coffee?'

'Yes. Rakisha sees auras.'

'I don't mean *see* in the literal sense.' Milly shook her head. 'Kerry is a man who is instantaneously hateful.'

Rosemary clattered about with the teapot and cups, keeping an eye on the woman as she did. Milly stopped talking and bent down to pat Sunny as the ginger tabby stalked past on her way to the windowsill. Once the tea was on the table, and Milly had taken a sip, Rosemary sat down opposite her. 'You said when I first met you that Kerry had a discreditable past.'

Milly sipped again. 'Oh, in my eyes he does. From the

moment he joined Jalopy, he was suspicious, if you know what I mean.'

'No, I don't.'

'Oh. Well.' Milly put her cup down and leaned forward. 'He gives off hints that he is forever pretending, whether that's pretending to listen, pretending to like you, or pretending to work. When he speaks to you, he never quite meets your eye. It's as if he's studying things in his peripheral vision, off to the side.'

Rosemary sipped her tea, listening intently.

'And he was often in places he shouldn't have been in.'

'Such as?'

'Well, his job was in stores, keeping track of parts. Remember, this was in the days before computers. He had to count the parts manually and keep note of them in the folder that hung off a nail on the back of the shed. That was so people could check if parts were on the shelf, or if they'd been ordered. The folder went to Colin at the end of the day so he could do the orders.'

'Kerry spent his days checking parts?'

'And cleaning up the second-hand ones. Our clients' cars often needed parts that couldn't be obtained new. Kerry's job was to keep track of old and new. He sometimes went to auctions and sales and bought bits and bobs. But he was never meant to be in the finance office.'

'But he was.'

'How did you know?'

'It's in your voice.'

Milly nodded, taking her cup up and sipping at the last of her tea. 'Yes, I saw him in Colin's office many times, frequently when Colin wasn't there. He always had an excuse. Putting the folder in there for Colin. Collecting the folder if Colin hadn't put it back. Looking for the folder when it was obvious it was on its nail.'

'What was the real reason?'

'I could never figure it out until the day of my retirement.' Milly's cup trembled as she placed it in the saucer. 'I went in to give Colin back my apron. He was in charge of ordering uniforms, you see, and we all had shirts and aprons and jumpers with the Jalopy logo. My apron was fairly new. I thought he could pass it on to a new employee. Well, Colin wasn't there. Kerry was. And he was putting letters into a manilla folder Colin had on his desk.'

'He'd been reading letters?'

'At first, I thought that was it. Then I realised he had papers in his hand that he wasn't putting back. He put them behind his back when I came in and sidled out sideways.'

'You didn't call him out?'

'No. No, I didn't, although I did tell Andrew later when he was interviewing us for the book.' Milly sighed. 'I *should* have called Kerry out, I had nothing to lose, it being my last day. But I was looking forward to waking up the next morning as a free woman, and I couldn't be bothered anymore with the likes of him. I felt bad when I found out what he'd done.'

Rosemary waited but Milly was temporarily lost in thought. 'Found out...?'

Milly startled. 'Oh, sorry. Found out that Colin had stolen parts of a 1935 Ford sedan.'

'Colin is a thief?'

'No, not at all! Colin denied it, with reason. He is an honest man. The trouble is, he couldn't explain where the parts had gone. The folder showed they had been received but there were no parts on the shelf. Even though the boss eventually put it down to an error, Colin nearly lost his job. The boss never fully trusted him again, so Lucy said.'

'That's horrible for Colin, but maybe it was a true mistake.'

Milly shook her head. 'It was no mistake. At the end of that last day, I went to my locker to pack up the bits and pieces I kept in there, and Kerry was lugging a huge duffel bag out the door. He just winked at me and disappeared outside. I remembered later the bag clinked, as if metal parts were banging against each other. He had stolen the parts, Rosemary, I'm sure of it. And it wouldn't have been the first time.'

Rosemary nodded slowly. It wasn't hard evidence, but it wasn't difficult to imagine Kerry's deceit. 'It's a big leap to think that Colin has been taken in for questioning for something Kerry has done.'

Milly sat straight. 'It's typical of Kerry's luck and Colin's *un*luckiness.'

Rosemary frowned. 'Why do you continue these jolly jaunts with former work colleagues, several of whom you don't like?'

Milly turned the cup in its saucer, making it squeak. 'It's hard to explain.'

'Try me.'

It was a few minutes before Milly answered. In that time, the sun went behind a wispy rain-free cloud, dimming the room. Milly's face shadowed, and her voice seemed disembodied when she finally spoke. 'You don't know what it's like because you are here, working happily, surrounded by people who like you. When I woke up the morning after I retired, I realised I wasn't a free woman. I was trapped.'

'Trapped.'

'Yes, trapped. Trapped by loneliness. I'd spent forty-five

years at The Jalopy Factory. My husband had died. I don't have siblings. My parents, who I looked after, were both gone. My little dog is my only companion but I didn't have him then. I woke up that morning and had nothing to do. *Nothing.*'

'You went out to find something to do.'

'You would think that would be the cure.' Milly smiled wanly. 'I tried. I got a job in a library shelving books. I volunteered with a few charities, but the people in them already had their friendship groups. I put my head down and worked at being charitable, and before I knew it, I was working as hard as I had when I was at the Factory. So, I stopped, and once again had nothing to do.' She waved her hand towards Goldmarket Road. 'These reunions are important to me because these people are the only ones I know.'

Rosemary poured Milly more tea. 'I get it.'

'Do you? Do you really see how I would prefer to hang out with people I know, even if they aren't the best people, than be by myself?'

'Of course.'

Milly smiled, a real one this time. 'Really?'

Rosemary held her gaze. 'Yes. Loneliness is truly awful.'

'Are you lonely?'

'No.'

'But you've been.'

Rosemary poured herself more tea but said nothing.

'Sorry, I shouldn't have asked.' Milly put a hand to her throat. 'But what to do about Colin?'

'I can make some enquires. A question first: have you seen Kerry today?'

Milly turned her head towards the kitchen wall as if she could see something. 'Isn't he next door?'

'No. He and Jasper have been absent all day. Has Kerry said anything to you or the other Jalopers about where he might have gone?'

Milly shook her head. 'The person to ask would be Colin but that's a little difficult at present.'

'Why Colin?'

'Because, despite their differences in character, the men stick together. Well, that only leaves Colin and Kerry now.'

'You think if Kerry said anything it would be to Colin.'

'Perhaps. Poor Colin had to put up with Kerry's rants.' Milly pushed her cup and saucer away and stood up. 'Here I am, enjoying a cup of tea with you when I really should be worrying about Lucy. I think I'll give her a call.' She took her bag from where it hung on the chair.

'Of course.' Rosemary stood as well. 'I'll see if I can find out about Colin. You stay here and I'll go into the shop to give you some quiet.'

While Milly fished her phone out of her bag, Rosemary took hers into The Preserved Mulbury. She stood at the door under the silent bell and called Honey.

'Hey, Mum. What's up?'

Behind her daughter's voice came others. Tallulah cooed in the distance while, even further back, Pearl was speaking loudly to someone Rosemary presumed was Ronnie. 'Is Ronnie working on a police case at present?'

'No. He's only taking insurance claims.'

'So, he doesn't know anything about the case of the man in the drowned dam? Even if he's not investigating it?'

'I don't think so. Why are you asking me? You should be talking to Ronnie directly.'

'I'm trying to be covert.'

'That's not your usual style.'

'No.'

'It's Pearl, isn't it?'

'What is Pearl?'

'You don't want Pearl to know you've asked Ronnie. He wouldn't be able to keep a secret from his mother.'

'Wouldn't he?'

Honey's sigh whooshed noisily down the phone line. 'You know he wouldn't. Ronnie is an open book, especially to his mother. She reads him like a tabloid newspaper.'

'Is that good?'

'I don't know. It is what it is.'

Rosemary listened for a moment to Tallulah. Close happy baby noises meant that Honey had picked her up and had her on her shoulder. 'How are you going with Pearl, Honey?'

'What can I say, Mum? She'll be going home soon and since her little breakdowns, I'm putting up with whatever she does which is mainly complain. When she's not saying how different the tearoom is to her beloved café.'

'Right.'

'Why did you want to know about Ronnie?'

'Colin's been taken in for questioning.'

'What for?'

'That's what I'm trying to find out.'

'Ask Kerry. He knows everything, or so he says.'

'Kerry and Jasper have been gone all day.'

'Where?'

'I don't know.'

'Did they take the boxes with them?'

Rosemary put a hand on the door, feeling the wood warm and reassuring. 'What boxes?'

'Kerry knocked on the door really early asking for a couple of carboard boxes. We get a lot from deliveries. He took two small ones. I saw him later putting them into his car.'

'Did he say what he wanted them for?'

'Books.'

'Books.'

'Yes, books. Hardly surprising, is it, if Jasper sells books. It was probably an online order and they were posting them.' Honey paused. 'You don't think it was an online order.'

'No. I'm sure it wasn't.'

'It wasn't books in the box, then?'

Rosemary thought about the pile of firsts in Jasper's special cabinet. 'Got to go, Honey.' She hung up, glanced back at Milly still on the phone, and went out the door. The blinds in The Read Mulbury were down, but she didn't need to go inside as the gap between them and the window frame showed the cabinet and its empty interior.

A squeal of a door, and Honey hurried out of the tearoom, clutching a gurgling Tallulah. 'What is it, Mum?'

Rosemary turned to Honey, her hands clenched. 'Kerry's taken Jasper to sell the firsts.'

NINETEEN

Rosemary rang Jasper every hour throughout the evening, receiving the same softly spoken voice message immediately every time, as if the phone was out of range. Milly had declined an invitation for dinner, and Mrs Lionel was at the Hubbards sharing a meal with the sisters, so Rosemary paced up and down the living room with only Sunny looking on. *You are disturbing my peace,* the cat seemed to say with her tail lashing.

'Can't help it, Sunny.' Rosemary rang Jasper's number again but hung up before the voice message ended. 'Something is not right.'

Twilight lengthened her shadow when she finally decided on action and walked across Goldmarket Road towards Patti and Gerry's house. The couple had bought a little miner's cottage next to the cemetery when they'd moved out of the shop under the veranda. Rosemary hurried up the steep hill and past the quiet graveyard to the house. A cheery glow exuded from the glass panelling over the door as she knocked. Gerry's heavy footsteps sounded and he opened the door. 'Rosemary! My, this is a surprise! Please, come in.'

Rosemary stepped inside, and for a moment was taken in by the compactness of the hallway with its whitewashed walls. She'd only been in the house once, and it was when Patti and Gerry had first bought it. The clearest thing Rosemary remembered was the damp smell of an unused building. 'You've cleaned it up.'

'The house? Oh, yes. We had a few structural things done, and the summer has helped air the place. Quite lovely now, isn't it? Just mind the box there. Patti's been collecting abandoned clothing from the bin at the cemetery. Rather an unusual habit, but you know Patti!' Gerry laughed. 'She actually found a lovely pair of men's Julius Marlowe's but far too big for me or I would have polished them up and had them for myself. What people throw out; it astonishes me.'

Rosemary peered into the box, noting the assortment of garments with a pair of dirty brown shoes on top, and nodded as she followed the little man down the skinny hallway to the extension built on to the simple cottage. Patti stood in the kitchen, rockabilly dress covered with a flowery half apron, holding a large spoon and about to serve up a creamy risotto. 'Oh, Rosemary! How gorgeous of you to visit! Have you had dinner?'

Rosemary thought of the few dry biscuits and cheese she'd consumed an hour ago. 'No.'

'Then share ours. Gerry always makes more than we need. We would love it if you would stay.'

'Unless,' said Gerry, his normally jovial face suddenly serious, 'there was something you specifically came to see us about.'

'There is.' Rosemary sat on the chair he pulled out for her. 'I'm looking for Jasper.'

'He's not home yet?' Patti plonked herself into a chair, her skirt puffing up as she did and settling slowly like a parachute coming in to land. 'That's odd. Didn't they say they'd be back tonight, Gerry?'

'No, but they didn't say they wouldn't be.' Gerry frowned, tapping a finger on his temple. 'I assumed it would be tonight because there was nothing said about looking after the shop tomorrow.'

'Right.' Rosemary smiled at Patti as she placed a plate full of mushroom risotto in front of her.

'Jasper will be okay,' said Gerry, sounding less than convinced. 'They're probably having a late dinner somewhere so they don't have to cook when they get home.'

Patti sat down. 'Did they tell you what they were doing, sweetie?'

'No, Kerry didn't say.' Gerry ate a forkful of rice, frowning slightly. 'Mind you, I wasn't listening at my full capacity because I was hurrying to get a box of odd socks down to the shop for you.'

Rosemary didn't bother to ask what Patti would do with a box of socks. She hoped they were well washed. 'No hints at all?'

'Let me think exactly what Kerry said.' Gerry put his fork down. 'He rang. I said hello. He said something like, "Gerry, old man".' Gerry looked at Patti. 'I'm sure I'm a good bit younger than Kerry.'

'You are, sweetie, by decades.' Patti reached across and gripped her husband's hand. 'And a good bit nicer.'

'Thank you. Then he said, "We're going out, Gerry. Mind the shop for us, would you?" And I said, "For how long, Kerry?" Then he said...' Gerry put his head down in thought. '"As long as it takes, old man."' He looked up. 'I guess that doesn't mean just one day, when you think about it.'

'Did you say anything else, Gerry?'

'Well, yes. After I'd said I'd open up, I just commented along the lines of I hope you have a great day with your son. Kerry said, and I remember this, "A great day, old man, yes indeed! A worthwhile day indeed." You know, *worthwhile* is an odd description.'

'It is, isn't it?' Patti poured Rosemary a glass of wine. 'Worthwhile sounds like a shopping expedition, not a lovely day out with your family.'

'Perhaps it was.' Rosemary ate a mouthful of creamy mushrooms thoughtfully. 'The firsts are missing from Jasper's cabinets. I believe they've gone to sell them.'

Gerry swallowed hastily and choked. When he'd finished coughing, he said, 'Sell the firsts? But they are so precious to Jasper! He would never sell them.'

'He thought he had no choice. Kerry has a letter signed by T. G. G. Duncan leaving the firsts to him.'

'What?' Gerry said hoarsely, and Patti rubbed his back until he could speak clearly. 'Jasper knew this?'

'Only when Kerry showed him the letter. And that was only after he identified himself as Jasper's father.'

'How odd.' Patti curled a segment of her apricot hair around her finger. 'It's all so strangely secretive. Jasper had no idea about his mother. Then he discovered she was an author writing under a pseudonym. Then he finds those precious books. Then Kerry turns up and they're his, not Jasper's. And Jasper finds his long-lost father. It's not the trajectory I thought Jasper's journey was on.'

'What sort of trajectory did you think Jasper would follow, my love?' asked Gerry.

'Well, I'm not really sure.' Patti's bottom lip wobbled for

a moment. 'I just thought that a kind soul like Jasper would discover the most wonderful things once he knew his mother was a famous author, and that his father would appear and be so regretful he hadn't known Jasper before, and they would live happily ever after.' She reached for her husband's hand. 'Like us.'

Rosemary turned to stare politely at the fridge as Gerry and Patti exchanged a noisy, risotto-laden kiss. Gerry chuckled as he noticed Rosemary. 'Sorry. But Patti is correct. Jasper deserves more than Kerry, even if he is his real father.' He narrowed his eyes at Rosemary as she began to eat her dinner again. 'Which I don't think you believe for one second.'

'It's too convenient.' Rosemary sipped her wine. 'Jasper and his sisters have been looking for clues to Jasper's real father ever since they found out T. G. G. Duncan's secret. Helena thought she had him but he disappeared once more. The documentary debuts and suddenly a man comes out of the woodwork claiming not only to be T. G. G. Duncan's lover but to be owed artefacts.'

'You're right, Rosemary. It doesn't make any sense.'

Patti shivered. 'But what do we do? Unless we get scientific evidence that Kerry isn't who he says, Jasper has to go with what he says. He probably feels the letter left for Kerry rather clinches it.'

Gerry leaned forward. 'It's too late, anyway. Once they sell those firsts, Jasper has lost them. They'll be sucked into someone's private collection.'

'Yes.' Rosemary finished her meal and sat back. 'Unless we stop it happening in the first place.'

'But how? We don't know where Jasper and Kerry have gone.'

Rosemary tapped her finger on her wine glass. 'Where would you go to sell precious old books?'

'Second-hand dealers specialising in books.' Patti frowned. 'Auction houses? Vintage shops? Space cowboy books are a niche, you know.'

'I guessed that,' said Rosemary. 'They wouldn't sell in the usual places.' She tipped her glass towards Patti. 'You know that world well.'

'What world?'

'The niche world. The speciality selling world. Your garments are niche.'

'Bespoke,' said Gerry. 'That's what we say, rather than niche.'

'Niche, nonetheless. Patti, if you wanted to sell something that wasn't mainstream, how would you even start?'

'The internet, obviously,' said Patti. 'I'd search it for relevant collection sites.'

'What else?'

'I guess I'd ask around.'

'Who would you ask?'

'People who sell bespoke items.'

'And how would you find them?'

Patti frowned and tapped an orange painted nail on the table. 'I'd start with people who sell ordinary items. For example, when I started repurposing old garments, I went to a few shops that sold vintage clothing for ideas on how to sell second-hand clothes. You remember those, Gerry?'

'Oh, yes.' Gerry shook his head. 'Some of those places smelled entirely of moth balls.'

'But it was useful, wasn't it, sweetie? In the end I discovered someone who mended vintage clothes and that gave me the idea for upcycling.'

'You're so clever, my love.'

'Thank you, sweet one.'

Patti reached for Gerry again and Rosemary put her hand up to delay the inevitable sloppy kiss between them. 'As Jasper doesn't sell clothing, where do you think he would start?'

'Oh.' Patti pulled back from Gerry. 'That's an easy one. He'd contact ordinary book dealers, wouldn't he? They'd surely be in contact with others who specialise in niche collections.'

Gerry chuckled again. 'That's ironic. Jasper is a type of book dealer, although I know he gets most of his books from the general public. He probably knows exactly who would deal with selling books like his mother's.' He stopped laughing when he looked at Rosemary. 'What is it? Have I said something wrong?'

'No. You've said exactly the right thing, Gerry.' Rosemary pushed her chair back and stood. 'I'm going to look through Jasper's shop for book dealer contacts.'

Gerry stood quickly, his chair falling backwards. 'Well, we're coming with you, Rosemary. I spent all day in The Read Mulbury without noticing anything that might have pointed to where Jasper and Kerry may have gone. We need not waste time looking in the obvious place when we could be doing a thorough search of other places.'

Patti reached for their plates and clattered them into the sink. 'Well, let's go! No time like the present!'

Outside, the air was still warm. As they hurried down the hill, Patti running lightly in her ballet shoes and Gerry lumbering behind, Rosemary noticed the light on in Robert Sparkling's window and a face silhouetted in it. She waved him down. By the time they reached The Read Mulbury's door, Robert had joined them.

Rosemary unlocked the bookstore door. It was dim and

quiet, although a night light shone in the living area for Snowy. The old dog wagged his tail as they surged in, and she gave him a quick rub of his tummy.

'I fed the old fellow before I left,' said Gerry. 'He seemed to expect it.' He paused. 'Rosemary, do you know where he kept his business contacts?'

'Most likely on his phone.'

'But this is Jasper we're talking about, sweetie,' said Patti. 'I think he would have had an old-fashioned paper address book or something like that.'

Robert sat on the couch next to the old dog, who thumped his tail in appreciation. 'Can I ask what we're doing? I'm struggling not to see this as a home invasion.'

Gerry briefed Robert as Rosemary went back into the shop to rummage under the counter. The shelves were full of Regency romances, most studded with bookmarks. Jasper's secret reading pile, obviously. From the tattered look of many of the books, they were his favourites. Amongst the reading matter, though, there was no address book. She went back to the living area where Robert and Gerry were still talking.

'I think you're going about this the wrong way,' Robert said. 'You're looking for how Jasper keeps his contacts.'

'Right,' said Rosemary, unable to keep the irritation from her voice. 'And you think that's wrong.'

'Correct.' Robert stood and went to the mantlepiece over Jasper's open fire. 'You should be looking at how other dealers give out their details. I mean, they don't grab Jasper's phone and enter their numbers. How do they communicate what they do? And I don't mean via their websites. What about at book fairs or in their shops? What do you take away when you visit them?' He took a business card from the shelf and held it up to show the logo of The

Read Mulbury—a person's face peering over a book—with a description of the shop on the back. 'This is what Jasper has. What would others do?'

'I imagine they'd have business cards as well,' said Gerry. 'Now, Patti has printed tea towels made from old bathrobes instead because she's very clever.'

'Thank you, sweetie,' said Patti from where she was rummaging through items on Jasper's kitchen table.

'Tea towels from a garment shop.' Robert nodded thoughtfully. 'That is clever. What would a book dealer have besides business cards?'

Rosemary spun around and ran back into the shop. She knelt beside the counter for a moment then rushed back in to where the others stood staring at her. 'Bookmarks,' she said, holding half a dozen in her hands. 'People dealing in books have bookmarks.' She fanned them out. 'Here are our clues to where Kerry and Jasper have gone.'

TWENTY

There was no point doing anything more until the morning. Patti and Gerry went home, Patti yawning as they slogged back up the hill. Robert stayed with Rosemary as she settled Snowy for the evening by taking him for a wander in Jasper's backyard. 'It is strange Jasper didn't ask for Snowy to be fed,' said Robert, standing with Rosemary on Jasper's balcony. 'That makes me think he'll be back home soon.' But they waited another hour with no sign of Jasper or Kerry.

Eventually, Rosemary took the bookmarks home and sorted them on the table, Robert behind her in the kitchen making tea. The disquiet she felt was like the morning Jasper closed his shop door and left for three months. Back then, he was clearly unsettled and going away seemed the only cure. To have him return looking worse than ever had been awful. To have him absent without notice again was chilling.

'Here.' Robert sat the tea on the table. 'It's not my greatest skill, brewing tea. My mum used to say a spoon for each person and one for the pot, but I never know what spoon size she was talking about. I used your wooden spoon.'

Rosemary frowned at him.

'Only joking.' He held up a teaspoon. 'I'm checking to see how worried you are.'

'What's your conclusion?'

'Fairly worried or you would have given me a look of disdain rather than crossness.'

'I've never looked at you in disdain.'

Robert laughed and poured the tea. 'Here. Have a cup and tell me what you're thinking.'

Rosemary sat, moving the two stacks of bookmarks away from her tea. 'Four of these bookmarks are advertising books, but two are dealers. One is in the city and the other is in a small town about two hours' drive away from here.'

'If it's a two-hour drive to the city, they'd be home by now if the dealer did business hours. If they left the city and drove to the other town, that would be how far?'

'About five hours.'

'That's a fair way to drive.'

'But if they knew they'd be gone that long, Jasper would have said something to Gerry.'

'Jasper didn't speak to Gerry. It was Kerry.'

'That's even worse.'

Robert nodded as he slid into the chair opposite Rosemary. 'There's a lot going on, isn't there? A prodigal father, a letter of ownership, a battered-looking Jasper.'

'You think Jasper looks battered?'

'In the sense that he looks unwell or worn down. He's sad. Definitely unhappy.'

'Yes.'

'Do you know why?'

'Turmoil. He wants to think he's found his father,

closing the loop on that mystery, but the father he's found is not the one he wants.'

Robert drummed his fingers on the table. 'Complicated.'

'Yes.'

He leaned back and put one arm on the back of the chair next to him. 'You don't believe Kerry is his father.'

'Do you?'

'I don't know. Families *are* complicated. Fathers particularly so.'

'My father was pretty straightforward.'

'Aren't you the lucky one?' Robert gazed into the distance. 'As much as I'd like to think Jasper's real father would be like Jasper, he may not be. Unfortunately, Kerry might be that mystery which should never have been solved.'

Rosemary slid the bookmarks over to Robert. 'Too late to contact them now.'

'That's for sure.' Robert eased himself upright. 'I'm going to head home. Didn't sleep well last night.'

'Why not?'

'Too much rustling going on downstairs.'

'Have you got mice?'

'No. I hope not, anyway. No, I've got Heather.'

'What?'

Robert grinned at Rosemary. 'I've got Heather working on her secret project well into the night. A bit of rustling but also lots of humming.'

'Do you know what she's working on?'

'Not a clue. She is spending more and more time on it, though.' He yawned. 'Patti knows. She sometimes helps.'

'Two lots of rustling and humming.'

'Patti dances and sings. It's a nice combination.' Robert

leaned over the table to squeeze Rosemary's hand. 'Jasper will be alright.'

'Yes.' She stood, sliding her hand out from his to walk him to the door. 'I'll make sure he is.'

TYPICAL OF LATE SUMMER, the day broke to a cacophony of kookaburras and magpies calling out over the long shadows in Rosemary's backyard. She was already awake staring at the ceiling with one hand on Sunny. The cat had her head buried in her front paws. She tucked herself further into the bed as Rosemary stroked her back. 'You can stay there but I have to get up.'

Sunny curled her head inwards in a show of, *I'm so glad I'm not human. Now please go away.*

Rosemary padded out to the kitchen and stood straining to hear any noise through the wall. It was early, but not for Jasper. Still, nothing stirred. On the other side of her living quarters, the radio was on in Mrs Lionel's kitchen, emitting a low indecipherable soundtrack to breakfast. Rosemary ate toast standing at the bench before heading to The Read Mulbury. Snowy greeted her from the couch, and ambled his way out the back door as she scanned the house for signs of Jasper. It was as it had been left, a comfortably messy place, albeit with a tinge of Kerry in a stack of tabloid newspapers spilling over on the coffee table.

With Snowy back on his couch, Rosemary locked the shop again, keeping the 'closed' sign in view. Gerry would not have time to tend to Jasper's shop two days in a row, even if he wanted to. She paused. Maybe she could run both shops for a while because surely Jasper would be back sometime today?

'Hi, Mum.'

Rosemary turned to see Honey clatter a sandwich board on the pavement. 'Opening early?'

'Only to the locals.' Honey wandered over to her mother, pulling her hair back into a ponytail as she went. 'Robert usually comes in. Kerry has been as well, much to Pearl's chagrin.'

'Why?'

'She reacts to Kerry for some reason. Practically hypes up to tornado-speed when he's around. No idea why.' Honey wiped her hands on her apron. 'Five days to go now.'

Rosemary studied her daughter. Honey's hair was its glossy self, but her face was unusually pale for this time of the season. 'Are you well?'

'Me? Yep. I'm good.' Honey ran her hand over her face. 'Well, Ronnie and I were up late discussing life. You know.'

'No.'

'You do know, Mum. Things that you and Dad would have talked about.' She paled further. 'Other than the fact he was about to take off and leave you. Sorry.'

'We certainly didn't discuss that.'

'Ronnie and I were talking about Tallulah, and our tearoom, and...Pearl.'

'Pearl is who's made you look like you haven't slept at all.'

Honey laughed. 'I guess so. On one hand...' Honey looked around but the street was empty '...she's a pain in the neck. On the other hand...'

'She's Ronnie's mother.'

'Not only that. She is actually a big help in the tearoom. She's efficient and works hard. She even has new ideas for cakes and tea mixes.' Honey sighed. 'I just wish she didn't carry on like she does. Whinge, whinge, whinge. It gets me down.'

'It would get me down, too.'

'Ronnie doesn't notice, because he's...'

'Her son.'

'*Amiable*, is what I was going to say. And sweet.' She grinned suddenly. 'I don't think I'm very sweet.'

'Sweet is an attribute not necessarily known to the Exeters.' Rosemary grinned back. 'It's best left to the Pattis and Ronnies of the world. We have other charms.'

'I hope so! Anyway, Ronnie doesn't want Pearl to go home. He thinks she's having some issues. I *know* she's got some issues. We all know.'

'You don't want her to stay.'

'We haven't room for her to stay with us. And I'm not sure I could put up with her complaints for much longer. It's complicated.'

'Yes.' Rosemary stepped forward and tucked a strand of her daughter's hair that had escaped the ponytail behind her ear. 'What would be the best scenario?'

'The best? The tearoom blossoms, and Pearl lives somewhere close where she could come and help if she wanted but without the moaning.' Honey put her hands on her hips, and her head to one side. 'Too fanciful?'

'No. One step at a time, though. Working out what's going on with Pearl is the starting place.'

'You're right, it is. She may need professional help if we can't help her.'

'What do you know about her café? The one she ran before Ronnie was born?'

'Next to nothing. Do you think that's got something to do with her...behaviour?'

'Yes. It wouldn't surprise me if it had everything to do

with her behaviour. It wouldn't take Ronnie a lot of work to figure out.'

'I guess not. He is reluctant to admit anything's wrong with his mother but he can't say she's normal.'

Rosemary thought about Geoffrey's reluctance to visit Pearl. 'Her normal is a bit trying for some.'

Honey laughed. 'Yes, I think she's always had a reputation for being outspoken. But still, this is worse than that, isn't it?'

'Yes.'

'Right then.' Honey clapped her hands together and turned to go back to the shop. 'Is Jasper still away?' she called back over her shoulder.

'Yes.'

Honey stopped and turned back. 'Kerry, too?'

'Yes.'

'That's odd.'

'Yes.'

'No, Mum. I mean that's odd when Kerry specifically said he'd be in to get a bee sting. I've made a few little ones for him.'

'When did he say that?'

'The other day when he was in. He said that he was going away for a little while but would be back to collect his bee stings before he left.'

'Left?'

'Yeah...' Honey came back to her mother. 'That's what he said. I thought he meant he was going with the other Jaunty Jalopers to something. I could be wrong, couldn't I? He may have meant *left* as in leave for good.' She frowned. 'But he wouldn't do that to Jasper. I mean, he's just come back into Jasper's life.'

'We think Jasper and Kerry have gone to sell the firsts.'

'What? But Jasper wouldn't do that!'

'He might have had to.' Rosemary filled Honey in on the letter.

'That is strange. A letter giving ownership to Kerry? How convenient.'

'You're thinking like me.'

'Well, it isn't hard. What makes Jasper think that the letter is genuine?'

'I don't think Jasper questioned it.'

'Did you get to see it?'

'Yes. I will admit, it looks genuine. It has the voice of T. G. G. Duncan and ends with her signature.'

'T. G. G. Duncan was a pseudonym. How can a letter have the voice of a pseudonym?'

'It matched the introductions she did for her later novels which explained the genre.'

'In what way did it match?'

'The words she used. A specific phrase or two.'

'Right. And the paper itself?'

'Of the era. And, before you ask, Robert said the pen ink was also of the era. We are talking about a woman who only died a few decades ago.'

'Still. Sounds odd. If the letter was written later in her life, why wouldn't she have left her firsts to her children?'

'The books were lost, remember. Jasper found them accidentally. Maybe she thought they'd never be found and wrote the letter thinking it would never be actioned?'

'Not a nice move, though. It doesn't sound like a thing a mother would do.' Honey pointed across the Square. 'Here's Robert.' She glanced at her watch. 'I'd better go back inside and get things going. Hey, Robert. The usual?'

Robert finished crossing the road and stepped up the kerb to hand Honey his reusable cup. 'Thanks, Honey.

Service extends to greeting your customers on the pavement now?'

'Only those who also buy cake.'

'Okay, well, I'd better have a slab of that orange almond one, if you don't mind.'

'Coming right up.' Honey gave Rosemary a quick kiss on the cheek and ran back to the tearoom.

'Lucky you,' said Robert, gazing after Honey.

'To have a baker as a daughter?'

'To have a daughter...' His voice trailed away. 'Any sign of Jasper?'

'None.'

'Have you rung the dealers?'

'Not yet. A bit early.'

'Then what will you do?'

'What do you mean?'

Robert peered inside the darkened bookshop. 'If they say they've seen him. What will you do?'

Rosemary frowned. 'I don't know.'

'I see.'

'You're being infuriating today.'

Robert smiled briefly. 'Add that to my list of charms.' He put a hand out to touch Rosemary's arm but let it drop before it did. 'Sorry. That was uncalled for. I can see you're worried about Jasper. He is a grown man, however, so whatever you think you should be doing is probably being overprotective.'

'You just moved from infuriating to condescending.'

'Sorry again!' He ducked his head, apparently absorbed in the destination of an ant hurrying across the ground.

Rosemary watched him for a moment, noting his reddened cheeks and folded arms. 'What is it, Robert? You're being odd.'

He shook his head but finally lifted it up to look at her. 'Do you want the truth?'

'Always.'

'Then I can tell you I'm a bit envious of your relationship with Jasper.'

'Envious. Do you mean *jealous*?'

'Jealous is such a teenage-y word, don't you think?'

'No.'

Robert smiled and shook his head. 'Well, I'm using the term *envious*.'

'I still don't know why.'

'You care about Jasper very much.'

Rosemary hesitated. When Jasper left three months ago, it had left a huge emptiness in the day. The bookshop was silent and empty, as if something truly awful and irreconcilable had happened. The weeks without Jasper had made her feel a restlessness that manifested in being unable to settle in the evening, to so many long walks that Mrs Lionel commented on Rosemary's shoe wear. But then, as he still hadn't returned after months, she started to get used to it, and that felt like betrayal. What if he'd never come back? The reality was she would've got used to that, too. 'Yes, I do. But...' She shook her head. There was no reason to explain anything to Robert Sparkling, but she couldn't help saying, 'He is my friend.'

'Yes. I'm sorry. I didn't mean anything by it.' Robert shrugged, and brushed back the hair from his face, a gesture that made Rosemary think of the teenager he had once been. She grimaced.

'You did, but let's leave it at that. You need to get your coffee before Honey thinks you aren't going in, and I need to get ready for the day. I'll let you know what the dealers say.' She turned around and went back into The Preserved

Mulbury without looking at him. As she closed the door, though, she glimpsed his face. 'If I didn't know better,' she said to Sunny, who was sitting on the windowsill looking out into the street, 'I'd say he was crestfallen.'

Sunny's tail flicked. *I have no idea why*, it seemed to say.

Rosemary had an inkling, but she pushed the thought away, gazing instead at the silent bell hanging uselessly above the door. It was an issue she'd yet to fix, adding to those other issues occupying her mind. And yet...

She went back to her kitchen and got the step ladder from the pantry, carrying it to the doorway and setting it up underneath the recalcitrant bell. This time, she took the whole thing down, turning it over in her hands as she balanced on the top step, and noting the heavy lines running through the brass dark with age. When it was a school bell, it hung on a chain outside the principal's office, and she rang it before class began. One of the saddest moments of Mulbury, Mrs Lionel had said, was when the sound of the bell disappeared as the school closed. 'Regular as clockwork,' was what Mrs Lionel had actually said. 'Then it was gone as if it had never existed.'

Rosemary climbed off the ladder and took the bell into her laundry, where she washed it in warm, soapy water before using a soft cloth to buff it. The bell shone warmly in her hands as she worked, revealing pits in its surface that spoke of stories she would never know. She finished, the old bell like a revitalised old friend, albeit a silent one.

She stared at it for a long time. It had been so dependable, alerting Rosemary to people coming and going from the shop. Now that it was silent, it was no longer a useful thing. Unless she could get a new knocker to work in it, was there any use rehanging it in the doorway of the shop? It had outlived its usefulness, and she'd got used to the door opening without the incessant jangling of an old bell.

Unless she could fix it.

Unless she could fix whatever was going on with Jasper. Because, she realised, being without his friendship was something she didn't want to get used to.

Rosemary put the bell on the dining room table and picked up her phone to ring the first of the book dealers.

TWENTY-ONE

The overcast day will keep the tourists at bay, Gerry thought, chuckling at the rhyme as he held the door of Honey B's Teas open for Patti. She gave him a warm smile and he felt his heart melt a little as it often did when his wife looked at him. 'What's so funny, sweetie?' Patti asked as he shut the door behind him.

'Nothing, really,' he said. 'I'm just happy to be with you.'

'What a darling man you are.' Patti touched his cheek lightly. 'Oh, I'm so looking forward to a bee cupcake.'

The tearoom was empty except for a couple paying their bill to Honey, and Pearl fussing around their abandoned table. Gerry took Patti's hand and they went to the counter to gaze at the array of cakes on display. Cuddles wagged his tail at them from his comfortable position next to the counter, and Patti bent to pat him before standing to look at the cakes again. 'Honey is at her very best,' said Gerry quietly. 'Just look at these!'

Alongside various cupcakes with blue-banded bees guarding their tops were iced apple cakes and chocolate swirl biscuits. Two larger cakes, one decorated daintily with icing roses and the other the shape of a cuddly teddy bear, sat under their own glass domes. A selection of teacups decorated the top of the counter, with a stout line of blue and black striped tea caddies at its edge. A lone, boldly floral teapot sat on a bench behind Honey and the customers as if waiting for something and, as Gerry watched it, Pearl pushed in behind Honey, snatched the pot and hurried into the kitchen.

Gerry nudged Patti. 'That was the teapot Pearl went under the table with.'

'Oh,' said Patti, craning past Gerry to look. 'I didn't catch it.'

The couple finished their transaction and went through the tearoom, chatting happily. 'Hello,' said Honey as they left. 'It's nice to see both of you at once. It's not often you get the time to drop in.'

'We know,' said Patti, swaying back and forth so her dress brushed the glass front of the counter. 'We were just saying how we don't see people as much any more. And now that Heather is with us, there's really no reason we can't have tea and cake more often. And see you and Ronnie. Oh, and little Tallulah, of course.'

'Ronnie's checking on her.' Honey glanced back through the kitchen but there was no sign of her husband. 'He's been there a while so he must be doing some work as well.'

A loud crash came through the door and Honey winced.

'Everything all right?' asked Patti, looking anxiously into the next room.

'Yes, it will be.' Honey ran her hand over her hair, pulling at the ponytail and letting it go so it bounced against her back. 'That's Pearl, probably finding fault with the oven door again.'

'It must be...interesting having your mother-in-law staying with you,' said Gerry.

Honey eyeballed him. 'I suppose you told Patti what happened with the teapot?'

'He did, sweetie,' said Patti softly. 'I think I might have a hint at what's going on for Pearl.'

Honey frowned. 'You do? But you didn't see it.'

'Can you come and have tea with us, Honey?' asked Gerry. 'Have a break and Patti can tell you her theory.'

Honey glanced at the front door but no one else had come in while they were talking and the pavement outside was empty. 'Okay then. I'll get us a pot. Would you like a cake as well?'

'Of course,' said Gerry, pointing to a pink cupcake almost hidden by the bee on its top. 'I'm assuming I can eat that fellow?'

'He's made of jelly covered in icing. I have a great mould Mum found for me online.' Honey grinned at Gerry. 'Think you can handle him?'

'My word, yes. Thank you, Honey.'

'And I'll have one of those swirls, please,' said Patti, pointing to the chocolate biscuits.

'Right, have a seat and I'll be over soon.'

Gerry and Patti took a seat at the front of the tearoom. It gave them a view to outside where only a handful of people wandered about Goldmarket Square, and front row seats to the comings and goings of Pearl as she reset the table, vigorously shaking out a new cloth and laying it firmly on the wooden surface and then placing a small vase of daisies in its middle. She frowned suddenly, removed the vase, took the cloth off, and exchanged it for another, and placed the flowers back before stomping out with the recalcitrant cloth over her arm. 'Clearly not happy with that one,' Gerry said.

'She has high standards,' said Patti. 'Nothing wrong with that.'

'No, unless it's driving Honey crazy.'

'Do you think it is, sweetie?'

Honey came towards them with a tray holding a squat teapot, three cups and their cakes, her face a thunderous shade of red. She sat the tray carefully on the table, and Gerry noted how her hands shook. 'Sit here,' he said, pulling out the chair to his right. 'Looks like you need a strong cup of tea.'

'I made up a Yorkshire blend.' Honey gave him a small smile. 'Sorry if it's too strong but, like you say, I need it.'

'I love a strong tea,' said Patti, picking up the pot and swirling it. 'Are you all right?'

Honey sighed. 'Yes, I'm fine really. I'm just having difficulties coping with Pearl's...'

'Officiousness?' suggested Gerry.

'I try not to label her but...' Honey nodded. 'That's what I think, not what I would say to anyone.' She put her hand on Gerry's arm. 'Please don't say anything to Ronnie. He loves his mother so much. I do, too, it's just...oh, I don't know. If only I had an explanation for why she's so over the top.'

Gerry glanced at Patti. She scrunched up her face, letting it fall back into pleasant features as she poured the tea and handed a cup to Honey. 'Well,' Patti said. 'I've been thinking.'

'About a new fashion creation?' Honey sipped her tea. 'Tell me, I'd love to hear.'

'Not about fashion, although I do think about it all the time.' Patti waved her hand in front of her face as if ten images of upcycled woollen blankets had just flashed before her eyes. 'I've been thinking about Pearl ever since Gerry told me about the incident under the table.'

'Oh.' Honey put her cup down with a thunk. 'You think she's officious and slightly mad?'

'Oh, no, sweetie. Not at all!' Patti leaned forward although no one else was in the tearoom. 'I think your poor mother-in-law is scared.'

Honey sat straight. 'What?'

'Patti knows about these things,' said Gerry. 'Patti, tell Honey what you told me.'

Patti gripped Gerry's hand as she told Honey about the people she used to care for in the mountainous retirement home. As she listened, Honey's face lost its anger and softened. She nodded slowly as Patti finished the story and sat quietly for a while. So long, in fact, that Gerry decided to eat his jelly bee and its cupcake roost. He'd only just finished when Honey stirred. 'Oh. Oh dear.'

'Yes,' said Patti, breaking off a piece of swirl. 'It sounds likely, doesn't it?'

'Yeah, it does.' Honey tucked a stray piece of hair behind her ear. 'It would explain a lot but what is she scared of? She hasn't experienced any wars or trauma of that nature.'

'Is there anything else you can think of?' Gerry waved his cake fork. 'A frightening incident of some kind?'

'Not that I know of. Not that Ronnie has mentioned, anyway, and I think he would if he knew of anything.' Honey glanced back towards the counter as Pearl marched back into the tearoom with a washing basket. 'The way she does things...it's as if she's on high alert.'

The trio watched as Pearl whipped off two other tablecloths and snatched serviettes. Gerry frowned. Pearl's movements were jerky and stiff, and she worked with her head high. When she couldn't find any other linen to remove, she marched back towards their living area, almost flattening Ronnie as he came into the tearoom with Tallulah against his chest, pushing the pram in front of him and nudging Cuddles out of the way. 'Really, Ronald.' Pearl scowled at her son. 'Can't you keep that pram near the front door so that it's not in everyone's way?'

Ronnie blinked at his mother but didn't try to help as she left the tearoom with the basket of tablecloths. He stopped in the middle of room, rocking the sleeping baby in his arms, staring after Pearl whose vigorous laundry noises filtered in through the open door.

'Ronnie?' asked Honey loudly. 'Are you okay?'

Ronnie moved his head slowly, keeping his eyes on the doorway until the last moment before switching his gaze to the three people at the table. 'Yes,' he said. 'I am. But I know why Mum isn't.'

Honey looked abruptly at Patti before turning back to her husband. 'What do you mean?'

'Her little...moments.'

'Moments?' Honey stood, reached for Tallulah, and settled the baby into her pram. 'The crashes under the table?'

'Yes.' Ronnie's voice went quiet. 'I know why.'

Pearl marched in again, Cuddles ducking away as she did, and swept up the pile of plates. She gave Ronnie a stern look. 'Shouldn't you be doing something useful, Ronald?'

Honey grabbed the pram's handle. 'We're just going for a walk, Pearl. Tallulah is unsettled today for some reason. Are you alright here?'

Pearl paused, glanced at the peaceful baby as Honey hurriedly flicked the hood of the pram down, and shook a hand at them. 'Yes, of course. You two get some sunshine. You're both so pale it's as if you've seen a ghost.' She turned back to her duties, chortling.

Honey beckoned to Patti and Gerry and flicked her head towards the door. Ronnie hurried to open it and Gerry helped him lower the pram down the step. They set off across Goldmarket Road to the hill on the right of the Square. The Exceptional Tree waved its branches as they went by, its enormous expanse meaning some leaves gently caressed Gerry's face as they went past.

'Right,' Honey said. 'What's going on?'

Ronnie looked at Patti and Gerry, and Gerry held up his hand. 'It's okay, Ronnie. We're as concerned as you are about your mother.'

'Yes,' said Honey, adjusting the pram's hood even lower to cover Tallulah better. 'Patti has a theory but you tell us what you're thinking first.'

Ronnie looked around as if someone else could hear them, but there was only a magpie stalking away to find a worm. 'Rosemary said I should look into Mum's behaviour, so I did a little digging. I was following my nose.'

'Following your nose to what? Your Mum's pretty clean cut.'

'To her café. It seemed the logical way to go.'

'Oh.' Honey jiggled the pram over a rough spot on the footpath. 'What did you find?'

'Mum ran a little café before I was born. It was in an outer suburb of the city, and sold bread, milk and newspapers as well.'

'Nice.'

'Yeah.' Ronnie chewed his bottom lip for a second. 'It was nice until some hooligans came in one day and robbed the till.'

Patti gave a quiet shriek. 'How horrible! Was she okay?'

'Apparently the police arrived to find her under one of the tables clutching a teapot.'

Honey stopped. 'Not our teapot?'

'They described it as a 1960s floral teapot.'

'Oh, sounds very much like ours.' Honey pushed on, slower than before. 'What else did they say?'

'The report recorded Mum's concern that the robbers wanted the teapot. In fact, one of them took it off its stand and went to go outside, but the other one told him to put it back.'

'Lucky.'

'In one way, I guess. They left with money from the till, although it wasn't much.'

And your mum? She wasn't hurt?'

'No. The police got her out from under the table and the teapot survived.'

They walked on in silence until they reached the top of the hill with its view across Mulbury. Honey put the brake on the pram and stared down at the rooftops of the shops along Goldmarket Road. 'Now I understand why she's attached to the teapot. But something seems to trigger her reaction.'

Ronnie checked Tallulah but the baby was fast asleep. 'I think I know what that is, as well.'

'What is it?'

'The last thing in the report was the words Mum said the robber yelled when he was made to put the teapot back. *Possessions give a man self-respect.*'

'No! Really?'

Gerry tipped his head. 'Are they significant words?'

Ronnie turned to him, worry creasing his forehead. 'They're what Kerry said the first time Mum met him.'

Patti put her hand over her mouth. 'So, the robber was Kerry?'

Ronnie shook his head. 'No. The man's dead now. But Kerry sounded enough like him to trigger Mum's reaction.'

'Oh, my goodness.' Gerry shook his head. 'Poor Pearl. The teapot in the tearoom might have been enough to remind her of that unfortunate event, but having Kerry say that... I do think Patti's theory is correct.'

'You said Patti has a theory.' Ronnie scratched at his head. 'What is it?'

Patti touched his arm lightly. 'That your mother is frightened, sweetie. The little moments she has, it's probably an ingrained reaction she can't control.'

Gerry saw tears well in Ronnie's eyes and took his other arm. 'It's okay, Ronnie. There are people that can help your mother, and we'll do all we can to support her.'

Ronnie shook his head, making the tears spill over and run down his face. 'I feel so terrible that I didn't know.'

'She didn't want you to know.' Patti linked her arm to his. 'You couldn't have known if she didn't tell you.'

Ronnie wiped at his face and smiled wanly. 'I guess you're right. But now that I do know, I have to tell her. I do. And then we have to help her.' He looked at Honey. 'Don't we?'

'Of course.' Honey pushed the pram and they started the walk along the cemetery. 'Of course.'

As Honey carefully manoeuvred the pram over fallen gumnuts, Patti and Ronnie took the lead, Ronnie still shaking his head. Gerry helped Honey over a particularly lumpy patch, and then walked beside her. 'Oh, Gerry,' Honey said softly. 'I feel so rotten.'

'You do?'

Honey shook her head as if in disbelief. 'I've been bad-mouthing Pearl since she arrived, and counting down the days until she leaves. How horrible am I?'

'But you aren't, Honey.' Gerry smiled at her. 'You were just frustrated, and fair enough. I hate to say it, but Pearl's right when she says you have a lot on your plate with a new baby and a new business. You didn't know about Pearl's past.'

'Yes. Yes, but now I do.' Honey's face took on a stubbornness that Gerry had only previously seen on a certain Rosemary Exeter. 'Pearl needs our help and, to be honest, we need her help. We'll just have to figure out a way to do it.'

Gerry nodded. 'You know, Honey Blossom? I have no doubt about that at all.'

TWENTY-TWO

Someone pushed open the door to The Preserved Mulbury, but it slammed against the ladder Rosemary had left under the bell, making an awful din. Rosemary saw Mrs Lionel peering around the blockage and she hurried to the door, hoisting her handbag over her shoulder. 'Hello?' Mrs Lionel called. 'What's going on?'

'The bell is broken. I'm going to fix it.' Rosemary yanked the step ladder aside and held the door for Mrs Lionel. 'I'm going to fix it.'

'So you said. So you keep saying.' Mrs Lionel eyed her friend. 'Everything all right, dear? You look *fierce*.'

'No. The bell's broken.'

'I may be old but I'm not deaf.'

'Right.' Rosemary let the ladder go and gave Mrs Lionel a small smile. 'Sorry.'

'Don't say sorry. It doesn't suit you.' Mrs Lionel pointed to the handbag. 'Going somewhere?'

'I'm finding Jasper.'

'He's still not home?'

'No.'

'Have you rung him?'

'Endlessly. No answer.'

'And how are you going to find him then?'

Rosemary brandished a piece of paper. 'Jasper and Kerry are going to Broken Books Inc to sell T. G. G. Duncan's firsts. I'm going there to track them down.'

'Where is Broken Books Inc?'

'Hutts Hill.'

'What makes you think they're there still?'

'Mr Houston from Broken Books Inc said two men were visiting today. Soon, he said.'

'How does he know?'

'They rang him after going to Autumn Leaves Antiques in the city. Autumn Leaves referred them to Broken Books.'

'There must be other book dealers.'

'Only two that deal with niche subjects, but Autumn Leaves focuses on the classics and not genre fiction. I need to go to Mr Houston's shop. I might catch Jasper. If not, I'll be able to trace him from there.' Rosemary put a reassuring hand on Mrs Lionel's shoulder, feeling the older woman relax slightly under it. 'You may not be hard of hearing but I suspect Mr Houston is. It was hard to communicate over the phone. Perhaps you could look after the shop for me?'

'No.'

The smile disappeared and was replaced by a sternness that only Rosemary could do well. 'But it's Sunday. You'll be here.'

'It is Sunday. As we know, we get good business on Sundays. But I won't be here. I'm coming with you.' Rosemary raised her hand to protest, and Mrs Lionel swatted it away. 'The world won't stop if we close our shops for a day. I don't trust you to do this alone.'

'What do you mean?'

'I assume Mr Houston is an older gentleman?'

'He sounded it.'

'Then you need me to talk to him on a generational level.'

'I can talk to him.'

'Yes, dear, you can. I suspect you'll ply him with blunt questions.' She chuckled. 'But I'll be the buffer. Anyway.' She indicated the shop. 'I haven't been further than Justin Gentleman's farm for a long time. I look forward to the trip. Hang on, and I'll get my bag.' When Rosemary kept standing there, Mrs Lionel nodded towards the outside. 'You start the car and I'll be there in a jiffy.'

A jiffy turned out to be more like 15 minutes. Rosemary shut the door of The Preserved Mulbury and headed towards her old blue sedan, but the three athletic Jaunty Jaloper ladies scurried across Goldmarket Road and into The Green Mulbury before Mrs Lionel could shut shop. Rosemary turned back and stood outside watching as the tallest of the three pointed forcibly down at her shoes before stabbing a finger at the shelf where Mrs Lionel displayed her stain removers. Mrs Lionel bent slightly to consider the footwear of each woman before selecting a product and brush from her selection and offering it to them.

Rosemary stepped closer to the door. Through its glass panelling, she could just make out the conversation.

'...guaranteed?' asked Barbara.

Mrs Lionel adjusted her glasses to peer down at the woman's bright green shoes. 'That's a nasty mark. What did you step in?'

'Dirt,' said Barbara, moving her foot away from Mrs Lionel's gaze.

Mrs Lionel shook her head. 'Not dirt. More like mud or manure. Have you been near either of those?'

'Manure?' said Karen, kicking off a shoe to sniff it in disgust. 'Hardly. Animals give me the heebie jeebies.'

'Mud, then.' Mrs Lionel took the shoe and examined it closely. 'It's been very wet lately. You've been somewhere with lots of swampiness.'

Barbara shrugged her shoulders. 'Perhaps. We walk a lot.'

'Do you?' Mrs Lionel handed the shoe back. 'Are your shoes new, then?'

'What do you mean?'

'They aren't worn at all. What a shame you went walking in such a boggy place.' Mrs Lionel moved to the counter. 'I'm sorry, I can't guarantee my cleaner will return them to their pristine condition but at least they'll be wearable.'

Barbara glanced at Karen. 'They'll get us through the jaunt.'

Rosemary waited until all three had paid and went back to the car, sliding inside and closing the door just as the three women came out. 'We'll throw them out when we get home,' said Barbara to Rebecca as they passed the car. 'Wretched farm.'

Rosemary kept very still but the packing room ladies didn't even glance her way. She couldn't catch what else they were saying but the disgruntled mumbling was obvious. The three disappeared under the shade of The Exceptional Tree, probably to attempt a shoe clean.

From the driver's seat, Rosemary saw Mrs Lionel doing something on her phone and then bending to talk to the floor. Not the floor; to Percy, the ghostly terrier. 'Now, Percy,' Rosemary imagined Mrs Lionel was saying, 'you're in charge. I just don't trust Rosemary in this situation. She can get a bit feisty when she's following a lead.'

Mrs Lionel collected her bag and quickly stepped out of the shop, silencing the frog standing guard at the doorway. She kept glancing back at the windows and almost missed her step as she slid into the passenger seat.

'Everything alright?' asked Rosemary.

Mrs Lionel shut the car door and stared at The Green Mulbury. 'Percy's standing in the window, looking out into the street. He misses Snowy, you know.'

'You're saying that Snowy sees ghosts, too?'

'I think he does. But it's a mystery as to why.'

'It's a mystery why you see Percy.'

'Not really.' Mrs Lionel adjusted her skirt, smoothing it down, before putting on her seat belt. 'Percy is my last link to Mr Lionel.'

'Mr Lionel gave you Percy as a pup.'

'Yes, just as he fell ill.' Mrs Lionel smiled sadly. 'Although Percy was mine, I think his presence kept Mr Lionel alive for far longer than he would have otherwise.' She glanced at Rosemary. 'Don't think I'm silly, but having Percy still around keeps me going as well.'

Rosemary turned to look straight at her friend. 'I would never think you silly.'

Mrs Lionel's smile turned happy. 'Thank you, dear.'

Rosemary started the car. 'Who were you texting?'

'Holly. She texted back *Have fun!* with one of those faces.'

'Emojis.'

'Yes, them.'

'The wonders of the modern world,' Mrs Lionel said. 'And the wonders of the ethereal world. We've covered a lot in the last few minutes.'

'Yes.' Rosemary clutched the steering wheel.

'Everything alright with you, dear?'

'Those women...'

'The ones who were in my shop? They wanted-'

'-shoe cleaner. I know, I heard them.'

Mrs Lionel smiled. 'Were you spying on them?'

'Yes.'

'I see.'

'Where do you think they got that mud?'

'Oh, I don't know.' Mrs Lionel shifted her bag on her lap. 'Somewhere with decent soil.'

'What makes you say that?'

'Well, as you know, Mulbury's topsoil was stripped because of the gold rush, leaving the town with practically nothing but stones and clay. Even if those women stepped in a puddle around here, the mud would be a light brown. This mud was dark. It probably had a lot of organic matter in it.' Mrs Lionel turned to Rosemary. 'What are you thinking, dear?'

'I'm thinking those women don't look like the sort to go hiking.'

'Is that what they did?'

'Perhaps.' Rosemary shrugged and pulled the car onto the road. 'We have a more pressing matter to attend to.' She turned up the hill.

They were level with Ravenshome when Robert Sparkling appeared in his doorway. He saw them and waved frantically. Mrs Lionel lifted her hand. 'Robert wants you, dear.'

'What for?'

'I have no idea. Aren't you going to stop?'

'No.'

'You should.'

'We'll be late.'

'We have all day.'

Rosemary sighed and braked sharply. Robert ran to the car.

Mrs Lionel wound down her window. 'Are you alright?'

'Yes.' Robert peered past her to Rosemary. 'Where are you going?'

'Broken Books Inc.'

'One of the dealers? Then I'm coming with you.'

'There's no need...' Rosemary stopped as Robert clambered into the back seat. She started the car up the hill again. 'I feel like a taxi.'

Mrs Lionel twisted around to see behind her. 'A chauffeur, don't you think, Robert?'

'A driver, I think. Like they have in movies when the President is going places.' He leaned forward and studied Rosemary's ear. 'Do you have one of those squiggly earpieces so you can talk to headquarters?'

She swatted at him. 'Sit back or I'll throw you out.'

Robert sat back. Mrs Lionel watched him in the side mirror. 'You knew about the book dealers, Robert?'

'Rosemary and I talked about where Jasper may have gone. She found some contacts in his house.'

'You know he has every right to sell those books.'

Rosemary glanced at her. 'Jasper has a right to sell them. Kerry may not have the right to the money.'

Mrs Lionel shifted so she could look at Rosemary without twisting her body. Rosemary frowned. She was sure that Mrs Lionel had more pain in her hips than she let on but would never worry anyone else about it. Stoicism was one of the more endearing, and challenging, qualities of her friend.

'This letter Kerry had.' Mrs Lionel shifted uncomfortably again, confirming Rosemary's suspicion. 'What makes you think it's not legitimate?'

'I don't think it's in character with what Jasper told us about his mother.'

'Jasper hardly knew his mother as an author. Not her secret, anyway.'

'But he *did* know his mother as a mother. He was raised by her. She was present in his life.'

'Why didn't she tell anyone she wrote books?'

Rosemary shrugged. 'We're talking about a time in history when mothers were meant to be good housewives and that's all. Perhaps she didn't want anyone to know.'

'Her husband must have known.'

'It's likely. Her books, though, really became a hit after she'd died.'

'Like Vincent van Gogh,' said Robert, his voice muffled by the sound of the old car.

'Vincent van Gogh didn't write space cowboy books.' Rosemary smiled to herself.

'Oh, ha ha.' Robert leaned forward again. 'You know what I mean. Hadn't he only sold one painting before he died? T. G. G. Duncan was just a lowly sci-fi writer until she died. Then she became a cult figure.'

'True.' Rosemary twisted her hands on the wheel. 'All the more a strange reason to leave your books to a previous lover if you didn't know they were going to be worth anything.'

'Maybe it was a joke,' said Mrs Lionel. 'Or an expression of whimsical love. A gesture that didn't mean anything more than a gift at the time.'

'Good thinking, Mrs Lionel.' Robert sat back. 'We really don't know.'

'I do,' said Rosemary.

'But how can you, dear? If Jasper can't see anything wrong with the letter, how can you presume you do?'

'It must be my uncanny sense of misappropriation.'

'Still not that much to go on.'

Rosemary turned to Mrs Lionel. 'That hurt.'

'Watch the road, dear. And, yes, you do have good instincts. I think, in this case, you might be coloured by your feelings for Jasper.'

Rosemary twisted her hands again but was silent. They drove for another ten minutes before Robert spoke up. 'Do you think that's the case, Rosemary?'

'What?'

He was quiet for another minute. 'Your feelings for Jasper-'

'I keep telling everyone. Jasper is my friend.'

'He's our friend, too,' said Mrs Lionel, looking straight ahead.

'Yes.'

'But?'

Rosemary accelerated as they hit a straight bit of road. She selected cruise control then set her hands firmly on the wheel. 'He's one of those friends you...need.'

Mrs Lionel reached out and patted Rosemary's tight left hand. 'Like I need you.'

'I need you, too, but I need Jasper *differently*.'

Mrs Lionel let Rosemary's words disappear without responding. Rosemary chewed her lip. She knew it was complex. Jasper was a kind, gentle man, loyal to the nth degree. He was dependable, too, and if you were in a pickle, Jasper was there. Or he had been.

'You'll be okay, you know,' Mrs Lionel said eventually.

'I am okay.'

'Good.'

From the back seat, Robert sighed. 'You'll be okay, too, Robert,' she said.

'Thanks?'

'Now that we're all okay, will someone answer my phone for me?'

Mrs Lionel jumped a little in her seat. Rosemary's phone was indeed ringing, an insistent quiet jangle reminding Rosemary of the lost doorbell of The Preserved Mulbury. 'It's Patti,' said Mrs Lionel. She picked up the phone and answered it.

'Oh, Mrs Lionel, sweetie. I was after Rosemary.'

'She's driving, dear. I'll put you on speaker phone.'

'Hello? Rosemary?'

'Patti. What's up?'

'I'm not actually ringing for me. I have Milly here. You know Milly. She wears Birkenstocks.'

Rosemary shook her head slightly. 'So do many, Patti, but I do know Milly.'

'Rosemary?' said a soft voice. 'I was looking for you to tell you about Colin.'

'We're away today. What about Colin?'

'He's back from the police station.'

'Is he under suspicion?'

'The police just said he should stay close for the time being.'

'How is he, dear?' asked Mrs Lionel. 'What a harrowing experience for him.'

'He's quite upset, but I think it's more to do with Andrew's death rather than the experience of being questioned.'

'You would all be upset about Andrew's death.'

'Well, yes, we are. Especially since the police say Andrew didn't drown but was strangled.'

'Ah.'

'You knew?'

'I suspected.'

Milly's breath quickened. 'This makes his death sinister. I mean, a drowned person could be an accident, but clearly strangulation is not.'

'Who else knows this in your group?'

'Lucy, of course. Barbara, Karen and Rebecca. Not Kerry because he's not here.'

'Yes.'

'Funny…'

'What's funny?'

'Oh.' Milly gave a short laugh. 'I could swear that those women were relieved Andrew died that way rather than drowning. But, anyway, Rosemary, that's not really why I wanted to talk to you.' The sound of close breathing echoed around the car through the phone's speaker.

'What is it?' asked Rosemary.

'It's what the police asked Colin. About Andrew. Horrible things.'

'Such as?'

'It's like they assume, because Andrew was single, that he was a horrible man. They asked about his relationships with his workers, how he behaved towards women, even what he ate for lunch.'

Rosemary nodded. 'They're trying to find a motive.'

'Funny way of doing it, belittling someone's character.'

'Why do you say that? Did Andrew behave badly at work?'

'No, not at all!' Milly's sigh was loud through the phone. 'And he could've. He could have taken advantage of things.'

'What things?'

'The fact that he was single, and many of us are. He might have had, you know, *flings*.'

'He didn't?'

'No! He was not that sort of man.'

'He was entitled to if he had a willing partner.'

'Yes, but, knowing Andrew, they wouldn't have been flings. More like *considerations* which would eventually lead to nothing.'

Rosemary rolled her eyes and Mrs Lionel tried not to smile. 'Right. So do the police have any evidence Andrew was a character of disrepute?'

'None at all.'

'Then what's the issue?'

More phone breathing, and a couple of catches as Milly went to speak. 'The packing room ladies said they were going to report him for stalking.'

'Did he?'

'Did he what?'

'Stalk them.'

Milly let out a huff of air that boomed through the speaker. 'No, of course not. They were just peeved.'

'Why?'

'He wouldn't be taken in by their flirting or desserts. He regarded them as silly creatures, but he was always polite.' The phone was quiet. 'That'll be it then.'

'What would be it?'

'Andrew humiliated the packing room ladies by not caving in to their charms.'

Rosemary looked at Mrs Lionel who shrugged. 'Right.'

'Don't you get it, Rosemary? Of course, those ladies reported Andrew for stalking and goodness knows what else.'

'You'll have to explain.'

Milly's voice wavered. 'They wanted revenge.'

TWENTY-THREE

Rosemary glanced down at the phone and pulled the car over to the side of the road. 'Sorry, Milly. We've stopped now. What is it that you want us to do?'

'Back Colin up, please. Andrew was a really lovely man. He wouldn't stalk anyone.'

'So you said.'

Milly harrumphed. 'Take my word for it. But, also, prove it.'

'That's why you're ringing.'

'Well, yes.' There were some mumbles through the phone as if Milly was talking to someone else before she spoke again. 'Patti said you're good at sorting out these sorts of things.'

Rosemary frowned. 'I'm not free to help you yet. We're trying to solve our own mystery.'

'You're looking for Kerry, aren't you?'

'I'm looking for Jasper.'

'Same thing.'

'Yes. That's why I'm not free.' Rosemary turned in her seat to take in her passengers. 'Neither are Mrs Lionel or

Robert.'

'Is there nothing you can do right now?'

Rosemary drummed her fingers on the steering wheel. 'No. There's something you can do, though.'

'Oh! Please, tell me what I can do to help poor Andrew's reputation.'

'Get a photo of Barbara's shoe.'

'What?'

Robert leaned forward, his eyebrows raised.

'Milly, get a photo of Barbara's shoe. From all sides. And the tread.'

'How do I do that?'

'Tell her you want to buy a pair.' Rosemary frowned. 'Flatter her. It will be easier than you think.'

The phone line was quiet for a moment. 'Alright then. Can I ask why?'

'No, not yet.'

'Okay then. I'll do it.'

'And Milly?'

'Yes?'

'Did Andrew interview all the Jalopers for his history?'

'Well, yes. I heard him say so.'

'Specifically, what did he say?'

'Oh, I'd have to think.' The phone was quiet for a moment. 'He said he had all the information he needed to make a compelling narrative. Yes, that was it. A *compelling narrative* sounded rather like a good read.'

'Did he ever show you anything he'd written?'

'No, he said he wanted it to be a surprise when it was done. All his information was in his notebooks.' Milly sniffed. 'I suppose we'll never see the finished product now. Well, was there anything else, Rosemary?'

'No. Don't forget the photo.'

'I won't.'

The phone scratched and snarled, and Patti came back on. 'She's gone.'

'Goodness,' said Mrs Lionel, resting the hand that held the phone on the gear stick. 'Is she alright, Patti?'

'I think so. She looks very determined.'

'She's quite upset about Colin.'

'Yes, she is. I saw her talking to Lucy outside, and the poor woman was very distressed. I think that's why Milly's so adamant that things are set right. Andrew was very dear to them, it seems.'

'Patti, do you still have the box of abandoned clothing from the cemetery?'

'Box? Yes, I haven't got to it yet. Why do you ask, sweetie?'

'Could you put the pair of men's shoes into a plastic bag? Try not to handle them too much.'

'Alright, Rosemary. And then what?'

'Once Milly has the photographs and you bag the shoes, get Ronnie to ring his Uncle Geoffrey. Give everything to him.'

'Goodness! Alright, I can do that.'

'Thanks. And keep an eye on Milly, Patti,' said Rosemary. 'And on Colin and Lucy.'

'Oh, I'm not sure I can. I have such a busy day here, especially with Heather...' There was a clicking noise as if Patti was tapping the phone with her nail. 'What about I tell Milly to take Colin and Lucy to Honey B's Teas? That way, Honey and Ronnie can look after them.'

'That's a lovely idea, Patti.' Mrs Lionel held the phone up again. 'What was that you were saying about Heather?'

A squeal shot down the phone. 'Oh my!' said Patti breathlessly. 'I must go. Jules has just turned up with a basket full of netball skirts she found at an op shop. Think of what I can make out of those!'

The phone call ended and Rosemary stared down the road. 'Do you have any idea what you could make from a basketful of old netball skirts?'

'Ponchos?' said Robert from the back. 'Scarves?'

Mrs Lionel chuckled. 'Patti will turn them into something glamorous.'

'Bespoke, at least,' said Rosemary. 'Something I wouldn't wear, in any case.' She started the car and moved it back onto the road. 'I think we're about forty-five minutes away from Broken Books.'

The road was quiet, so they zoomed without distraction down its narrow, asphalt length, Mrs Lionel occasionally commenting on the condition of the cows in the paddocks or the growth of noxious weeks on the side of the road. Rosemary heard the expertise in her voice, and wondered whether her friend missed the busy-ness of farm life and the warm breaths of the dairy cows Mrs Lionel had as company for many years. But even Mrs Lionel fell quiet as they reached Hutts Hill.

The town was smaller than Mulbury and there was no resemblance to Mulbury's thriving hustle. The few houses they drove past as they slowed for the main street were dull and unkempt. Dried grass matted fence lines and paint peeled from weatherboards. They turned left to enter the town centre and saw shop after shop boarded up and empty. The only sign of life was a tiny general store that housed a post office and sold ice-creams, and a grand red-brick building across the road with a dilapidated swinging sign that read 'Broken Books Inc.'

'Well, at least that business has survived,' said Mrs Lionel quietly.

Rosemary turned the car to park outside Broken Books. 'Do you think it's open?'

'Surely, dear, you looked that up before we drove all this way?'

'Yes. Broken Books Inc is open seven days a week, 52 weeks of the year.'

'Poor proprietor,' said Robert, rattling the door handle but unable to open it. 'Rosemary, this car...' The door flung open, its edge scraping on the kerb.

'Careful, Robert Sparkling,' said Rosemary, getting out. 'It's the only car I own.'

'Time to take care of that.' Robert pushed himself up from the seat, slammed his door shut, and helped Mrs Lionel out. 'What is the name of the fellow that owns the store?'

'Mr Houston.'

'Okay, then. And is he a whiskery gentleman with a long grey braid down his back?'

'I have no idea.'

'So, we don't know whether that's him, then.'

Rosemary looked where Robert had indicated. A man sat in the window of Broken Books Inc, sorting papers on a table that had been wedged between two bookcases. When he leaned back to reach for something behind him, he disappeared into the darkness of the shop, but as he came forward again, his scrappy white beard brushed the top of the table, and the tail of a thin, white plait poked over his shoulder. A pair of glasses pushed into his nose, one arm missing. From the way he sighed and placed a piece of paper into a cardboard in-tray to his right, Rosemary had no doubt this was Mr Houston.

'Is he expecting us, Rosemary?' asked Mrs Lionel.

'No.'

The older woman looked around. 'No sign of Jasper or Kerry.'

'They might have been already. Over the phone, Mr Houston said visitors were coming in with a special collection. He told them he wouldn't really be able to help them until he'd consulted his fellow dealers in the city, which wouldn't happen until Monday.'

'What happened next?'

Rosemary stuffed the car key into her skirt pocket and walked towards the door of the shop. 'That's what we're here to find out.' She pushed on the Broken Books door.

A sound like one hundred cats screaming nearly bowled Rosemary over. She ducked her head instinctively, although the noise seemed to be coming from the bookcases on either side of the entrance. Mrs Lionel, close on Rosemary's heels, stumbled backwards and Robert caught her. They hurried in behind Rosemary. The door swung shut. The screeching stopped.

'What the blazers was that?' said Robert, rubbing the side of his head.

'The worst doorbell I've ever come across.' Rosemary put her hand out to Mrs Lionel. 'Are you alright?'

'Yes. Thank you.' Mrs Lionel put a hand on her chest. 'My heart is nearly back to normal.'

Thumps came from a room to their left and the whiskery gentleman appeared in the doorway. 'Yes? Hello? Is someone there?'

'Yes,' said Rosemary, stepping forward. 'Surely no one can creep in here and surprise you.'

'Eh?' said the man. 'You'll have to speak up.'

'I said,' said Rosemary loudly, 'no one could possibly sneak in here with that noise you've got at the front door.'

The man put his head down and chuckled. 'Remarkable, isn't it? My grandson did that for me. I needed something I could hear from the back room.'

'Wouldn't a ding dong do?' asked Robert.

'Ding dongs and pretty door chimes are for those who aren't serious about preventing theft.' The man shuffled back into the room, heading for his chair in the window and sitting down heavily. 'I've had my share of stolen goods. No more. Since I had that alarm, I haven't lost one paperback. Not one old journal. Not one encyclopedia.' His head went down and he laughed again. 'They even tried it this morning and were stopped in their tracks.'

Robert frowned and glanced at Rosemary. 'You had thieves come in here today?'

'Not thieves. Potential thieves. Men trying to sneak their way in and take my Shakespeares. I heard them come in.'

'How do you tell the difference between customers and thieves if everyone gets assaulted with that noise as soon as they open the door?'

The old man lifted his head and stared at Robert. 'I can smell them.'

Robert shook his head but said nothing more. Rosemary didn't blame him. The man continued to stare until Robert's face took on a ruddy glow which brightened to scarlet after the old fellow leaned forward and sniffed heartily. Robert flinched. 'Everything okay with me, then?'

'You smell of oil and wood shavings. They're honest smells.' Mr Houston sat back. 'That one this morning, he smelled of mildew.'

'I imagine there's a bit of that around old books,' said Mrs Lionel.

Mr Houston straightened in his chair. 'Oh, my lady, I

didn't see you there.' He stood hastily, knocking his chair backwards. 'Would you like a seat?'

'No, thank you.' Mrs Lionel smiled politely. 'I have two perfectly good legs to stand on.'

Mr Houston nodded but remained standing, staring at Mrs Lionel. He lifted his hand and smoothed his beard, unsuccessfully trying to capture its wispiness. 'You, my lady, smell like sunshine on peaches.'

'Thank you,' said Mrs Lionel without turning a hair. 'That's very kind.'

Rosemary cleared her throat and Mr Houston glanced at her. 'So,' she said. 'You had two men come in here this morning, not to steal your Shakespeares, but to sell you some books. They smelled of mildew.'

'No.'

'They didn't come in here?'

'Oh, yes, they did. But one smelled of mildew. He was large.' Mr Houston spread his arms wide. 'The other, no, he smelled of eucalyptus.'

'That's my washing detergent,' said Mrs Lionel.

'With a hint of bergamot.'

'That's my tea,' Rosemary said.

'Would you like tea?' asked Mr Houston, once again staring at Mrs Lionel. 'I have some...' He looked around his desk as if a tea-cosied teapot and an empty teacup were hidden under his papers.

'No thank you,' said Mrs Lionel. 'We've come to ask about the gentlemen who visited you this morning.'

'Long gone.' Mr Houston waved his hand as if brushing away fog. 'Someone rang me about that.'

'I did,' said Rosemary. 'I rang you. You said some men were coming to sell you books.'

'Yes, yes.' Mr Houston sat down, remembered Mrs

Lionel, and stood up again, indicating his chair. She smiled and declined with a wave of her hand. 'They had some firsts. Good condition, not perfect. Worth something, worth quite a lot. Auction, I said. Best bet for those niche books. Someone out there could pay a lot of money.'

'So, they went away?'

'I sent them away. They weren't happy. Well, Mildew Man wasn't.'

'Why?'

'Oh!' Mr Houston shuffled around to be closer to Mrs Lionel and once again offered her his chair. Mrs Lionel's smile thinned as she shook her head. 'Well, that big man kept insisting that I take the books and approach the auction house on his behalf. He even gave me a letter to show provenance. Quite thick, isn't he? I told him about my toes but he didn't get it.'

Rosemary crossed her arms. 'Your toes.'

'Yes. Bandy, they are, hard to walk on. See?' He shook his foot and his shoe shot off, revealing sockless feet and a row of gnarly toes.

'Looks very painful,' said Mrs Lionel, leaning forward to inspect them as the others took a step back. 'You should visit a podiatrist.'

'What's one of them?'

'They're a health professional who take care of feet. This town may even have a visiting service.'

Mr Houston gazed at Mrs Lionel with watery eyes. 'No one's ever suggested that to me. You must be an angel.'

'No.' Mrs Lionel bent to pick up his shoe and handed it back. 'I was a nurse and so I know things. Put your shoe back on to protect those toes and tell us more about why you think the man was thick.'

Mr Houston spent a moment spearing his foot back into

his shoe, wobbling furiously until Mrs Lionel guided him into the chair. 'The man,' he said at last. 'He wanted the books gone, you could see that. He was pushy. Almost had a hissy fit when I said for the third time I couldn't take them, I'm not an auctioneer. It was like he wanted to see the back of them. Gum Tree Man piped up then. Asked very politely if I could mind the books, put them somewhere protected for a while. Seemed happy when I said I could bung them in the safe until they worked out their next move.' Mr Houston scratched his head, pulling his braid around to play with its end. 'Odd pair. Couldn't work out whether they were friends or not.'

'What happened next?' asked Robert.

'They went outside and had it out there.'

'What do you mean?' Rosemary glanced out the window as if Jasper and Kerry may have still been there. 'Had it out?'

'They fought.' Mr Houston raised his fists and punched the air a few times.

'They had a physical fight out on the street?'

The whiskery man hit the air a few times more, then lowered his arms. 'No. Not physical. Might have been better if they had.'

'Why?'

'Well, you know how these nasty wordy arguments go.' Mr Houston looked from Rosemary to Robert to Mrs Lionel, blushing slightly as he caught the older woman's eye. 'Lots of shouting. Crude, rude and unappealing, I'd say. Yes. Preposterous.'

'A fist fight could have been cleaner,' said Robert.

'Yes, yes. And the younger one might have won that.'

'He didn't win the argument?'

'Mildew Man did, I think. He stood over Gum Tree

Man and yelled, then...' Mr Houston shot his arm out and pointed down the road.

'He left? Without Jasper?'

'Jasper? That's a rock.'

'Jasper is the one who smelled of my washing detergent,' said Mrs Lionel. 'The other man was his father.'

Mr Houston shook his head. 'No, no, no. Not his father.'

Rosemary frowned. 'How do you know?' She held up her hand as Mr Houston went to speak. 'No, don't tell me. They didn't smell the same.'

Mr Houston's nose twitched. 'What an odd thing to say.'

'You're the one who's fixated on smells.'

'You're rather spicy, like a pickled onion.'

'Sorry?'

Mr Houston sniffed. 'You are peppery.'

Mrs Lionel stepped forward, gently nudging Rosemary back. 'Tell me, please, Mr Houston. What made you think the pair weren't related?'

'Call me Horatio, my lady, if you would.'

Mrs Lionel smiled 'Thank you, Horatio.'

'And I can call you...?'

'Mrs Lionel, if you don't mind. Now, what was it you noticed?'

Mr Houston's mouth wobbled before he said, 'I didn't see anything while they were here, but when they started with those words on the footpath, I thought I'd heard them before.'

'You'd heard them arguing before they entered the shop?'

'No, no. The words Mildew Man said: that he "hated putting on his old set of habits again".'

'What did he mean, dear?'

'I don't know what he meant, lovely lady, but I'd read those words before.'

'You've read them.'

'Yes.' Mr Houston stood and shuffled over to the bookcase nearest the door. He pulled a tatty book from the shelf. 'Patricia Highsmith, such a writer. This is her book about Mr Ripley.'

'*The Talented Mr Ripley.*' Rosemary nodded. 'I see what you mean.'

'I don't,' said Robert.

'The book is about a man pretending to be someone else.' Rosemary tipped her head to one side. 'Although, surely what you saw must have been more than a quote from a fictional book.'

'It was Gum Tree Man's reaction. I was watching, you see.' Mr Houston leaned over and tapped the window. 'They were right there. Gum Tree Man—Jasper, you said?—had this look.' He passed his hand over his face, revealing open-mouthed shock as his hand dropped away. 'He must have recognised the phrase as well. He knew from that moment. It was as obvious as a termite hill. He realised the one in front of him was not who he said he was.'

Rosemary glanced at her friends. Robert widened his eyes and shook his head slightly. Mrs Lionel, though, had a tight mouth and was twisting her hands together. 'What happened after the man left?'

'The man called Jasper headed the other way.'

'To where? There isn't much activity in this town.'

'This town has exactly the right amount of activity it needs,' said Mr Houston. He smiled at Mrs Lionel, showing a row of gappy teeth. 'If only it had a podiatrist.'

'Horatio,' said Mrs Lionel. 'Where do you think Jasper would have gone?'

'Well, my lady, my guess is he started walking back the way he came. Mildew Man had the car. He drove in that direction.' Mr Houston jerked his thumb to the right. 'He was alone in his car.'

'How far is the nearest big town?'

'It's twenty kilometres back. A long walk.'

Mrs Lionel grabbed Rosemary's arm. 'I don't understand why he didn't contact us. We would have come and got him. He didn't even answer your phone calls.'

Mr Houston shook his head. 'There's no mobile phone reception around here, lovely one. Nothing for miles around.'

'It's more than that,' said Robert. 'He'd just realised he was swindled by a man pretending to be his father. Finding his father was the whole purpose of his time away from Mulbury and he'd thought he'd achieved his goal.'

'Yes,' said Mrs Lionel, gripping Rosemary's arm more tightly. 'Even though Kerry wasn't the father Jasper had imagined, finding him was the closure Jasper was seeking.'

'You both think he doesn't want to be contacted?' Rosemary shook her head. 'I don't get it.'

'He needs time to himself, Rosemary,' said Robert gently. 'He'll contact you when he's ready.'

Rosemary studied Robert's face. He was looking somewhere over her shoulder, lost in thought. 'I'm holding you to that.'

Robert turned his gaze to her. 'You can do that.'

'Wait,' said Mrs Lionel. 'If Kerry isn't Jasper's father, he isn't the owner of those books, even if that letter states he is.'

'What letter would that be, my lady?' asked Mr Houston, bobbing slightly.

'Kerry had a letter from the author bequeathing the

books to him. It included phrases specific to T. G. G. Duncan, and she'd signed it.'

'Oh, the letter that proved provenance. But you think now it was a fake, wise one?' Mr Houston sniffed quietly. 'O Peach Scented One.'

Mrs Lionel frowned. 'Yes, and that's quite enough, Horatio. The letter was a fake. Do you have it?'

'Would it have been in a white envelope?'

Mrs Lionel glanced at Rosemary, who shrugged. 'It may be.'

'There's an envelope in the safe with the books.' Mr Houston shook his head, so the thin braid whipped his back. 'I put it there when the fellows had gone, just as instructed.' He peered at Mrs Lionel. 'I am a trustworthy soul.'

Rosemary sighed. 'It was a very good fake, obviously. It fooled Jasper. And me.'

Mr Houston chuckled and Mrs Lionel tipped her head towards him. 'What do you find funny, Horatio?'

'It sounds like Mildew Man's done a Lee Israel. Do you know that story, my lady?' Mr Houston looked around his shelves and pulled another book out, handing it to Mrs Lionel. 'Lee Israel wrote letters pretending to be from famous authors and sold them as authentic. She was very good. Wrote them just like the author would because she studied how they worded things. Clever, she was. Clever, clever woman.'

'She fooled a lot of people who should have known better?'

'Oh yes. People can be so easily fooled.' For a moment, Mr Houston was mortified. 'Not you, Mrs Lionel. Not you.'

'That makes me feel better,' said Mrs Lionel. 'But I don't like that Jasper was duped.'

Rosemary was quiet. Her chest felt tight, and not only

because a simmering rage for Jasper's deception was lodged there. An idea was forming, one that made more sense the more she considered it. She crossed her arms and wandered off to look at Mr Houston's bulging bookshelves.

'Careful, Pepper!' Mr Houston stretched his hand to the ceiling. 'Touch that bookcase and the roof will cave in. It's the only thing holding the place together.'

Rosemary studied the ceiling where the top plank of the bookcase acted as a truss to a very saggy ceiling. 'You have so many books here,' she said. 'But I imagine these represent only a handful of what has passed through your hands over the years.'

'Correct,' said Mr Houston. 'Millions, I've had. Billions, even, as I am very old as my toes demonstrate.' He waved a hand at his lower leg as if the presence of gnarly toes were the only indications of growing older.

'And you would have correspondence with major auction houses filed among your many papers?'

'Eh? Correspondence?'

'Letters, then.'

'Letters? My word, yes. All the important auction houses in the world have sent me letters.'

'Over many years for the billions of books you've had?'

Mr Houston screwed his face up. 'No need for cheek, young lady. No need. I have scores of letters from auction houses. Scores.'

Rosemary smiled. 'Then I think I have a solution. Kerry is not the only one who can pen a counterfeit letter. How about we dupe the duper?'

TWENTY-FOUR

Mr Houston's bookshop was more of a maze than Rosemary had imagined. The stacks of paper on the table under the window were only a fraction of the papers spread across a roll-top desk at the very back corner of the building. To get to it, Rosemary had to weave between bookcases, step over shonky piles of novels, duck under sagging racks of comics, and push between two piles of boxes that contained, said Mr Houston, pulp fiction yet to be sorted. She was very glad the proprietor didn't have an open fire as a heater, or she doubted he would have made it through the winter without burning the papery place down. Broken Books Inc made The Read Mulbury look like a commercial bookstore in a shopping mall.

Thinking of The Read Mulbury almost pulled Rosemary up. She hesitated in front of some science textbooks, hearing Mrs Lionel and Mr Houston chatting distantly at the front of the shop.

'Okay?' asked Robert, wedged behind her between protruding anatomy atlases.

'Yes.' Rosemary ploughed on and finally made it to the desk. 'You start on the drawers and I'll go through the top.'

Robert stared at the rows of drawers supporting the elegant, rolled hardwood top. 'What are we looking for again?'

'Annotated letters from auction houses. The ones that show personality, and not form letters.'

'Why?'

Rosemary pushed the desk top up, revealing tiny pigeonholes stuffed with old envelopes. 'So we can imitate them. We must be authentic in our fakery to fool a cheat.'

Robert laughed. 'Anyone hearing that sentence out of context would be completely baffled.'

'We have a context, Robert. Get on with it.'

Still chuckling, Robert pulled open the first of the drawers and pulled out its contents. There was no room to sit down so he leaned against a bookshelf and used the spare centimetres above the rows of books to sort papers. Rosemary started on the pigeonholes, removing letters from their envelopes and stacking them into piles.

After about twenty minutes, it became obvious there were two main auction houses that treated book dealers as individuals. The letters from Westerlies were formal but personalised, and those from Scones were as chatty as a social media post. Rosemary scanned the pile of Westerlies and saw they were written by a Mrs Brenda Bass. Mrs Bass used a typewriter with a fading ribbon, and always signed her full name and title. The correspondents from Scones varied and letters were printed on colourful letterhead. For that reason, and for the overpowering feel that Scones employed interns who came and went, Rosemary put those letters back in their pigeonholes. 'The best ones are from West-'

'-erlies,' said Robert at the same time.

'Mrs Bass?'

He nodded. 'Brenda is the one.'

'I've got letters here from over three decades.'

'Same.' Robert shuffled through his find and held up two piles. 'These are from the early days and these are more current. I imagine that Mrs Bass has been present throughout the whole life of Broken Books Inc.'

'What does she call Mr Houston to start with?'

'Mr Houston.'

Rosemary singled out a letter. 'She starts to cross out the formal title about ten years' ago. "Horry" is written in blue ink.'

'Show me.' Robert peered at the colour. 'Nothing fancy there. Standard office blue ink. What's the last letter you have?'

'It's dated this year. It's a reply to Mr Houston's entry into an auction. He's selling a leatherbound copy of *The Odyssey*. She's very happy to accept it on behalf of a regular customer.'

'That doesn't sound very personal.'

'Then she writes that she hopes his feet are feeling better and recommends rubbing peppermint lotion into his toes.'

'Seems like his feet have been an ongoing issue.'

'He must know her well to talk about his feet.'

'Not necessarily. We knew about them without fifteen minutes of meeting him.'

Rosemary flicked through the letters. 'Here's something better. *Dear Horry, thanks for the book* blah blah. *We have orders from Mrs Truscott for pre-War Encyclopedia Britannicas, particularly G-H* blah blah.' She ran her finger down the page. 'Here. *Have you tried adding washing soda to your wash? I soak any ink-stained clothing in it first and hang the garment in the sun. I also avoid wearing white while handling old books.* She's giving him laundry advice. That's personal.'

'And occasional cooking advice. Listen to this: *Marinate the meat overnight and it will be softer once cooked which will be better for your dentures.*'

'She's a modern-day Mrs Beeton.'

Robert brandished his letters. 'So, we'll copy her style?'

'Indeed.'

It took ten minutes to weave back to the front of the shop where Mrs Lionel was quietly listening to Mr Houston as he indicated his feet, which were once again out of his shoes. Rosemary waved the letters at her, smiling at the look of relief on her friend's face. Mr Houston stopped talking as they approached. 'We found your correspondence with Westerlies. We think we can imitate Mrs Bass.'

'Oh.' Mr Houston nodded. 'Mrs Bass has been there for many years.'

'So we gathered.' Rosemary handed the letters to Mrs Lionel, who read a few and smiled.

'There is one problem with all this,' said Robert, watching a magpie peck at the ground outside. 'We can write the letter but we don't know where Kerry's gone.'

'To their accommodation from last night?'

'Most likely. He'll be waiting for tomorrow when Mr Houston can contact the auction house.'

'He could be anywhere from here to the city.'

'But he won't be. He'll be close in case Jasper comes back first.'

Robert turned to the proprietor. 'Mr Houston, where can people stay overnight around here?'

Mr Houston scrunched his face up to think. 'There's

aren't any motels or hotels, no sirree, not around here.' He thought further. 'Try The Eerie, Carol's bed and breakfast place. It's a little way up the road and is never booked out because you need to drive up a rocky driveway. Doesn't suit city cars.' He tilted his head to look outside. 'Yours would be okay, Pepper, because you couldn't wreck it any more than it already is.'

Rosemary opened her mouth to debate that issue, but Mrs Lionel put her hand on her arm. 'Thank you, Mr Houston. Now, dear, do you have a typewriter we could use to write a letter from Mrs Bass?'

Mr Houston blushed. 'A typewriter? Yes, my lady, I have my trusty Olivetti. Right this way.'

Mr Houston limped his way to another area of the bookshop where he had a small kitchenette complete with kettle, computer and an ancient typewriter acting as a paperweight for a pile of newspapers. 'I'll get you some paper.' He bowed slightly to Mrs Lionel and left the room.

'Right.' Mrs Lionel lifted the typewriter from its pedestal and placed it on the little table in the middle of the room. She sat down, fiddled with the roller, and worked the return lever. 'I'm ready to go.'

'I can type,' said Rosemary.

'No doubt you can but I'll be better at it than composing a fake letter. You and Robert can dictate to me.'

'You have a lot of faith in us,' said Robert, grinning.

'I do, dear.' Mrs Lionel peered around them to look into the shop where they could hear Mr Houston still rummaging for paper. 'You'd better read all the letters you have to get a feel for the topics Mrs Bass discussed with Mr Houston. She might surprise you.'

Rosemary put the pile of letters on the little kitchen benchtop and leaned back on it to read. Robert lounged on her other side and shook a letter to read aloud. '*Dear Hr Houston* crossed out *Horry. Thank you for the advice you have for sale a collection of signed Peter Temple hardbacks. Unfortunately, we already have an allotment to sell and so will be rejecting yours.* Harsh.'

'Keep reading, dear. I like Mrs Bass. She sounds decisive.'

'*Your silverfish problem is a perpetual one in the book world. I understand insect bombing may help, as will regular book hygiene.* No chance of that.'

'Mrs Bass's faith in Horry would seem unrequited.'

'*As for Mr Valencia...*' Robert straightened. 'Why does that name ring a bell?'

'Keep reading,' said Rosemary, her own letter forgotten.

'*As for Mr Valencia, he is once again asking to be advised of any rogue* War and Peace *first editions coming through dated before* 1890. *He has also added to his order any blank journals of mid-price range. It appears he is writing a history of his workplace and would prefer to do so in vintage notebooks with a fountain pen. Mr Valencia is nothing short of rather vintage himself.*' Robert lowered the paper. 'Andrew Valencia, the dead man?'

'Could be.'

'Did you say Andrew Valencia was a collector?'

'Kerry admitted it himself.'

'So, this Mr Valencia is our dead Mr Valencia?'

'We can't presume.' Rosemary turned to the stack of letters and began to flick through them. 'What date is that letter?'

Robert straightened the page. 'Two years ago.'

'Long enough ago to have finished a draft of his history.' Rosemary tapped the letter Robert held. 'Maybe there's more about him. He sounds like a regular customer.'

Robert took more and for a minute the only sounds in the bookshop were the flick of discarded letters, the sliding in and out of chest drawers as the search for paper continued, and the occasional twitchy sigh from Mrs Lionel. 'Here,' said Robert. 'He's mentioned again. *Mr Valencia is keen to acquire early editions of Miles Franklin. Alongside his penchant for orange sport jackets he has told me about is a newly discovered need for early European Australian writers.*'

'A man with distinctive taste,' said Mrs Lionel.

'Indeed,' said Rosemary. 'His orange jackets are indicative of that.'

'I've found a few more.' Robert fanned the letters out in his hand. 'He was a regular customer.'

'Antique and vintage books are a niche market,' said Rosemary. 'And niche is what book dealers love.'

'Niche is nice,' said Mrs Lionel. 'One of my customers told me that when I sold her a cake of honey and rose hip soap. She had a thing for honey.'

'Odd, don't you think?' Robert took a few paces forward and back. 'We come out here chasing Kerry and end up with Andrew Valencia.'

'Not so odd,' said Rosemary. 'I imagine Andrew's interest in old books filtered into his workplace. It usually does. For example, I know a lot more about lavender's medicinal properties since working next to The Green Mulbury and I've grown lavender for years.'

'True,' said Robert. 'Quiz me about the uses for discarded hockey socks and I'll tell you all Patti knows about them.'

'Knowledge you never thought you wanted.'

'Or needed,' added Mrs Lionel. 'But you're correct, Rosemary. Talk in the lunchroom inevitably reveals people's home interests. Kerry must have known, as did all his work colleagues, the value of special books.'

Mr Houston appeared in the doorway of the kitchenette, some long strands of hair floating free of its spindly braid. 'Found some, my lady.' He thrust a reem of paper towards Mrs Lionel. 'It was at the back of the bottom drawer of my third cedar cabinet. I knew it was somewhere safe.'

Robert delivered the paper to Mrs Lionel, who stacked it neatly next to the typewriter before tucking one sheet behind the roller. 'Rosemary, show me how Mrs Bass starts her letters. I'll do the front piece while you think of more words.'

Rosemary set the letter down and Mrs Lionel busied herself copying the capitalised wording of Westerlies Auction House. The firm clack of the typewriter steadied Rosemary's mind and when Mrs Lionel looked at her expectantly, it was easy to begin.

'*Dear Shackle, Shackle and Bunt,*

Regarding your sale of T. G. G. Duncan's speculative fiction writings, including the first edition first printing of the Forces and Horses *series, as part of her husband Mr Anton Lu's late estate...*'

'Who are Shackle, Shackle and Bunt?' asked Mrs Lionel, typing furiously.

'Solicitors. Now gone, along with any incriminating records, or lack thereof. I'm trying to show they are acting on behalf of their client who had possession of the books at his death.'

'Did he?'

'No idea. And neither will Kerry. But you can't deny that Mr Lu would have inherited his wife's items, including any books.'

Cross out Shackle, Shackle and Bunt,' said Robert, his hand out to stop Mrs Lionel. 'Pen in Tomas, Wentworth and Amelia.'

'Who?' said Rosemary.

'Good names, eh?' Robert grinned at her. 'Looks like Mrs Bass knew the solicitors well.'

'Good idea,' she said, and stepped back from the typewriter. 'Let's keep going.'

They worked for a while, Mrs Lionel using the eraser tape in some sections as they changed the wording, until they had a sound letter from Mrs Bass noting the sale of her first edition books to a private collector dated after the death of Mr Lu, with a handwritten footnote carefully penned by Rosemary explaining the benefits of niche collectors and their propensity to keep collections for the term of their natural lives.

'This doesn't explain why the books were found in a box of donated novels.'

'Clearly the collector died and people didn't realise the value of the books.' Rosemary shrugged. 'All we're trying to do is to show Kerry's letter doesn't add up.' She took the letter from Mrs Lionel and folded it carefully before reaching into her pocket for the car keys.

Robert stood up straight from where he was leaning on a bench. 'What are you going to do with it?'

Rosemary glanced at Mrs Lionel, who nodded. She turned back to Robert and squared her shoulders. 'You both stay here. I'm going to show Kerry.'

'Now?'

'No.' She jangled the keys in her palm. 'First, I'm going to get Jasper.'

TWENTY-FIVE

Jasper Lu walked as steadily as he could along the side of the road. The edge of the asphalt was broken, and he stumbled occasionally, silently cursing his flimsy shoes. Occasional trucks roared passed, their trailers rattling like the dry bones of dinosaurs. Dead grass rustled in a slight breeze and he watched it warily, for it was the kind of foliage he imagined snakes lurking in. Every now and then, he glanced at his phone but it was still out of range, and the text he'd sent Rosemary last night to feed Snowy had not been delivered. Despite that, despite the dangers of walking along a dry county road, despite the aches beginning in his calves as he walked, he felt freer than he had for three months.

Three and a half, if he thought more carefully about it. There'd been his exit from Mulbury, which had felt like a charge into the unknown. It had been exciting at first. Rakisha's sister had dropped him at Helena's, and Helena was unusually animated. She was convinced she'd found his biological father, and her excitement—so removed from the nasty digs she often sent his way—was uplifting. But it didn't remain. The man she'd discovered disappeared, if there had ever been a man in the first place. Helena grew sullen. Jasper moved to be with Iris.

Iris, his younger half-sister, was her beautiful self, but she was busy with her family and work and all the things that made up domestic life. He'd stayed with her, and mostly felt in the way. The city, too, blared at him. It was always lit, always noisy, and smelled odd. At night, lying with the window open for fresh air, Jasper imagined his little home in Mulbury, where the night sounds were thumps of possums on the roof, fox yaps, and Snowy's snores. And how he missed that dog! Snowy hadn't done much but sleep for a few years now but he was a solid comfort, an ever-wagging presence of love.

Love.

Jasper trudged on.

Then the documentary was released and suddenly the goal of his current life—to find his father—was met. But Kerry was not what he expected. What had he expected? A warm, loving book nerd perhaps, someone who regretted not knowing his son? Someone to embrace as a father figure. Instead, there was Kerry. Instead of resolution, there was disillusion.

'Hey, hello!'

Deep in thought, Jasper hadn't noticed the cyclist coming up behind him. He stopped on the road level with him.

'Car broken down?'

Jasper shook his head. 'I decided to walk into town.'

The cyclist, a lean tanned man in yellow athletic gear and wearing a small backpack, glanced up the road. 'From where? Hutts Hill? Bit of a way to go to Birdton. Do you think you'll make it?'

Jasper touched his face. It was hotter than he'd realised

and sweat ran down from his temples. 'I guess I forgot that it was summer.'

'Yeah.' The cyclist reached down and pulled a water bottle from the bike frame. 'Here. Drink up.'

Jasper took the bottle and drank its contents gratefully. There was some kind of electrolyte in it, making its taste tangy. 'Thanks,' he said, handing it back. 'I didn't realise I was so thirsty.'

The cyclist smiled kindly, making his face crease so Jasper saw he was older than he'd originally thought. 'Something on your mind?'

'You could say that.'

The cyclist studied him for a moment, and Jasper had a growing sense that he had seen the man before. Perhaps it was the cycling gear as lots of cycling groups sped through Mulbury. 'What about I go on and get my car so I can give you a ride into town? Unless you want to hitch a ride on the back of my bike.'

Jasper looked at the thin piping of the road bike and turned back to the grinning cyclist. 'I'll pass, if you don't mind.'

'Okay then.' The cyclist put his toe back into the shield of his pedal. 'Stay in the shade and I'll be back in about twenty minutes. Take this.' He handed Jasper the small backpack. 'There's more drink in there. And a book, in case you like reading. I might be a little while. Alright?'

'Alright.' Jasper reached out to shake the man's hand. 'Thank you.'

'No worries. My name's Ken.'

'Jasper.'

'Keep in the shade, Jasper.'

Jasper watched as Ken shot off, the bright flashes of road gear gradually fading into the distance. Now he had pointed the heat out, Jasper felt hot and itchy. His long shorts had chafed the tops of his knees, and his toes felt blistery. His neck, no longer protected from long hair, was burnt. He left the road and stood under an ironbark tree, carefully checking the ground for bush residents before crouching down to lean on its trunk to wait, opening the backpack and drinking more salty energy drink. There was a paperback at the bottom of the bag and he idly noted its worn pages and creased cover. It was either a favourite or very pre-loved, and Jasper smiled as he closed the bag.

Without the distraction of walking or an appetite for reading, Jasper couldn't help but revisit his last encounter with Kerry. The man who called himself his father—Jasper could only think of him as Kerry, not Dad—was so insistent they sell the firsts that finally the unease Jasper had been feeling since he'd first met him blossomed into something resembling a blaring siren with flashing lights. *What,* he asked himself, *was he doing*? Selling his mother's books to the highest bidder like they were someone else's treasure? He was T. G. G. Duncan's son, for goodness' sake! Letter or not, he couldn't do it.

Kerry clearly could. They'd stood on the pavement outside Broken Books Inc after Mr Houston had taken the books as if they were duellers in Victorian times. In fact, Jasper was convinced Kerry would have fired before the count of three if only he'd had a pistol in his hand. It was too much. 'I'm not having anything to do with it,' he'd said to Kerry. 'You take them, sell them, whatever. I can't do it.'

'Yes, you can, boy.' Kerry's voice, usually so jovial, had an edge to it. 'You need to verify where you'd found them, otherwise it makes me look like a...'

'Thief.' There, the word was out.

Kerry flushed a beetrooty purple. 'She gave me these books. I have the letter to prove it.'

'I've seen it. Should be enough, then, for you to sell them without me.'

'No, no, no. I need you with me...son.'

The word fell flat. Jasper had shrugged. 'I'm going back to Mulbury. You can do what you like.'

'Well, you'll have to walk then.' Kerry tapped his pocket where keys jangled. 'I've got the car.'

'Good luck with it. I don't need you.' And Jasper had turned on his heel and walked away.

It felt much longer than twenty minutes before a white four-wheel drive with an expansive bike rack on its rear door appeared. Ken leaned out of the window. 'Right there, Jasper?'

'Yes, I'm good.'

The cyclist jumped out of the car. His bright top had been replaced with a white T-shirt, although he'd kept his cycling shorts, and had a pair of light runners on. Jasper guessed he was probably a similar age to Kerry but that was where the resemblance stopped. This man was wiry and lean, with dark eyes bright against his olive skin. 'Yes, I'm fine.'

'Come on, then. I've got more water in the car.'

Jasper stepped into the front of the big car and took up the water bottle from the seat. 'Thanks,' he said as he drank it.

'No worries. Right to go?'

Jasper nodded. Ken jumped into the driver's seat and sent the car onto the road.

Town was only a short drive away, and Jasper felt he could have walked it. On a cooler day. If he had water. After all, he had all the time he wanted and the further he walked from Hutts Hill, the further away he was from Kerry. As they swept into the main street, Jasper saw a row of well-maintained shops, and a car yard of new vehicles the same make as the one he was sitting in. 'This town's going okay.'

Ken laughed. 'Oh, yeah. It's flourishing, thanks to the tourist industry. It used to depend on sheep and wheat farms, but those days were numbered long ago.'

'We're a long way from anywhere.' Jasper turned to check the shops along the main street, which seemed to be mainly cafés. 'What brings the tourists in?'

'Gin. Bespoke distilleries.'

'Really?'

'Yes.'

'People in town work at these distilleries?'

'Some. The others are in local businesses.' Ken turned the car into a side street and made their way to the back of the car yard. 'This is mine.'

'You own a car yard?'

Ken laughed. 'I'm as surprised as you!'

'Sorry, I didn't mean to sound surprised. I should know that first impressions never stack up.' Jasper felt his cheeks warm further. 'That sounded even worse.'

Ken smiled widely. 'Oh, don't worry about it. I understand. I look like I should be retired and I was. I'd been retired for years from being a real estate agent, but I shifted here and took the business over when my brother died. I felt I had to keep it going for him.' The smile vanished. 'He died last year. My only family.'

Jasper was quiet as Ken parked the car and turned it off. 'I'm sorry about that.'

'Yeah. Me, too.' He shrugged one shoulder as if trying to

shift something off it. 'Well, here we are. Come in now and you can organise to get back to...where, exactly?'

'Mulbury.'

'Mulbury? That's a fair distance. What brings you out here?' Ken held up his hand. 'Sorry. Shouldn't pry.' He opened his car door. 'Come and I'll get you another drink. What do you feel like? Beer, soft drink, something harder?'

Jasper hesitated. 'I wouldn't mind a cup of tea.'

Ken laughed again, chuckling his way out of the car and leading Jasper into the showroom of the car yard. Jasper followed behind, smiling at the warmth in Ken's voice. There was something about the older man that made Jasper feel relaxed, a sort of acceptance at the strange situation Jasper found himself in. It only increased when Ken went straight to a kettle at the back of his open office and Jasper saw a whole row of tea canisters sitting on the bench. 'I don't mind a cup of tea, either' said Ken, waving his hand along the row. 'What's your medicine?'

'Earl Grey, if you don't mind.'

'Like the old bergamot, eh?' Ken switched the kettle on and pulled a small teapot from the cupboard. 'How about you use the phone on the desk, and I'll make us a brew?'

Jasper pulled his phone from his pocket and looked at its signal. 'It's okay, I've got service again.'

Ken nodded and pointed to the vast space in the showroom taken up by only one car, an unusually coloured mauve sedan. 'It'll be better in there.'

Jasper walked out to stand next to the vehicle and connected to his contacts. He could ring Gerry, or Robert or even Franco and they'd be there as soon as they could. Jules, too, and any of the Hubbard sisters. Patti would pick him up, also, although she'd probably take time to finish what she was doing first. They all had cars, and they'd all be happy enough to drive hours to get him. But there was only one person he really wanted to see. He dialled Rosemary.

'Where are you?' she asked without acknowledging his greeting.

'In a car yard.' Jasper walked back to the office area. 'Sorry, Ken, but where are we again?'

Ken grinned. 'Birdton.'

Jasper repeated the name. 'I'm wondering if...'

'I'll be there in ten minutes.'

'What? How come?'

'It's a long story and one that you feature in.'

Jasper frowned. 'Have you been following me?'

'No, because you didn't say where you were going. I had to work it out.'

'And you worked it out.'

'Obviously.'

'Where have you been?'

'Visiting a Mr Houston from Broken Books.'

'Oh.' Jasper closed his eyes.

'Yes. We know all about your fight with Kerry.'

'Oh.'

'Is that all you can say?'

Jasper glanced at the office, where Ken was carrying a teapot and two mugs to a little round table. 'No.'

Rosemary's sigh disappeared into the road noise through her phone. 'See you shortly.' She hung up.

Jasper lowered his phone and stared at it for a moment. She'd been concerned about him. The thought made his heart race a little. Concern for a friend or for something else?'

'Are you alright, Jasper?'

Ken stood a little way off, looking at him in much the same way Mrs Lionel did at times, especially since Jasper had returned to Mulbury with...that man. 'Yes,' he said, sliding the phone back into his pocket. 'She's coming to get me.'

'She?' Ken shook his head vigorously. 'Sorry, prying again.' He scratched his head. 'I'm not usually like that. I must be getting old.'

'It's okay. Rosemary is coming to get me. She's a good friend.'

'A good friend. I see.' Ken smiled, his look soft. 'Tea's ready.'

They walked to the table where Ken had also put out a packet of chocolate biscuits. He offered one to Jasper as they sat. Jasper took one, suddenly aware that it had been some time since he'd eaten. The sweet milk chocolate coupled with the tea was exactly what he needed, and he ate three biscuits without hesitation.

Ken had been quiet all that time. As Rosemary's old blue sedan pulled up in the street, and Jasper turned quickly, he spoke again. 'It's hard, isn't it?'

Jasper watched as Rosemary stepped out and gazed around before noticing him in the showroom. She started her brisk walk towards him. 'Hard?'

'When they can't return your love.'

Jasper choked on the last of the biscuits and took a big swallow of his tea before looking at Ken. 'Sorry?'

'It's okay. I know. I recognise it because it happened to me, too. They want to love you back but it turns out their feelings are somewhere else.' Ken leaned back in his chair. 'Don't be like me, Jasper.'

Rosemary slid open the showroom door, closing it with a thud behind her. 'What do you mean?' asked Jasper, his eyes on the woman coming towards him, wispy threads of hair pulled from her braid the only sign that she was perhaps more disturbed than normal.

'Accept your relationship for what it is and move on.' Ken's voice was so low, Jasper barely caught it. 'Don't be lonely like me.'

'Jasper,' said Rosemary, arriving at the table and spearing him with a look that was at once cross and concerned. 'Have you finally worked out what's going on?'

Jasper looked back at Ken, whose sad smile broadened into real mirth at the sight of Rosemary standing with her hands on her hips. 'Hello, Rosemary. The answer is yes. Yes, I have.'

TWENTY-SIX

Rosemary studied the men in front of her. They were sitting at a table drinking tea, of all things. The sharp aroma of bergamot made her nose twitch. She waited a bit longer, but Jasper didn't offer up anything else. His face was a deep red, and not because he was embarrassed. He was clearly sunburnt, with matching red knees and chapped lips. The way he took a large swig of his tea made her suspect he was dehydrated as well. Rage at Kerry simmered in her head, making her vision momentarily blurry, but Jasper poured himself another cup from a chipped teapot that was nonetheless a lovely Brown Betty with a deep caramel glaze. As he sat the pot down, she pulled out the chair next to him and lowered herself with a thunk. 'I'll have a cup of that.'

The older man leaped up and moved to the back of the office for another cup with an agility Rosemary had expected with one so lean and wiry. His lower legs were hard and hairless, signs of a serious cyclist. His face, too, had a bronzed outdoor look with paler sunglass-marked circles around his eyes. His dark eyes, though, were kind and amused as he delivered a cup to the table and sat back down to pour her tea. 'I'm Ken,' he said, pushing the full drink towards her.

'Rosemary Exeter.'

'Pleased to meet you.' Ken indicated Jasper. 'I didn't expect you to arrive so quickly.'

'I was nearby.' Rosemary sipped her tea, noticing with some surprise the rich quality not normally associated with car showroom beverages.

'Who else is at Broken Books?' asked Jasper quietly. 'Is...?'

'Mrs Lionel and Robert have stayed with Mr Houston. No sign of Kerry.'

'He won't be far.'

Rosemary watched as Jasper fiddled with the handle of his cup. 'No. He'll stay close to those books of his.'

'They aren't his.'

She shrugged. 'Good. You understand that.'

'He has that letter...'

'Fake letter. Don't worry. We're matching it.'

Jasper looked up. 'What do you mean?'

'He's not the only person who can pass off a con. We now have another letter stating the books were left to your father.' She handed the letter to Jasper who opened it and started laughing.

'Rosemary, you are amazing!'

Rosemary nodded once and put her cup down. Ken was turned politely away from the conversation. 'We are dealing with an imposter,' she said to him.

Ken nodded, as if imposters turned up every day. 'I see.'

'And a murderer.'

Jasper jerked at Rosemary's words, knocking his cup, and spilling some tea on the table. 'What?'

Rosemary glanced at him and then at Ken, who'd

forgotten to be polite and was leaning forwards, elbows on the table. 'He killed Andrew Valencia.'

'How do you know?'

'I have a strong suspicion. The evidence will be in Andrew's journals.'

'You have his journals?'

'No.' Rosemary sipped at her tea. 'You do.'

'I do?'

Rosemary put her mug down. 'You had two boxes of books in the car with you to take to Broken Books.'

'Yeah... well, one. Mum's firsts were in one.'

'And the other?'

Jasper shrugged. 'I don't know. Kerry put them on the back seat and I just assumed they were the books he'd brought with him.'

'The leatherbound journals he brought with him when you both came back to Mulbury.'

'He had some leatherbound books.' Jasper frowned. 'How do you know they were journals?'

'He left one on your kitchen table, unfortunately a blank one.'

Jasper nodded slowly. 'I tried not to touch anything of his. They made my skin crawl just knowing he'd held them.'

'Pity.' Rosemary sipped her tea. 'You might have discovered his secrets sooner if you'd read what another person thought of him.'

'Ooof,' said Ken, hiding behind his mug.

'It's alright,' Jasper said to him. 'Rosemary always says it like it is. I should have been more curious instead of...'

'Trusting,' said Ken.

'Naive,' said Rosemary at the same time.

'Both those.' Jasper rubbed at his head. 'Find Kerry, find the evidence, I guess.'

'I'll contact Geoffrey and tell him what I know.'

Jasper ran his hand through his short hair. 'Yes. But he'll be hours away.'

'We can't let Kerry go.'

'Rosemary...'

'What?'

Jasper ran his hand through his hair. 'He's dangerous.'

'You're just coming to that conclusion now? You've spent nearly every moment of the last few weeks with him.'

'Yes, I've just come to that conclusion.' Jasper glared at her. 'Some of us aren't as astute as you.'

Rosemary let her shoulders slump. 'It's nothing to do with astuteness, Jasper,' she said softly. 'Some of us didn't have as much hanging on Kerry being who he said he was.'

Jasper hung his head. 'I'm an idiot.'

'Don't be ridiculous. You are the least idiotic person I know.'

A small smile ghosted Jasper's mouth. 'I don't know why, but I feel so much better when you're cross.'

'I'm sorry for interfering but you ran from a murderer?'

Rosemary had nearly forgotten Ken was there. He had his elbows on the table, leaning forward with an intensely worried look on his face that reminded her of someone else. Perhaps another car salesman? It was doubtful.

'I didn't know at the time,' said Jasper, twirling his cup around. 'I mean, I should have but I was taken up with the thought he was my father.'

'He's not your father?'

Jasper shook his head. 'No. It's very clear to me now.'

'You don't know your father?'

Jasper shook his head once more.

'Okay,' said Ken, sitting back. 'That's sad.'

'It's not really.' Jasper gave a short laugh. 'I had a good

father who raised me, but somehow you always want to know your actual origins.' He pushed his cup away. 'You know how it goes, though. I should have let sleeping dogs lie.'

'Why is that?'

Jasper eyed the man in front of him. 'When you're desperate for something, anything will do.'

Ken nodded. 'Will you keep looking?'

Jasper turned to Rosemary, who kept very still. Outside, a magpie warbled, its sound muffled by the thick, showroom glass. 'No.'

Rosemary smiled and resisted the temptation to grab his hand. 'You'll stay in Mulbury?'

He frowned and tipped his head to the side. 'Where else would I go?'

'Right.' She ducked her head to cover up the way her smile had grown to a grin and checked her phone. 'I'll ring Mr Houston to tell Robert and Mrs Lionel I've found you, and then we'd better get going.'

'Going where?'

'To find Kerry.'

Ken startled. 'And Kerry is the murdering man?'

'Yes.'

'And you're going to find him?'

Rosemary stood, waving her phone. 'Yes. I'll call the police and explain, and then we'll track Kerry down so he doesn't escape.'

'Is that really your job?'

'Of course it isn't, but we can't let him get away.'

Ken stood as well, shaking his head. 'You sound so confident, it's like you've done this before.'

Jasper turned to Rosemary, then pushed his chair back to stand up. 'You don't know the half of it,' he said to Ken.

'Well, how can I help?'

Rosemary tucked the strands of loose hair back into her braid. 'You can't. Thanks for the tea.'

She walked towards the door, noting the little mauve sedan in the middle of the showroom and the way it caught the light streaming in from outside. She went to say something to Jasper, but found he was still at the table, talking to Ken. He put a hand up, spoke for a little longer, then hurried to Rosemary. 'Ken's going to Broken Books to see the others.'

Rosemary opened the door and stepped out into the beating sun. 'Why?'

'He was keen to help. He did help, Rosemary. I would have ended up bitten by a snake or run over by a truck if he hadn't collected me.'

'Rubbish.' Rosemary opened her car door and sunk into its hot depths. 'You're too clever for that.'

'Well, dehydrated at the very least.'

'That I can see. Not the cleverest to storm off without water on a hot summer's day.'

'I wasn't thinking very clearly.'

'Right.'

Jasper waited while Rosemary rang the police before they climbed into the car. The engine roared in protest when Rosemary turned it on, and she shook her head before turning to Jasper. 'Geoffrey is on his way to Broken Books as a starting point. Kerry will be close because he'll want to go back and get the books from Mr Houston once the auction house has been notified.'

'I suppose he could be where we stayed last night. I don't think they have many bookings.' Jasper gripped the door handle. 'Mr Houston shouldn't give the books to Kerry without me being there.'

'Mr Houston can only act on the proof that he has, which is the letter. Given his own choice, I think Mr Houston wouldn't give Kerry the time of day.'

'He doesn't trust him either?' Jasper stared out the window. 'And how does he know Kerry's untrustworthy if I couldn't figure it out?'

Rosemary beeped a raven wandering out on the road, and it shuffled its way back to safely. 'Mr Houston has special powers.'

'What?'

'He thinks Kerry smelled bad.'

From the edge of her vision, Rosemary saw Jasper's mouth open. Instead of saying something, though, he burst out laughing. '*What?*'

'Mr Houston thinks Kerry smells like mildew.'

'And that makes Kerry bad?'

'Wouldn't it make anyone bad? Who else do you know who smells like mould?'

Jasper's laugh turned into a fit of giggles. 'No one I know. Really? He said Kerry smelled?'

'And you, too. In fact, all of us.'

Jasper couldn't speak. His laughter, something Rosemary realised she hadn't heard for months, filled the car and made her smile. She started chuckling herself.

Jasper gasped some words out. 'And me? Was I mildewy as well?'

'No. You were like eucalyptus leaves.'

He nodded, wiping at his eyes and waving at her. 'You?'

'Pepper. Mrs Lionel is a peach, and Robert wood shavings.'

It was enough to keep Jasper giggling for the next ten minutes. Every time he stopped, it was only a second before he started up again. In the end, Rosemary pointed to the glove box. 'Tissues in there.'

Jasper wiped his face and settled down, pulling out his phone and finding a map. 'Rightio. I think he'll be at that place we stayed at last night. The Eerie?'

Rosemary pulled the car over and leaned over to look at the map. 'He'll be waiting until Mr Houston opens in the morning to make the call to the dealers. He's in no rush to take the books now as Mr Houston believes in the letter. Kerry wouldn't want to be taken in for stealing just as he finds a bit of money.'

'Here it is,' Jasper said, zooming out the map. He turned the phone around to show Rosemary. 'It's about five kilometres north on the next road.'

'Right.' Rosemary turned the car back onto the road. 'Let's go get our murdering mildewed friend.'

The road to The Eerie was potholed and skinny. Rosemary turned on to it warily. The car rattled obscenely and at the first glimpse of the house she pulled it to the side as close to the tree line as she could get and wound down the window. 'I think we've found him.'

Kerry's booming voice carried across the paddocks above the sounds of moaning ravens and warbling magpies. Jasper was out of the car first, with Rosemary close behind. They followed the sound to find Kerry standing in a driveway gesticulating wildly. The woman he was talking to looked bamboozled, and Rosemary felt certain she was either being talked out of something or talked into something. Rosemary turned to Jasper. 'This is where you stayed last night?'

'Yes.'

'Your landlady doesn't look happy.'

'Her name is Carol and she doesn't.' Jasper chewed his lip. 'What do we do?'

'We go get him.'

He swallowed. 'Should we wait for Geoffrey's team?'

'Probably. No.'

'Then let's do it.'

Rosemary tucked the car keys into her pocket and started the walk up the gravel driveway. Despite the cheery bed and breakfast sign on the gate, the house was run down and badly in need of attention. The woman standing next to Kerry echoed the nature of the house, and the downcast sit of her shoulders indicated that having Kerry's patronage was not going to further her fortunes.

Rosemary caught the last of his sentence. '...and so, dear lady, you won't get any money from me!'

'But you stayed in my accommodation last night without any complaints.' Carol's voice was weak. 'You should pay for the next night if you're staying.'

'Yes,' said Rosemary, catching the attention of both. 'You should, Kerry.'

The large man pulled back from his stance over the woman. 'Rosemary.' He smiled widely at Jasper. 'Jasper, my son.'

'Not your son.'

'What's that, son? Can't hear you for the overwhelming presence of a busybody.' Kerry narrowed his eyes at Rosemary.

'I'm not your son.' Jasper's voice rang out clearly.

'Ah.' Kerry turned his back on Carol, who hurried away towards the house. 'That's your conclusion, eh? Despite the evidence.' He shook his head sadly. 'Your poor mother would be horrified. Think of her, Jasper. Think how she'd be.'

'She'd be horrified that a total stranger used her books to dupe her son,' said Rosemary.

'I cannot see,' said Kerry slowly, 'this is the case. Jasper, *think.* How would I have that letter if it wasn't your mother's wish?'

'Talking about letters...' Jasper pulled the envelope from his pocket. 'Mr Houston remembered something after we left. It was lucky Rosemary turned up so he could give it to her to give to me.'

Kerry came closer. 'What is it?'

'It's a letter from a Mrs Bass of Westerlies auction house.'

'Who? I don't know a Mrs Bass.'

'No, but Mr Houston knows her well.'

'As did Andrew Valencia,' added Rosemary.

'Andrew Valencia? Andrew Valencia?' Kerry's lips tightened. 'What's Andrew got to do with anything?' He shook himself slightly. 'I mean, poor man. It's terrible of you to bring him in on the conversation. Outrageous!'

'He deserves to be in the conversation, though.' Rosemary tilted her head. 'Especially since he was writing the truth in his history of The Jalopy Factory.'

The sun was directly in Kerry's eyes, but Rosemary saw his sideways glance at his car. She looked as well, noticing the cardboard box full of leatherbound books on the back seat. 'That man...' Kerry said quietly.

'You mean Andrew? Andrew Valencia, who knew all about your thievery from the factory? Who understood how a thief could turn to other crimes, such as being an imposter for monetary gain?'

Kerry stepped across her line of vision. 'You are a particularly annoying woman, eh? Very annoying. You remind me of that Andrew Valencia and his endless, endless questions. But he's gone now, eh, so you have no proof. No proof of anything you've said.' He put his hands out to Jasper. 'Eh, son? She's making it all up.'

Jasper stood still. 'Not according to this letter.'

'What?' Kerry leaned forward to snatch the letter from Jasper's outstretched arm. He read it quickly, shook the page, read it again.

'Interesting content?' asked Rosemary.

This time when he stared at her, his eyes were narrowed against the sun. Or was it that they were narrowed as he thought of a shrewd way to get himself out of the tangle he appeared to be in? Rosemary reckoned the latter. She waited patiently for whatever he did next.

'Where are the books in question?' Kerry's tone was breezy, as if he was only mildly interested, although Rosemary caught the quick intake of breath that finished his question.

'Where we left them,' said Jasper before Rosemary could stop him. 'Safely locked up waiting for the police,' she added.

Kerry folded the paper. 'And why on earth would police need to be contacted about a bunch of old books?'

'They form part of the story.'

Kerry stepped towards Rosemary, slipping the letter into a back pocket. 'Do they just? A tale of intrigue and innuendo, no doubt, fired by someone with a jealous imagination.' He tapped her arm. 'Don't like it that Jasper has a daddy now. Someone who might take him away from you, eh? Do you, eh?'

Rosemary felt her cheeks warm, although it could have been because of the foul breath issuing from Kerry. 'I would love Jasper to find his father if the man appreciated what a fine son he had. If the father was a hideous, money-grabbing conman, I would prefer him to remain absent.'

'Hmph.' Kerry turned to Jasper, his face morphing into a smile. 'What do you say, Jasper, my boy? Do you believe the dreadful story that has come out from those annoying ex-work colleagues and your *friend* here has taken up to support her own mission.' He placed a hand on Jasper's shoulder. 'Remember, son, she didn't contact you for three months when you left.'

'Rubbish.' Rosemary crossed her arms. 'I was giving Jasper some distance.'

'You could have rung me,' Jasper said softly, looking at the ground. 'You had my phone number, and Iris's.'

Rosemary felt her chest thicken. 'True, I did. You didn't contact *me* so I didn't contact *you*. I thought you needed time away and I also knew Iris would let us know if she was worried about you.'

Jasper lifted his hand but didn't turn to her. 'She would have.'

'Right. But you expected me to contact you anyway.' Rosemary sighed. 'I'm sorry. Of course, I should have.' The thickening in her chest spread to her throat as Jasper finally caught her eye. The pain on his face made her feel sick. She grabbed his hand and held on tightly. 'I have never been so sorry in all my life.'

He squeezed her fingers. 'I have never been so lonely as I was in those three months.'

'Oh.' Further words wouldn't form in Rosemary's head. She could only see the man in front of her, forlorn and weary. Instinctively, she pulled him into a hard hug and was insanely happy when he instantly tightened his arms around her back.

'Excuse me. Excuse *me*.'

The words finally penetrated the hug and Rosemary dropped her arms to see the landlady of the bed and breakfast pointing down the driveway.

'I'm not going to get my money if that man leaves, am I?'

The revving of an old car made Jasper and Rosemary spin around. Kerry took off in a cloud of dust down the winding track. 'He's going to Broken Books,' said Jasper, one hand clutching the top of his head.

'Then we are, too.' Rosemary sprinted for her car, waving away the landlady's protests, and jumping in just as Jasper did. The sedan coughed a few times then revved angrily, and she swung it around to follow Kerry.

It was difficult to see through the heavy layer of dust but Kerry's occasional red brake light showed the way. At the base of the hill, both cars went left onto the bitumen and finally Rosemary could see clearly.

'Careful,' yelled Jasper over the road noise as they hit a pothole, making the car shudder.

'I'm being careful,' said Rosemary, concentrating on keeping the car straight as more potholes loomed. 'They really need to fix this road.'

'I'll write them a sternly worded email when we finish here,' said Jasper, hanging on to the arm on the door. 'It's disgraceful we can't enter a car chase without our vehicle bottoming out on the road.'

Rosemary glanced at him. Despite the dreadful realisation he'd come to, Jasper looked more like himself than he had since he'd returned. Bits of hair fell over his forehead, swept wildly around by the air rushing through his open window. He kept trying to brush it back but it wasn't long enough to go behind his ears. Colour once again warmed his face, probably from his sunburn, but it made his dark eyes stand out. And was there a sparkle in them? A hint of the old, carefree man who loved his dog and his Regency romances?

'What are you grinning at?' Jasper grabbed the seat as they thumped into another hole.

'Absolutely nothing.' Rosemary steered quickly around the shreds of an old tyre. 'We don't have the right to smile, not with us chasing a murderer.'

'You're right.' Jasper's smile creased his eyes and he laughed as a raven took off out of their way. 'This is crazy!'

The outskirts of town loomed and finally Rosemary slowed the car. She met the speed limit right on the sign and gripped the steering wheel tightly. 'He's gone.'

'No.' Jasper pointed to the right. 'He's there, parked around the corner.'

Rosemary screeched the car around one hundred and eighty degrees, ignoring the crunching, grinding noise as the old sedan battled to cope. She pulled up right outside the door of Broken Books Inc, glimpsing Mr Houston in his window seat staring up at a large, looming figure over him.

'Where's Mrs Lionel?' said Jasper as they leapt from the car.

'Safe. With Robert. I hope they've gone to get a drink from the shop.'

They ploughed into the bookshop, shoulders jamming in the book-laden corridor, screeching cat alarm deafening. Rosemary pushed her way passed Jasper and flung around the corner in time to see Kerry wielding a large thesaurus at Mr Houston. The older man cowered in his seat and tipped his head to see Rosemary. 'Mildew Man is here! Help!'

Rosemary leapt at Kerry, catching his arm and sending the thesaurus flying. She had the advantage of speed but not of weight. Kerry brought his arms down around her, locking her arms to her side. He kicked out at a shelf of domestic noir and sent the bookcase crashing down, trapping Jasper out of the area.

'Rosemary?' Jasper's voice was thin through the debris. 'Are you okay?'

'Oh, shut it,' yelled Kerry, holding Rosemary tightly. 'Useless man. Glad you're no son of mine!'

Rosemary huffed. 'Got you.'

'What does it matter now?' Kerry squeezed her tightly and she gasped. 'Where are the firsts?' he hissed in her ears.

'Why would I know?' she forced out against his restrictions. 'I don't own the shop.'

'This old man says they're in his safe. Where's the safe?'

Rosemary wriggled madly but Kerry only held on tighter. She was wedged between his solid torso and strong arms and could hardly breathe. 'Let Mr Houston go and I'll take you to it. I know the combination.'

'Just tell me where it is.'

'You won't find it.' Her words were strangled. 'Not in this mess.'

That seemed to make sense to Kerry. He loosened his hold and Rosemary took a few deep breaths in and out before gesturing to Mr Houston. 'Crawl out,' she said. 'Go under the shelf.'

Mr Houston glanced down at the gap under the crime novels. In the corridor behind them, Rosemary heard Jasper scrabbling to move books out of the way but his efforts only seemed to cause more book avalanches. 'I can't,' said Mr Houston. 'My toes...'

Rosemary nudged him roughly with her free foot. 'Mrs Lionel will rub them when you get out.'

Mr Houston's face brightened. He dropped awkwardly to his knees and crawled slowly to the little gap. 'Help!' he said into it. A pair of hands reached in to grab him under the arms and yanked the man through. As he went, books collapsed after him, closing the tunnel, but Rosemary heard his final yell: 'Watch the roof!'

Kerry yanked her around so she faced the dirty front

window and put his foot up on the desk to brace himself. The old blind had dropped in the commotion and hid the view of outside. 'Nice boots,' said Rosemary, panting. 'Although dress shoes would match your outfit better.' She felt Kerry still for a moment before he tightened his grip.

'I've been wanting to get you alone, yes, indeed,' said Kerry, his hot breath on her cheek.

Rosemary wriggled but he had her fast. 'I'm not interested in a man like you.'

'And I'm certainly not interested in a nosey, cunning woman like you.' He gripped her more tightly. 'I need those books.'

'You'll never be able to sell them now.'

'Oh, you'll see, you'll see. Private collectors of the right kind often feel above the law.'

'I didn't mean you wouldn't be able to *sell* them. I meant *you* wouldn't be able to sell them.'

Kerry went still. 'You aren't talking about the letter, are you?'

Rosemary twisted, trying to free her neck a little. 'I'm talking about how difficult it would be to sell a set of niche collectable books in goal.'

Kerry moved his arms slightly, crushing her ribs and Rosemary couldn't help but gasp. 'What are you talking about?'

'You strangled Andrew Valencia to stop him revealing truths about you.'

He let the pressure off her torso and Rosemary took a big breath in just before Kerry's bicep pressed against her throat. 'What truths are you talking about?'

Rosemary grabbed his arm but her grip was weakened by her limited movement. 'The Jalopy Factory thievery.

Conning Jasper. There are probably others. Andrew wrote about them in his journals, didn't he?'

Kerry was quiet for a moment, although the noise in Rosemary's ears increased as the pressure against her throat tightened. She blinked to clear her vision but blurriness remained. 'You are an interfering witch, my girl,' he hissed in her ear. 'I should squeeze your throat like I did to Andrew Valencia but I don't think I'll have to. It will be a shame when you are accidentally crushed by that horrible old man's desk.' He kicked the solid desk, sending a flow of papers to the rubble on the floor. 'But first you need to tell me where the books are.'

'There's a crowd outside,' wheezed Rosemary. 'You'll never escape.'

'Oh, I think I will.' Kerry laughed shortly. 'That crowd will be too interested in saving you to bother about me.'

As if on cue, Jasper's panicked voice came through the pile of books. 'Rosemary? Are you alright?'

'She's good, just grand,' said Kerry, but not loud enough for anyone but Rosemary to hear. 'Now, my girl, where are those books?'

The humming in Rosemary's ears grew louder and she fought to take in more air. Kerry's arm eased a little and she gulped in a reviving lungful. 'I feel I'm going to faint...' She let herself collapse in his arms, and Kerry eased his hold. With the slight freedom, she scrambled around and rammed into him, catching him off balance. He staggered back towards the bookcase holding the roof up. 'Jasper! Get out!' Rosemary ran back as far as she could in the refined space. 'It's going to let go!'

Running footsteps faded just as Kerry crashed into the bracing bookcase. There was a mighty crack as the wood gave way. His arms flung up as he went backwards. The top plank ripped from the ceiling, letting a shower of building debris fall. A split-second later, the truss broke as well.

Rosemary crouched down, clutching her head, as one hundred years of bird nests and ceiling plaster rained down and buried her completely.

TWENTY-EIGHT

Rosemary came to slowly and found herself on her back. There was no sound but the ringing in her ears. The weight of what felt like a tonne of books pressed her to the floor. She moved her hips slightly and a book slid a little from her stomach, letting her breathe more easily. She kept her eyes shut, straining to hear what was happening in the world above. Gradually, her ears picked up the high-pitched scream of police sirens and shouting. She lifted her arms a tad and felt another book slide but it jammed against others, trapping her completely. There was nothing else she could do so she relaxed, keeping her eyes closed to concentrate on what else was going on.

There was a rumble of books nearby.

Kerry protested.

A familiar law enforcement officer gave calm directives.

Kerry protested louder.

Someone called her name.

The heavy spine of a leather-bound dictionary sat on her nose but she couldn't move it. Strangely, the pressure and the delicious smell of aged paper grounded her to her surroundings. A voice called her name again. Some minutes later, the books were lifted carefully away, the dictionary coming off last to reveal a pale, tight-faced Jasper. 'About time,' said Rosemary, blowing dust from her face.

Jasper crouched beside her, his elbows on some John le Carre thrillers. 'I thought you were dead,' he said. 'Why aren't you dead?'

'Do you want me to be dead?'

His face drained of all its remaining blood. 'No, of course not! It's just I don't know how you could have survived this.' He waved his hand across the remaining books on her legs. 'There are 30,000 books in this shop, 10,000 in this front section alone.'

'Trust you to know that.' She sat up slowly, feeling bruises burn from the cascade of those thousands of books. Jasper held out his hand and she took it to help her stand, feeling more pain the higher she rose. Dizziness rocked her for a moment as she straightened completely and she closed her eyes, feeling Jasper's arm strong across her back. 'I need that.'

'Did you say you need me?'

Jasper's voice was close to her ear. She opened her eyes to stare straight into his. 'Jasper, you don't realise how much I need you. *I* don't realise how much I need you.'

A smile split his face.

'You are my closest friend.' She brushed hair from her face. 'Besides Mrs Lionel.'

The smile began to droop. 'A friend?'

'Best friend.'

He pulled back a little. 'But no more than that.'

'Jasper.' She put both her hands on his upper arm. 'That is so much. *So* much. I've had romantic love before and it didn't turn out so well.' She shook Alasdair's image from her head and clutched Jasper tighter. 'I love you better than that.'

'It's better?'

She held his look, watching him as his brow furrowed. 'Of course it is. It's stronger and not subject to whimsical changes of mind. How about you come back to Mulbury and be my best friend again?'

He was silent.

Behind him, Rosemary saw Kerry being led by Constable Christopher to a patrol vehicle parked against the curb. An emergency vehicle turned up, and orange-overalled figures jumped out and ran to them, helping Jasper to step her over the rubble and onto the path away from the disaster. Mr Houston was already there, sitting on an upturned crate with Mrs Lionel brushing the dust from his beard. She straightened to come to Rosemary, who waved her back to the admiring Mr Houston. 'Is everyone okay, Jasper?'

'Everyone's fine, as you can see.' Jasper settled her on an upturned bin. 'We're most worried about you.'

'No need.' Rosemary leaned her hands on her thighs, breathing in the clear air of the dry summer. 'I'll be good once I've had a shower.' She pointed at the police car. 'What about him?'

'Robert's explaining the situation to Geoffrey. Apparently, they have enough evidence to arrest Kerry. Something about shoes?'

Rosemary smiled to herself. 'They'll need to talk to the packing ladies first.'

'Who?'

'Rebecca, Barbara and Karen. They didn't report Andrew Valencia to the police for stalking but they did lead him to the dam.'

'They did? Why?'

'Retaliation. He'd rejected every one of them. They wanted to scare him and had him go on a walk to Justin Gentleman's dam.'

'That's retaliation?'

'Andrew Valencia was scared of water. I imagine they may have been the ones to push him in.'

'But he didn't drown. He was strangled.'

'Yes. They only prepared him for what happened next. Or, should I say, *who* happened next.'

'Kerry.'

'Yes.'

'So, they knew what happened?'

'I doubt it. Nasty though they are, killing someone is not their style. Too messy.'

Jasper shook his head as if the information was too much. 'But you know Kerry murdered him.'

'He had motive and we have his shoes.'

'We do?'

'Specifically, Patti does. She has evidence the footprints at the dam consisted of the packing room ladies' green walking shoes and a particular pair of brown Julius Marlowe's formerly owned by Kerry Carruthers. And he admitted strangling Andrew to me. I'd say there is enough for Geoffrey to work with.'

Jasper nodded slowly, his eyes on the patrol car as it pulled away.

'Jasper?'

He turned back. 'Yes?'

'You didn't sound convinced when you said you would stay in Mulbury.'

He looked away, running a hand through his hair in another attempt to tuck a short strand behind his ear, before turning back. 'Mulbury is my home, Rosemary,' he said firmly. '*You* are my home. If best friendship is what we have, then how lucky am I?' He laughed ruefully, the action warming his face and brightening his eyes. 'And, besides, the day is long.'

She smiled, clapping her hands on her thighs. 'Right.'

He blinked. 'Right, what?'

'We have a mission.'

'We do?'

'Yes. We have to find your father.'

'We do?'

'Well, don't we?'

He rubbed his eyes. 'No. It didn't turn out so well last time. I should have known the family curse would still be with me.'

Rosemary stood, noticing Mrs Lionel studying her. She nodded and looked around at the small crowd gathered on the edge of the footpath. It included the weathered car salesman with the kind, dark brown eyes. 'Forget the curse, Jasper. I have a strong feeling it will be alright this time.'

Mulbury seemed extra quiet once the Jaunty Jalopers left. The normal array of tourists pattered around town with not a sinister thought in their heads, or so Rosemary hoped. It was oppressively hot, and she switched her ceiling fans to high and opened as many windows as possible to let the hot air circulate. A roll of thunder in the distance promised a change in the weather but the heat continued throughout the day, and she was glad when it ended.

The door to The Preserved Mulbury had only been shut five minutes before there was a strong knock on its wood panelling. Rosemary was halfway through slipping on a cotton house dress and snagged her braid on its zip in her haste, forcing her to tug the hairband out. She combed her fingers through her braid as she went to the door, opening it with a scowl and a cascade of long waving hair massing around her upper arms. Two men stood on the pavement under the veranda, one with his mouth open at the sight of her and the other with a slight smile. 'Jasper,' she said. 'Robert. To what do I owe the pleasure?'

Robert held a large plastic container in his hands. He lifted it up. 'From Mrs Lionel.'

'What is it?'

'She said to tell you it's Justin's jumbleberry summer pudding.'

'Did she say why she's giving it to me?'

Robert lowered the dish and tipped his head a little to one side. 'Because you're hosting tonight's Monday dinner.'

Sunny chose that moment to lean against her mistress's leg, pushing hard against it as if to say *Commiserations*.

'Dinner.' Rosemary shook the rest of the braid out, sending long dangles of hair down her back. 'I'd-'

'-forgotten.' Jasper held another container up. 'It was to be expected, Roman said. He's donating Caesar salad material.' He shrugged one shoulder to show the cooler bag hanging off it. 'Chicken in here.'

'Right.' Rosemary twisted her hair into a quick braid. 'You'd better come in and help me get ready.'

Robert gave the dessert to Rosemary. 'Sorry, can't now but I'll be back. Set the table for two extras.'

Rosemary elbowed the door open and held it for Jasper as Robert walked back the way he'd come. Jasper stopped in the doorway and looked up. 'You fixed it.'

'Fixed what?'

He nodded his head at the ceiling. 'The bell.'

Rosemary tilted her head as well. The bell resounded with its usual firm jangling but it was so familiar she hadn't registered the noise. She smiled. 'Yes. I found the knocker behind a jar of kasundi relish in the window display. I fixed it.'

'Knew you would.' Jasper stepped inside. 'It's a habit of yours.'

'What is?' Rosemary followed him into her living area where Sunny had retreated to the windowsill.

'Finding lost things and fixing them.' Jasper unpacked his load into the fridge and finally turned to look at her. 'I haven't said a thankyou yet.'

'Friends don't need to say thanks for anything.'

'Oh, I think they do.' He came forward and put his hand on her forearm. 'So, I will. Thank you for supporting me through…' He twisted his mouth '…what happened.'

'I expect you would do the same for me.' Rosemary lifted the bowl. 'Can I put this down now?'

Jasper laughed, a clear happy sound she hadn't heard for months. She grinned and thrust the bowl at him as the door jangled loudly again.

'Mum!'

Jasper took the pudding and Rosemary headed to the shop where Honey was pulling Tallulah's pram up the step. 'No Ronnie? No Pearl?'

'Ronnie took Pearl back to the city.' Honey adjusted the pram hood over the sleeping baby. 'She's agreed to see someone about her episodes.' She stood and stared at Rosemary. 'I feel bad, Mum. I was hard on Pearl.'

'You weren't to know.'

'I suppose.' Honey wriggled her shoulders. 'I said to Ronnie that perhaps Pearl should live nearer to him, maybe even help us in the tearoom on a more permanent basis.'

'Would you be alright with that?'

'Yes.' The young woman shrugged. 'Although I would like her to live somewhere other than in our spare room.'

Clamouring at the door made both turn. Holly, Hannah and Heather stood on the pavement under the veranda, their arms linked together. They were talking rapidly to each other, Holly sounding like she was listing things for

Hannah who answered by talking over the top of her big sister. Heather, in the middle and wearing a backpack, was chanting cheerfully to a lively tune.

'Hi,' said Honey, making the sisters fall quiet for a moment. 'Is something up? Other than...' She nodded at Holly.

'It's my last Monday dinner for a while,' said Holly, pulling Heather into her side more firmly.

'And Robert has hired someone to replace her,' said Hannah, moving closer to Heather so the youngest sister was wedged between her siblings.

Heather smiled. 'Holly's going away with Toffee.'

'I know. That must be sad.' Honey glanced at Holly, who looked pained.

'A little,' said Heather. 'Holly will come back.'

'Yes,' said Holly. 'I'll be back to visit as soon as I can.'

'No,' said Heather.

'No?' Holly sounded stricken.

'That's not what I mean.' Heather freed herself from both her sisters as Mrs Lionel's frog heralded the older woman's exit from The Green Mulbury. 'You'll be back.'

As Heather waltzed over to Mrs Lionel, Holly shook her head at Hannah. 'I swear that girl is part Nostradamus.'

'Why?' Hannah put her hands on her hips. 'Are you coming back? You haven't even left.'

'I don't see me staying away forever so Heather is probably right.'

'Jeepers,' said Hannah. 'I get used to one change and you tell me another.'

Holly rolled her eyes. 'I don't want to be too predictable.'

'Too late for that.' Hannah barged into the shop. 'Oh,

that's better. It's a bit hot out there. Anything I can do to help, Rosemary?'

'Jasper's in the kitchen so go and see.'

Hannah practically ran into Rosemary's living quarters, not, thought Rosemary, because she was dying to see Jasper, but more because that's how Hannah moved. Honey followed with the sleeping baby, and Holly nipped in to hold the door for Heather and Mrs Lionel, who came after more sedately. Before she could shut the door, Rakisha ran across the road shouting, 'Wait, darling! Wait for me!'

'Who else am I expecting?' Rosemary said quietly to Mrs Lionel as the older woman stepped back to allow Rakisha to rush in with her bangles clashing noisily.

Mrs Lionel peered into the living area. 'Patti and Gerry, and Robert. Roman and Jules have visitors, and Franco is trying a new bread recipe. Kelly said...' She paused. 'Kelly isn't coming, either.'

'Right. I can just imagine what Kelly said when she realised dinner was here.'

'Well, dear, you two have this odd rapport.'

'Her fault.'

Mrs Lionel started for the kitchen. 'I'm not getting into *that* on this fine evening.'

Rosemary smiled to herself and took the door from Holly, who led Rakisha away. She looked through the door for Robert but couldn't see him or his mysterious guests. The bell jangled happily as she shut the door and jangled noisily again as Patti and Gerry appeared and she had to open it. 'Thank you, Rosemary,' said Gerry as he stepped inside. 'So lovely to be out of that heat.'

'I second that, sweetie.' Patti gave Rosemary a fleeting cheek kiss before following her husband inside.

In the kitchen, dinner was being prepared without her

assistance. Holly and Hannah were assembling the Caesar salad while Jasper set the table. Mrs Lionel and Heather had found cream in the fridge and were taking it in turns to use the hand whisk to whip it. Honey stood with Gerry and Patti, who cooed over the pram. Rakisha was talking to Sunny. The cat sat elegantly on the sill with only the tip of her tail moving, staring at the tie-dye-clad woman with such steely eyes that a lesser, or perhaps a more aware, person would have shrivelled.

Rakisha spotted Rosemary watching her and beamed. 'Your kitty cat, darling, is so precious! She has this beautiful amber aura I only see in intelligent animals. You're so lucky, darling, to be in the home of this gorgeous feline.'

'I always thought Sunny was in my home, not me in hers.'

Rakisha laughed, brushing away the floating tendrils of hair from her face. 'Oh no, darling! The cat always owns the home.'

Rosemary glanced at Sunny, who lifted her chin as if to say *You shouldn't be surprised.*

'Oh,' continued Rakisha, gazing back at the ginger tabby. 'I do hope my new friend has an aura of rich colour. It's a risk when you've only met someone a few times that they aren't who they seem to be.' She turned to Rosemary. 'But what do you think, darling? Have I made the right decision?'

'About what?'

'About my new house guest, of course, darling. What else?' Rakisha clapped her hands together. 'And here she is.'

Rosemary swung around to see Robert entering her living quarters, closely followed by Justin Gentleman. 'Mumblemumble,' the farmer said in greeting.

'And to you, Justin. Welcome. You've never been to a Mulbury Monday dinner before.'

Justin waved his hands around, indicating with much waggling how busy it is on a farm at dinner time. Or, at least, that's what he might have been indicating. Robert clapped him on his back mid-flow and steered him towards Jasper, who was pouring drinks.

'You've got Justin Gentleman staying as your house guest, Rakisha?'

Rakisha blinked rapidly at Rosemary and shook her head in wonder. 'I don't think so, darling, not unless I've missed something and I so rarely miss anything.' Before Rosemary could contradict her, Rakisha pointed at someone entering the room. 'Here she is, darling. Milly's my house guest.'

Milly stood uncertainly in the dining room, hands clasped and feet together. Rakisha scrambled over to her and stopped a few inches away. 'Oh, look, Rosemary, darling. Milly is green, a beautiful fresh grass green.'

Milly blanched.

Rosemary shook her head as she went to the two women. 'It's your aura Rakisha's talking about.'

'Oh.' Milly gave Rakisha a small smile. 'And is grass green good?'

'Darling, it's perfect.' Rakisha ran her hand over Milly's head, grabbed her hand, and peered at her palm. 'Green means you have love in your heart and empathy for others.' Her bangles rattled as she dropped Milly's hand and raised her arms. 'You and your darling doggie are very welcome in my home!'

'Thank you,' said Milly. 'It's very kind.'

'No.' Rakisha grew solemn. 'It's destiny.'

'Right.' Rosemary reached for Milly's arm and guided

her towards a chair at the table. 'Sit with someone more logical tonight. You'll get enough of Rakisha if you're staying with her.'

'Do you think I'll be okay?'

'With Rakisha? Without a doubt.' Rosemary glanced at the other woman, who had darted over to Mrs Lionel and Heather and was tasting the cream from the edge of the bowl. 'She must be fluorescent green. All heart, despite her eccentricities.'

'I know I'll be okay with Rakisha but thank you for that description. I was wondering whether you think I'll be okay with the job?'

Rosemary started. 'Job?'

'At Mulbury Feeds. Robert has asked me to work with the Hubbard sisters to grow the garden side of the business. Well, *two* sisters. One is leaving, apparently.'

'Do the sisters know?'

'Oh yes, they interviewed me.' For the first time since Milly entered the room, her face relaxed into a smile. 'Lovely young women, aren't they? Extraordinary, what they've achieved. Holly has a real business head, Hannah is so full of energy, and Heather is very talented. Have you seen those birds of hers?'

'If that's what you think, you'll be perfectly suitable to work there.' Rosemary could hear the sisters talking together again, with Holly giving instructions which Rosemary was sure Hannah wouldn't need to remember. 'Congratulations.'

'Thank you.' Milly beamed at Rosemary. 'For the first time in many years, I feel excited about the future.' She chuckled. 'And I won!'

'You won. What did you win?'

'The Jolly Jaunt! My job was the most original thing to

come from our outing!' She laughed and turned to sit down. She glanced back at Rosemary. 'And didn't the packing ladies hate it.'

Now that everyone was there, Rosemary set about serving Roman's delicious Caesar salad. The chef had been generous to a tee, and most people had second helpings, including Holly, who kept looking wistfully around the table as if storing the memory for another day. Rosemary collected her empty plate and spoke low into her ear. 'You're doing something for yourself, Holly. It'll be okay.'

Holly looked up with a glint of tears in her eyes and blinked them rapidly away. 'Thanks, Rosemary. I know. I probably won't be away forever.'

'You won't.' Heather patted her sister's shoulder.

'I know you keep saying that...hey, what are you doing?'

Heather had pushed back her chair and was now standing on its seat, her backpack in her arms. The conversation at the table stopped as the diners stared up at her. 'Are you right there, Heather?' asked Robert.

'Yes.' Heather pulled something out of the backpack, letting the bag drop to the floor. 'This is for Holly when she comes back.'

'Wait.' Hannah stood up so quickly, her chair fell over backwards, making Sunny crouch low on the windowsill. 'Are they Mum's dresses? And have you made them into...'

'A wedding dress,' said Mrs Lionel slowly. 'Is that it, Heather? You've created a wedding dress for Holly.'

Heather held up the garment, letting its cotton folds fall in an ivory flow to the floor. 'Yes.' She stooped and held it out to her, sister. 'For you, Hol.'

Holly stood slowly, and took the dress, folding it carefully over her arm and caressing it lightly. 'It's the most beautiful thing I've ever seen, Heather, but Toffee and I haven't even discussed getting married.'

Heather jumped lightly down from the chair. 'When you come back. You'll need it then.'

Holly shook her head slightly and smiled up at Heather. 'You made this and two weeks ago you couldn't even sew. What a creative sister I have.'

The dress crushed in between Heather and Holly as the two sisters hugged, and was squashed even further when Hannah joined in. Patti gave a little squeal and clapped her hands.

'A special project indeed,' said Mrs Lionel, smiling at the seamstress. 'You have an apprentice, Patti.'

'Oh, no, Mrs Lionel.' Patti grabbed Gerry's hand. 'This is the student outdoing the teacher. Heather is a natural.'

Rosemary took the plates into the kitchen, smiling at the happy hum of conversation. Honey was feeding Tallulah, rocking the baby slightly and smiling at the people around her. Robert leaned over to Rakisha as she tried to explain something to him about, Rosemary thought, auras or destiny or perhaps incense sticks. Patti joined the sisters to show Milly the fine stitching that pieced the precious material together, and Gerry turned to Mrs Lionel, gesturing at the dress and then at his head, as if he couldn't get over the production of such a bespoke dress. Only Jasper was quiet. He sidled his way out of his chair and came over to Rosemary as she stacked plates into the dishwasher. 'Can I help?'

'No.' She closed the dishwasher door. 'Everything's done.'

He nodded then shook his head. 'Not everything.'

Rosemary frowned at the bowls in front of her, the pudding and the cream. 'Yes, it is.'

He leaned his elbows on the kitchen bench and linked his hands together. 'No, one thing left, although it's going to take time.'

'Jasper, we've been through this. You're my friend-'

'I'm not talking about us, Rosemary.'

'Oh.' Rosemary stared at him. 'You aren't?'

'No.' Jasper stood up again, giving her a lopsided grin. 'We're good. One thing isn't, though.' He tugged at the hair growing over his ears. 'I hate this short style. I'm going to grow it long again. What do you think?'

Rosemary crossed her arms, tipped her head on the side, and said, 'I think that's the best idea you've had in a long time.'

ACKNOWLEDGMENTS

A Jaunty Jam was borne out of the experiences of working in teams with all the foibles that accompany social interactions.

Thanks to my editorial team and ARC readers who help me see what I should be seeing but just can't.

All remaining errors are entirely my own.

ABOUT THE AUTHOR

Juno Harvey lives in Victoria, Australia, with her family.
She makes jam on the weekends and works in a university
during the week.

Want to join Juno's Reader's Team?
Go to www.junoharvey.com and receive a free story!

https://www.junoharvey.com/

Books of light...and shade.

www.ingramcontent.com/pod-product-compliance
Lightning Source LLC
Chambersburg PA
CBHW020353120726
47904CB00002B/546